At The Touch of Love

A Novel by Sierra Kay

ISBN: 978-0-9848477-9-2
At the Touch of Love

Sierra Kay

This is a work of fiction. Names, characters, businesses, places, events and incidents are either the products of the author's imagination or used in a fictitious manner. Any resemblance to actual persons, living or dead, or actual events is purely coincidental.

To my parents, who've transitioned from this earthly plane. And, I am sorry, dear parents, for the pre-marital sex in this book. I blame public schools. LOL.

PROLOGUE

"I don't understand why loving that girl has to equate to marriage." Rose Ellison's anger resonated in her voice, as much as she tried to control it.

She leaned forward on the salmon armchair. "You think marriage is about love and poems and romantic notions. Marriage is a financial institution. A man in your position would do well to remember that. Enjoy, but keep your exit strategy."

Rose wanted to kick the white table in front of her, but that wouldn't do. Raising her eyes to the twenty-foot ceilings, she stopped just short of rolling them. Another thing her father drummed into her. She wouldn't act pedestrian. Rose was born a Dobson. This house in Burr Ridge had nine bedrooms, eight bathrooms and most importantly, no mortgage. It was owned by the Dobson estate. If you think about it, for all intents and purposes, so was she. That's exactly what her now deceased father wanted.

This ongoing argument with her only son, Daniel, ended far too many of his visits. Rose surmised it could be because of one of two reasons. Either she really didn't like his fiancé, Telia, who was also the mother of his two children, Shelley and Rocky. Or, it could be because she loved pissing him off. Maybe both.

"Mother, I'm not going to keep going over this with you. It's a moot point. She won't say yes. So why keep rehashing?" Daniel ran his fingers through his dark brown hair, pressed his thin lips together and glared at her with the only part of him that revealed he was a Dobson—his cobalt eyes.

Rose tilted her head, assessing him. "Yes, I don't know if I should like her or despise her for thinking she was too good to marry you."

Daniel Ellison, Jr. broke out into a mirthless laugh, again sounding more like Daniel Ellison, Sr. "Well, Dad did say the only true emotion that you ever displayed was anger. So you probably despise her."

The statement caused Rose's nostrils to flare. He dared bring up that man in her presence. That man he worshipped like the second coming of Jesus, stole her money during the divorce by having the gall to demand alimony, and then he stole the favor of her only child.

"She just quit her job. She changed her mind about working. What if she changes her mind about marriage?" Rose implored.

"Mother, please," Daniel pleaded.

She modulated her voice while inspecting her nails. "You know we wouldn't have this conversation at all if you changed the terms of the estate. You can give me direct access to my inheritance, and then you wouldn't have to drop off an allowance every month, like I'm a child incapable of managing my own finances."

That was the crux of the issue. It wasn't that her son visited. It's why he visited. As if she needed him to babysit her. A house full of servants that she manages quite well, but her father left Daniel the contents of her bank account.

She shouldn't have been surprised that, Matthew Dobson, left the complete Dobson estate to his only grandson. The only positive thing he ever said about Rose was, "Well, at least she's pretty."

Rose leveraged her beauty to marry Daniel's father. Genius level intellect, handsome, but for some reason, he had an altruistic streak that refused to be motivated by money. Even the millions her father dangled in front of him weren't enough for him to give up medicine and manage the vast Dobson fortunes. Unfortunately, her son had inherited that gene. Even with millions at his fingertips, he insisted on living off what he made as a dermatologist.

At the Touch of Love

Even after the divorce, Father respected both Daniel Ellison senior and junior in a way he never respected her. But … at least she was pretty.

"Change the will?" Daniel's voice cut through her inner thoughts. "And miss the opportunity to visit with you every month? Now, what kind of son would I be?"

"If you marry her, will you at least get a prenup?" Rose implored.

"Mother it's not about the money," Daniel said through gritted teeth.

Rose laughed. Arrogant bastard. "There are a very privileged few who can ever utter that statement and mean it. And they're all wealthy."

"Mother, she doesn't even know what it means to be a Dobson," Daniel explained. "She has no idea the amount of money in those accounts. And she will never know. Money corrupts people."

An adage from his father. Daniel Senior actually thought that is why their marriage didn't last. In addition to being pretty, she was a damn good actress. She had pretended to be exactly the kind of woman he needed. Eventually, that act wore thin.

Rose will admit the one good thing about the relationship between Dan and Telia was their daughter, Shelley, possibly even Rocky, though it was too early to tell with him. But Shelley would be the prize of the family.

Even now, the six-year-old showed more promise than both of her parents. With her sharp intellect and flawless logic, Shelley absolutely had Dobson blood running through her veins.

She was beautiful now. When she grew, she'd be glorious. Mrs. Ellison would make sure of it.

"So where is she tonight? Out on a date perhaps" Rose inquired, trying for nonchalance.

"Echo's birthday is today. Telia is taking her out to dinner," Daniel explained before walking over to the intercom and calling the children. "I promised the kids ice cream tonight."

"Daniel, you may hold the reigns today," she stated. "You think that gives you power, but know, battling me isn't wise."

"Of course not, Penelope." Daniel enunciated each syllable. "Wouldn't think of it."

Only two groups of people called her by her given name: her enemies and those soon to become enemies. Friends chose her middle name. To everyone else, she was Mother, Ma'am or Miss.

As Daniel slammed out of the front door behind his children, Christoff Lawry stepped into the drawing room. Christoff had worked for the Dobsons since Rose's teenage years. He served as the butler, bodyguard, driver, man Friday and everything in between. His razor-sharp perception missed nothing, and he found a way to solve even difficult problems. He always held Rose in high esteem and would do anything to ensure her well-being. Loyalty like that didn't exist these days. Take Daniel for example.

"Anything I can do, Ma'am?" Christoff inquired, his deep voice echoing in the near empty room.

"I'm fine." Rose waved Christoff off. He disappeared as quickly as he arrived. She needed to think without distractions.

Rose stared at the closed door. A will was only as good as the lawyer that drafted it. She stalked down the hall to the office. She'd find a way to wrench control from Daniel one way or another.

At the Touch of Love

CHAPTER
1

Echo Sherise Charles died on the same day she was born. She was born April 27, 1981, at 1:37 a.m. at Beth Israel Hospital in Boston to defense attorney Gregory Charles and stay-at-home mom Grace Charles. Echo's heart stopped on April 27, 2002, at 8:29 p.m.

She checked the caller I.D. wanting to be sure of the exact moment she received the call. She wanted to be totally aware of the specific minute she passed out; the precise time she came to as someone else—someone who could handle the fact that her parents were laid out on a slab in a morgue in Chicago, 500 miles away.

Echo wasn't in the car that killed her parents on that day in April. Hell, she wasn't even in the same state. She'd entered the final week of her last semester at the University of Pittsburgh. She returned from the library after finishing her last take-home exam to join her roommates in their efforts to "blow off steam" and celebrate her birthday.

While her parents were probably screaming at the drunk driver speeding towards their car, she was laughing at her roommate's jokes. While her parents' black Saab crumbled under the impact of a blue Cadillac, she was shaking her ass to the sounds of Prince's "Let's Go Crazy" blasting from the apartment stereo. While her dad ricocheted in the interior and her mom was thrown out of the window to land on the concrete yards away, Echo had kissed a boy she didn't really like. She merely thought he was kind of cute.

When she received the call, she passed clear out. When that call came through, the voice on the other end spoke to dead air. The world had faded out of focus and she opened her eyes as someone picked her up from the floor. She didn't remember what the caller said. They were gone—just like that. What only child survives something so tragic? If loneliness doesn't make a person check out on life, guilt surely will.

Today, at the celebration of her thirty-fifth birthday, she did the world a favor and remained in her little one-bedroom condo, paid in full by the generous insurance policy left by her parents. Today she was more than just an orphan. She was an unemployed, single orphan, with no job or relationship prospects whatsoever. Not surprising, since she was a ghost, after all. But it still hurt as if each breath pulled at the seams of her heart.

Dressed in White Sox booty shorts with matching baby girl tee, she listened to every depressing song available on her iPod, letting the tears run slowly down her cheeks. She made an unsuccessful attempt to watch the 50-inch flat-screen television hanging above the fireplace.

Even with an excessive amount of movie channels, she couldn't find anything that held her attention. Right now, all she wanted was to burrow deep into the navy couch in the dark and let depression take her for a ride. That's it and that's all. She didn't figure it was too much to ask. It was her birthday, after all.

A noise from the front door snatched her attention. She picked up the remote and turned the music down. With her luck, it would be some masked, hockey-stick-yielding, mute character from the horror movies coming to get her. Normally, it only went after people getting freaky or investigating some house they should have avoided, but there was always the exception.

Taking a deep breath, she leaned towards the door, ears perked for anything out of the ordinary. The jingling of keys! Those crazy horror movie killers didn't have keys. Telia Nicole Arthur had keys. Damn. Damn. And double down on the damn.

Echo believed someone should have a backup key just in case. Telia held the position of sister, even though they didn't share a drop of DNA between them. Some days, like today, she proved to be as irritating as she heard real siblings could be. Telia would be wanting to celebrate Echo's thirty-fifth birthday, not realizing her presence would only make Echo feel worse.

Telia wore a quick and permanent smile, while Echo was more reserved. Echo's held onto her moods tighter than a baby holding her mother's pinky. Her bestie radiated positivity like heat from the desert sand. Echo found solace in a hot drink and a quiet corner with a good book. However, they found a kindred thread in the sixth grade that has yet to be snapped.

Balloons entered before Telia's red bottom heels could click clack along the cherry hardwood floor. The burgundy wrap dress draped on her fit form and gave more than a little peek at her ample cleavage. No one would guess she was the mother of two children.

The fact that she refused to marry her permanent beau, also known as the father of her children, contributed to the perception that she lived the single life. Telia swore she didn't want to dampen the heat of their relationship with something as mundane as marriage.

Echo supported Telia through her parent's bitter divorce, which left a scar so deep and permanent, not even Dr. Dan Ellison, a dermatologist, could find it to smooth out the rough edges. But Dr. Dan's name was tattooed on Telia's heart. When they were in the same room, you could feel their energy following the other around like shadows in the sunlight.

The Tiffany ring sparkling on Telia's left hand provided evidence of Dr. Dan's dedication to his babies' momma. The first time Echo saw it she mumbled under her breath. "Women have given up their last name for a chicken dinner, and your tail refuses the man who has given you two children, a fabulous house in Old Town and a Tiffany ring."

Telia's dark brown eyes flashed fire. "I heard that."

Echo glared back saying, "Good."

Today, those eyes held a determination that told Echo whatever excuse she could come up with would fail harder than the housing market in 2008. Telia would celebrate Echo's birthday regardless of whether Echo participated.

"Surprise," Telia shouted complete with cheerleading spirit fingers.

Echo struggled with the effort of turning her lips up into a smile, "Hey."

Telia lifted her left eyebrow. "Wow. That was, well, anticlimactic to say the least."

Echo slowly breathed in and out trying to fit the broken eggshells of her psyche back together. Echo felt like someone had taken her spirit, let all the air out, and left it in on a dark closet shelf to collect dust. She was a failure. Telia would dismiss everything that Echo felt as wrong and do her best to make Echo feel better. Echo wasn't in the mood to feel better. She was in the mood to wallow.

"Girl, I'm fine." Echo moved to embrace her bestie. Echo's five-foot-six-inch, thick-thighed body was a contrast to Telia's five-foot-eleven-inch, lean frame.

"Then why are we listening to this?" Telia waved her hand as the forlorn voice of Tank singing, I Can't Make You Love Me floated through the air.

Echo trudged over to the docking station and switched it off. "For your information, some of the most beautiful lyrics are in what you call sad songs."

Telia draped herself on the couch in the space Echo recently vacated, forcing her to find another spot to plant her weary body. "Yes, so you've told me before. However, you know what else is beautiful?" Echo grimaced, which didn't stop Telia from continuing, "A good meal at a five-star restaurant."

Sighing, Echo ventured a steely "That's nice, but I think I'm going to stay home tonight."

"Oh, you think you have a choice," she snapped with a smile that wasn't warm or comforting. "That's so cute. I'll be right back with your outfit."

Echo flipped the bird at Telia's retreating back. She didn't want to get dressed. She didn't want to go out. She didn't want to get up off the couch. She didn't want it. Didn't. Want. It.

"I see you," Telia shouted from the bedroom.

No way in heaven was that even remotely true.

Telia always got her way. For once, Echo planned to speak her mind. She would not leave the house tonight. She had a date with her bathtub, a bottle of Moscato, moody love songs, and her bed. Telia be damned.

CHAPTER 2

Telia paused and inhaled, expanding her lungs as far as they would go before exhaling. It would be easy to sit on the couch, let Echo lean her head on her shoulder and absorb the depressing songs piped through the speakers. But, she'd tried that approach for years. It would only serve as an express elevator to depression for both of them.

Telia assessed Echo's apartment finding that the air was heavy with depression and darkness rolled off Echo in waves. It almost brought Telia to her knees when she walked through the door. Birthdays were hard for Echo. Her parents dying that horrible way had a great deal to do with it. But coupled with that recent unexpected "downsizing,"

Telia knew Echo was going to be depressed but this … this was over the top. It wasn't just the heavy air and the down-in-the-dumps music. Echo's heavy heart etched in every facial line along with baggy eyes and dried tear tracks on her cheeks.

Telia desperately wanted to throw every window open and push all this … this weight, this negativity out and wish it good riddance. Unfortunately, she'd have to push Echo out of the window along with everything else.

This year, she would try tough love, and hope that she was tough enough not to gather Echo in her arms. She would have to be resilient. Life was too precious and way too short to devote so much energy to the dark emotions that consumed Echo like a man-eating plant.

Telia gathered her inner bitch, grabbed a few form-fitting dresses and marched back into the living room armed with cotton, silk, and polyester ammunition.

The white Calvin Klein creation embellished with gold zippers that followed the curves of Echo's body would be perfect. Until Echo turned up her nose. "It's April in Chicago. It's too early for white."

Echo tried it. The whole seasonal thing as an excuse. Yes, she did.

"It's never too early for classic style and to stand out in a crowd," Telia countered, holding out a black jumpsuit with silver embellishments. "White does that. And we are in the middle of a warm spell. It might snow tomorrow, but tonight we pick up men."

Echo stared at Telia as if she had grown a second head along with a third tit. Telia glanced down to make sure she hadn't. "Remember Dr. Dan," Echo challenged.

"Yes. When you have the Mona Lisa in your possession, you don't go trolling for kindergarten craft projects. But tonight, I'm on the catch-and-release plan." Telia's eyes twinkled with mischief.

Echo shook her head at her friend, but mostly at the black romper with a sheer skirt that brushed the floor.

"You would know if you took Brandon out for a spin," Telia teased.

"Don't bring him up again. He's so irritating. And don't try to change the subject," Echo warned.

Holding out yet another dress that was more revealing than the last one, Telia added. "I told Dr. Dan that tonight I'm going to flirt with strange men."

Echo's jaw dropped. "You told him."

"Yep," Telia confirmed with a wide grin, laying the dress beside the other rejects.

Echo leaned in. "What did he say?"

"He laughed and told me, 'Have fun.'" Telia frowned as though suddenly realizing that what he said wasn't quite right. "Cocky bastard." She did a little shimmy before adding, "I know you haven't quite warmed to Brandon, but also note that I offered you my brother Remy."

Remy—tall, dark, and handsome. If Echo married Telia's brother,

At the Touch of Love

they'd be real sisters. Though she'd been dropping hints at both Echo and Remy since high school, they both shut down that conversation every time Telia opened the door. Couldn't blame a girl for trying, and trying.

But she believed that Brandon would be a better pick for her best friend because unlike Remy, Brandon's hazel eyes followed Echo around the room like tractor beams. Not to mention, the added bonus of his gorgeous face propped up by a chiseled body. Plus, the man's intelligence flowed with ease and would match Echo's wit word for word.

Lifting her eyebrows up and down mischievously, Telia sang, "Remy is a financial planner. He has a job with benefits."

Echo frowned in disgust. "That's damn near incest."

"Well," Telia added. "I won't tell the preacher if you won't."

Echo smirked, not a belly-shaking, window-rattling laugh, but a smirk.

"Why are you in tonight?" Telia asked, as if she wasn't sitting across from her best damn friend watching her valiantly trying to put glue between the cracks in her façade.

"What am I supposed to do when my birthday is on a Wednesday?" Echo shot back. "I'm celebrating this weekend. Aren't you supposed to be across town with your permanent beau and kids?"

"Are you kidding?" Telia leaned against the love seat aligned across from the couch. "I asked Shelley if she was going to miss me. She stared at me like I had asked if Mickey was a mouse and said she'd see me in the morning. You'd think I'd get a bit more love from my five-year-old daughter, but no. She's fine. She has her daddy. That's all she needs."

"And how's my godson?"

"He's chatting up a storm," she answered smiling as she pictured her jolly little man who would celebrate his first year in five weeks. "Half the time, I don't know what he says, but I'm guessing it's important. He'll be talking clearly soon if only to tell off his sister."

Telia did a happy dance, which she was told reminded people of a mix of the funky chicken and a touchdown dance. "I can't wait."

"So," Echo plucked at her blanket, "for all you know, I could've been out clubbing or getting very intimate with some cute stranger."

"Girl, please," Telia scoffed. "I'd probably have to come over with that cucumber from sex ed to give you a refresher." She winked. "For the record, had I heard some strange noises coming from your room, I would have left the balloons and high-tailed it out of here. I won't get caught in between my best friend and a booty call."

Fat chance of that happening. Echo clung to the negativity like a security blanket. Somebody would have to pry it from her cold, cramped hands for it to feel some sense of freedom.

"Plus, in addition to your birthday, I quit my job. Yay! I decided I'd rather be stared at by my husband than the creepy frequent flyer guy who's always on my route," Telia stated with a flourish. "So, we're celebrating your birthday and my liberation from the race de la rat," she finished with her version of a Spanish accent. "Tonight, we dine."

Echo produced a cheer so listless it almost pulled Telia into her own depression. Something had to be done. Telia wasn't opposed to breaking a few of Echo's fingers if it meant she would release her hold on this death spiral. That wouldn't help.

Echo had been screwed in more ways than one, and not with that sex-ed cucumber, either. What happened at Echo's job this year pissed Telia off more than she let on. Well, Telia had more than a few choice words to say about Echo's former boss in the Marketing Department at Corgan Financial Management. She wasn't so silent about her feelings on that subject.

Telia spent many an hour ranting to Dan about the unfair treatment and racist practices. She unleashed a tirade to Echo about fighting back, maybe getting a lawyer, but Echo got all Rafiki from the Lion King, saying that whole, "What is meant to be will be."

Echo had a pretty good leg up on a discrimination lawsuit, and now that she was out the door, she'd rather wallow than take stock of her life and move in a direction that would benefit her in the long run.

"You know that Cymbalta commercial," she said, focusing on her friend. "Depression hurts. Cymbalta can help. I think it's time you tried to get a little help around here."

Echo rewarded Telia with another smirk; and for a minute, Telia thought she was going to be blasted for that suggestion. Instead, she grimaced

At the Touch of Love

and said, "You know, I tried. When I went for my yearly check-up, I asked my doctor about it. Even with the ten million side effects, I figured, why not?"

For a minute, Telia's heart lifted at the thought that her friend had been proactive at getting a handle on things.

"He suggested that I see a shrink."

Telia let the silence run for a minute before quietly asking, "Did you?"

"Really, Tee? If I'd seen a shrink, gotten the good medication, and still sat here on this couch tonight, then I'd sue."

"Well, maybe we will find a cute, single male shrink that will want nothing more than to unscrambled the mind Echo," Telia winked. "and find you so intriguing that he forgoes billable hours just to hear the sound of your voice."

Echo's replied. "My life is not now, nor has it ever been a romance novel."

Telia snorted at that truth. "Valid point. I know that depression was the highlight of your day, but I'm here now, and it's not going to be the highlight of mine. So, for your birthday and my liberation, I'm going to select a fabulous dress," Telia ticked her to do list off her finger.

"Beat back Mother Nature and her ugly children with some makeup, get you all fierce to infinity; take you out to a very expensive dinner courtesy of our favorite doctor, and show you how turning thirty-five is supposed to be done."

Defeated, Echo's head lowered. "Tee, please. Just go home. That's not what I want."

"Baby, I can't bear to see you like this," Telia responded in a soft tone.

Echo shrugged, "I know. That's why I didn't invite you over here. I didn't ask for you to bring balloons. Or take me out. Or try to cheer me up. Just leave me alone."

Telia stood, went to the curtain and whipped them open. "You didn't ditch me in high school—too late now."

Telia advanced on Echo. "Fine. I get it. Life isn't firing on all cylinders right now. Your parents died. You lost your job. You don't have a man." Telia added. "But you're beautiful, intelligent and you don't even have to work. Come Echo. Let's kick the moping to the curb and live."

Echo's shoulders tensed. She stood as her voice rose to a shriek. "I don't mope. I date. I used to go to work. I had a happy life three weeks ago."

Telia stomped her Louboutin heel.

"Bull! I've known you since sixth grade. I knew you before the crash, and I definitely know you after. You sparkled before. Sometimes it still peeks out when you're not concentrating on ... the D-word. Echo parted her lips to speak, but Telia held up her hand to shut her down.

"You had this audacity before. You've always been snarky, but before there was a daring behind it all," Telia explained. "People were drawn to you. Now, you just block people out. You're all shut down."

"Really? You're giving me life advice?" Echo retorted. "You? You with the perfect man and the perfect kids and the perfect life.

Running around pretending that you're a flight attendant because you love your work and you love to travel. And that job is just a cover. I'll own up to mine. My parents died on this day in African American history."

Telia's jaw clenched. "Perfect is a misconception. At least I'm not afraid to let people in. At least I'm living my life."

Echo shouted, "As you so eloquently put it, 'Bull.' You're not living your life. Your life is at home with your man and kids. That's life. You're doing everything, but. You cling and run, face and avoid. You're like Two-Face on Batman. Grow some balls. Marry that man already."

Telia's skin flashed with a crimson color at hearing those words from a friend. She planned to tell Echo over dinner that she should spend the rest of her days as Dan's wife. However, she'd brushed him off so many times, he didn't bother asking anymore.

What if her window of opportunity slammed and shut firmer than a nun's thighs? She nodded at Echo. "   Touché, heifer. That's some real truth there. Doesn't it feel good to get all cozy with some truth?"

Echo eyed her best friend with suspicion, as if she didn't quite know what to do with someone who should be upset, but for some reason wasn't.

"Ahh, my dear Echo," she whispered, "I'd rather you be pissed at me than whatever that shit you were doing when I got here. Hell, I can deal with

At the Touch of Love

pissed. So where are we going to eat?"

"You ...." Echo closed her eyes, sighed, opened them and glared. "What the hell? Arrrgghhh. I hate you." She waved her off. "Dr. Dan can have you."

Telia laughed, and the sound dissipated the heavy air smothering the room. "He does." She added a sexy body roll. "Any way he wants to."

Telia's cell rang and vibrated in the purse she'd left on the couch. Echo and Telia locked eyes. Then Echo said, "Ohhh. Tell whoever's calling to kiss your fantastically toned rear end." Echo rummaged through Telia's purse. Telia tried to reach around her, but Echo blocked her with her butt.

Echo answered laughing, "Hello?" She stared straight into Telia's eyes and responded, "Yes, this is Telia Arthur. How may I help you?"

Echo's body froze, her eyes round with shock, her breath caught coming at uneven intervals.

Telia snatched the phone. "Hello, hello. What happened?"

"Ms. Arthur, Dr. Ellison and your children have been in an accident."

CHAPTER 3

Brandon Hall leaned his six-foot-one-inch physique against the door frame and closed his eyes for a second as the buzz of the emergency room surrounded him like bees in a honeycomb.

He realized the description was more accurate than he first thought. Nurses, doctors, technicians, and other hospital personnel moved quickly and efficiently attending to patients.

Normally, he didn't work in this department, but they called him in on a case. Since they needed the coverage, he agreed to stay, which was happening more and more often.

That's what happens when everyone else had husbands, wives, and families waiting.

Unfortunately, those weren't part of his existence. He could go home and pretend to be interested in television. There did seem to be an uptick of good shows. Who was he kidding? One of these days, he was going to have to get a life again.

If working in a hospital taught him one major thing, it was to seize the day. Although he loved his job, covering for everyone else's shift, on top of his own, wasn't a life. Marrying Susan Gayle had been the starting point for disaster. Coming to work was infinitely better than going home.

Susan's entire life had centered on the desire to marry a professional; so it wasn't like she could complain when he spent so much time at work. He just told her the hospital was short-staffed, when, really, their staffing levels were fine. The problem was he had run out of patience for constant demands and ultimatums.

If that wasn't enough, four months ago his G-Ma died. Most children attached themselves to one parent or the other. He loved his parents, but G-Ma was his soul-mate. Anytime she giggled, he knew she was doing all types of wrong. Dementia had stolen her giggle. Some days she wasn't sure if people were laughing with her or at her. That cut her to the core—him, too.

In some ways, he understood that death relieved her of the misery in which her mind began to trap her. But not having her to talk to everyday hurt like sawing off an appendage with nothing but a bottle of whiskey to drink and a leather strap to bite.

It didn't help that last month he found evidence that Susan had taken out a small insurance policy on his G-Ma naming herself as the beneficiary. He'd been searching for evidence that it was illegally attained, but he couldn't find a trace. And that was the kind of woman with whom he tried to build a life.

The home of his best friend, Dan, had become his other sanctuary during the marriage, after the divorce, and G-Ma's death. Dan's wife, Telia, was a flight attendant so she was often out of town a great deal of the time. He could camp out, play with the kids, and exist without a woman who needed a bottomless pit of attention and money.

Brandon's house, before and after the divorce, was filled with unspoken recrimination and resonated with failure. Dan's house was always full of energy and laughter and love.

Brandon had shared a house with a woman who could run Satan himself out of the room. He knew it was bad when two little, rambunctious children provided more peace than the place he called home.

The blaring sound of someone leaning on a horn outside, along with the common noises of the emergency room, broke into his trip down the best-to-be-forgotten memory lane. He needed a break. Maybe he'd see what Dan was doing tomorrow. Hell, maybe one day, he'd throw a line for Echo, and see if he could finally reel her in.

Telia's sister/best friend brought out the devil in him. He constantly poked at her verbally, sometimes physically, if she tried to ignore him. He felt like a high school kid who pulled the pigtails of his crush; yet at the same time afraid was that she would respond, because then he'd have to allow her into his heart.

After Susan, the weight of another failed relationship would bow his back, if not break it. Even so, thoughts of Echo floated freely in his mind night and day.

He longed for companionship, and Echo's quick wit fit the bill. Yet, he hesitated.

When the familiar sound of an ambulance and the increased bustle of activity that was associated with its arrival began, he stretched, mentally preparing for another night of submersion into the ER hive. What he wasn't prepared for was a familiar cry clawing through his conscience and putting a vice grip on his heart.

"I want my mommy. Where's my daddy? I don't want you touching me. You're not my doctor."

That sounded like Shelley. What's Dan's daughter doing here?

Brandon pushed his way past a technician into the section with three adjoining bays. Sure enough, Shelley Ellison was sitting on a gurney with her hands on her hips, eyeballing the nurses like she was as grown as the ones standing in front of her.

He almost laughed at the nurse making the cooing noise and trying to distract Shelley with a toy. He didn't have the heart to tell them no matter how many soft, soothing noises they made, his goddaughter wasn't going to go down without a battle or some answers, ones he needed himself.

Brandon walked into the bay. "Shelley, love?"

Shelley turned, ready to do battle with yet another adult, until she laid those bright blue eyes on him. Her face crumbled and tears made a rapid descent down her round face. "Uncle Brandon."

He rushed forward and the two uniform-clad nurses gave him a wide birth as he captured the feisty little minx in his arms. She held on with a grip tight enough to cut off his air supply. " Shhh, Baby," he cajoled. "It's okay. It's okay."

Shelley's eyes were glassy with collected tears. "Is my daddy okay?"

Brandon settled her in the center of the bed. "Is Dan here with you?"

Shelley nodded. "They made us come in a different ambulance. She," Shelley pointed and glared at a red-haired, wide-eyed nurse, "said my daddy was here, but won't let me see him."

Dan processed the information. If they didn't allow Shelley to see Dan or ride in the same ambulance, there was a good reason."

"Well, I'm sure they have the best doctors with him, Shelley, love." Brandon declared.

Shelley leaned closer to him and whispered, but it was still loud enough for those nearby to hear. "But, what if it's one of the hacks Daddy talked about?"

The burgundy stained lips of a nearby nurse quirked, but she didn't say anything. It seemed that everyone, even a six-year-old, knew that all doctors weren't created equal.

Rubbing her curly hair, he said, "I promise you. It's not a hack. Now, I need you to let the nurse check you out."

Shelley glared at Nurse Kent and then flickered a questioning look at Brandon.

He leaned forward and whispered. "No, she's not a hack either." Holding up two fingers, he added, "Scout's honor."

A blonde nurse held Rocky against her bosom and the baby "pimp" nestled in tight. His thumb firmly stuck in his mouth, lashes spiked from tears, and eyes wide with curiosity at the scene unfolding before him. Since he was more settled than his sister, Brandon didn't interrupt them.

He went back to Dan's bay, and was careful to stay only in viewing distance as the doctors and nurses worked around him. The terms unconscious, head trauma and CT scan fell from the lips of the dark-haired emergency room doctor. His friend was in trouble.

Come on, Dan.

Brandon strode past the action and made sure the curtain to Shelley and Rocky's bay was firmly shut before they wheeled Dan past them in an unconscious state. No child should see that.

Where the hell was Telia?

CHAPTER
4

"Echo? Echo!"

The frantic sound of her name came from seemingly far away. Mom. Dad. No Tee. This time it's Tee.

Suddenly, she was jerked back to the current reality from the explosion of pain on her right cheek. She focused on Telia who was screaming her name. Unfortunately, no sound would slip past Echo's lips. Telia raised her hand, poised to strike.

"No. Yes. What?" she drew back, bracing herself for another blow. "What do you need?"

"Don't you dare," Telia screeched, shoulders heaving trying to keep her emotions at bay. "Don't you dare shut down on me."

Echo nodded. Shut down. Don't shut down.

"We have to go to the hospital. My family…" She blinked twice as though trying to focus. "Please, Echo."

Echo cocked her head at Telia's pleading eyes and distraught facial expression. She had to go. Where did they need to go again?

Telia threw up her hands and turned. She's leaving. We have to go.

"Wait, Tee. I'm coming." Moving forward was like walking through fog. She had to be stronger, quicker. She had to shore up her sanity. She would manage for Tee. "I just have to my find my purse, my jacket, my shoes."

Telia stopped at the door, tapping her left foot in an impatient rhythm against the bamboo hardwood. Echo grabbed her things and shuffled towards the door. She would rather trudge through the depths of hell than go to the hospital today. Who was she kidding? This was the depths of hell.

As Telia peeled out of the driveway, Echo prayed, God, please give Tee strength to get through the horrors of this day. Please protect her family from the pain that I've had to live through.

Tee needed help and right now. And God was her best option, since it certainly didn't seem to be a best friend who kept experiencing flashbacks of the day her parents were killed.

Echo leaned her head against the window as Telia shot toward Lake Shore Drive, which would take them north to Lincoln Park.

The gravelly voice on the other end of the call they received five minutes ago, took Echo back to that day fourteen years ago when she heard the news about her parent's accident. "Miss Charles, this is Officer Klein from the Chicago Police Department."

With those few words, she knew. She knew, and didn't want to hear any more. She had been the emergency contact for her parents ever since she turned sixteen years old. Her family had a long line of only children.

As much as her parents tried to have other children, Echo was the only baby that lived to term. With the three other failed attempts in their past and a successful birth with Echo, they stopped trying. The result was too painful and in her mother's advanced years of forty, it was too dangerous.

Their death shoved Echo out of the cocoon of their love and protection. For the next eight months, her life was on autopilot. She completed everything that was required of her by their lawyer, Attorney Jones, and then spent the rest of the time at home crying herself to sleep. She gave the lawyer power of attorney to do whatever he wanted.

He could have taken her for every cent and she wouldn't have known until he was skiing in the Swiss Alps. Fortunately, the man her parents had chosen to take care of their affairs had been so scrupulously honest that he made Abe Lincoln look like a hustler.

Echo never made it to her graduation ceremony. Telia tried to change her mind, but what was the point? She couldn't imagine sitting in the auditorium among a sea of proud graduates who were busy searching the stand for their parents. And when they walked across the stage, there would be cheering and clapping from their families. The graduate would smile proudly knowing they accomplished something significant.

The only thing that would be significant about the day Echo crossed the stage is that two seats, which should have been occupied by her family would be empty. And the only one clapping would have been Telia trying valiantly to make up for the fact that Echo's parents weren't there. Knowing Telia, she would have brought noisemakers and everything. The woman did love attention.

Things progressed to a point where Echo only had so many hours of face time that she could tolerate before the tears would come no matter where she was or what she was doing. In her lawyer's office one day trying to figure out what to do with her parent's house, tears slid down her cheeks like a sled down a hill.

Attorney Jones reached over the desk and handed her a tissue, but didn't stop her side of the conversation. She cried so often that if she stopped every time, she'd never get out of bed. She cried through most of her conversations in those days. So, he reached out to Telia, who now lived two hours away.

Telia came to Echo's place the next day and dragged her through all the paperwork that was part of wrapping up her parents' lives. "Girl, your life's ambition cannot be huddling under your comforter crying all day. You know your parents wanted more than that for you."

Echo had sniffed between outbursts. "I shower every day."

"Yeah, but putting on the same clothes is a dead giveaway that you're not quite right." Telia had countered.

Now Echo, who still wasn't 'quite right' in the passenger seat fourteen years later, was praying they would make it to the hospital without another accident. Cutting her eyes to her friend, Telia's focus was on the curves of Lake Shore Drive, as she whipped the dark gray Porsche Panamera at near break-neck speed.

Echo's prayers shifted from the Ellisons to praying the cops, usually hiding on the entrance ramps, now had someplace else to be. If not, they were about to have an O.J. chase moment for real, because Telia wasn't about to slow down for a ticket when her family needed her.

Glancing at the speedometer inching up again, Echo sent up another prayer and grabbed the "oh shit" bar situated right above the passenger side window. As Telia wrenched her car into a hard turn and the tires squealed, Echo slammed her eyes shut. Best if she didn't see the danger coming. A morbid thought raced through her mind ....

If we get into an accident, who was there to call?

CHAPTER 5

Echo tried to keep up with Telia who dashed through the glass emergency room doors.

Telia addressed the triage nurse between breaths. "Dan ... Dan Ellison? Doctor? My children? My family? Do you know what happened to my family?"

As the nurse opened her mouth to speak, Brandon maneuvered her. "Telia?"

Echo glanced up to see Brandon Hall and her breath caught at the sight of him. Even amid an emergency, he appeared magically delicious. If his infantile mind ever aligned with that body, she'd have a hard time keeping her panties on.

She managed to see as far as the forest green shirt covering his flat stomach, since he was much taller than her five-feet-six inches. She had to make the effort to lift her head to see that handsome face the color of rich caramel, green eyes and neatly trimmed beard.

He was a Lenny Kravitz type, earring and all. His strut overflowed with the kind of swagger that made a woman think of leather pants and guitars. Echo swore he purchased all his shirts from Baby Gap. The way they hugged his pecs left every orifice watering.

She and Telia shared a high-five about him before. She didn't much feel like high-fiving anyone right about now.

At the Touch of Love

Their observant, but comedic, conversations had taken place over a year ago, when he was still married to the woman they both merely referred to as "The Crazy One." That broad was so nuts that she had a Planters factory in her head. Echo figured he was a bit off for marrying a woman who can kiss you with one breath and verbally shank you the next.

If he hadn't lost his sanity before that marriage, then it certainly went missing in action by the time it ended. His presence at the moment was explained by the fact that he was an anesthesiologist at St. Augustine, where Dr. Dan also had admitting rights. And right now, he was Telia's lifeline, and Echo's by default.

"Brandon! Thank God. What happened?" Telia managed to get those five words out then broke down crying at that point. Evidently, she'd used up all of her calmness to get them to the hospital in one piece.

Brandon draped his arms around Telia and guided her to the waiting room. He sat her down and rocked Telia as if she were a mere child needing a hug. "Come on, now," he crooned between her loud wails, which attracted the attention of the nearby patients, families, and staff. "You need to pull it together. Let me tell you what's going on. Shush now."

As Brandon raised his eyes his view landed on Echo who quickly leaned over and put her elbows on her knees, inspecting the floor until Telia managed to gain some of her composure. Echo could feel Brandon's eyes boring into the top of her head, as he continued his efforts to comfort his best friend's wife. After a couple of minutes, Telia lifted her head from his shoulder.

"I'm sorry Brandon," she stated. "I've been crazy since I got the call. I didn't know what to think. I didn't get any details other than they're alive and on their way here."

"They're here. Everyone's alive. That's the good news. Shelley and Rocky are hanging out in Pediatrics. But, we have to go to Dan first. The doctors are prepping him for surgery."

Clasping Telia's left hand, the one sporting that ice-skating-ring-sized rock the man had given her, to nudge her into a legally binding relationship. "He hasn't regained consciousness yet. I'm glad you were able to get some crying out of your system because you're going to need to keep it together for what's next." He perused Echo behind her as he said, "It's a good thing that

Sierra Kay

25

Echo's here."

Echo forced her eyes to remain glued to a particular spot on the floor, instead of rolling in their socket. Even in her manic state, Telia would recognize that Echo's body was physically there, but her mind was a crapshoot.

"I'm so glad that you were here," Telia said to Brandon. "Were the kids conscious, responsive?"

Brandon gave her a sad smile. "Yes, they're fine. I'm just glad that I was on duty. Shelley kept asking me about Dan. She had a fit when she had to leave the emergency room without him," Brandon explained. "When she started crying, Rocky started crying, too. She knows something is very wrong. I haven't given her any details. I had another call or I would've gone to Peds with them. Plus, I knew you would be here soon. Shelley's going to need some answers. She's a quick one."

"I hear you." Telia took a deep breath, and her shoulders visibly relaxed. "Let's get Dan into surgery."

Brandon caught Echo's stare. She merely shifted her eyes so that they landed on the tips of his shoes. "I'll let them know you're on your way."

Echo followed Telia out of the emergency room, only to feel a pinch on the upper part of her arm. Brandon leaned down as she passed, "Get your head in the game. She needs you."

Her nose flared along with her anger. She didn't need Brandon telling her what to do. She didn't know him like that.

As they stepped into the elevator, Brandon stared after them, as he listened to a red-haired nurse who cornered him and seemed to be talking a mile a minute.

"Hey, Tee. You know everything's going to be okay, right?" Echo attempted to support Telia, but it sounded weak to even her ears.

Telia grabbed her hand and held on as tightly as she once did when they had played Red Rover in grammar school. "It has to be, doesn't it?" Telia pressed the button that would lead them to the pediatrics floor. "Listen, I need you to check on the kids while I'm dealing with Dan. I'll be there as soon as possible. I can't … he can't go into surgery …," She trembled from the impact of the words. "I need to see him before they take him in. He has to know he's not alone."

She hugged Echo and ran off the elevator before Echo had time to decline the offer to take on two children who could run rings around the average adult.

Echo arrived at the nurse's station. "Excuse me."

The nurse lifted her eyebrows in an unasked question, as though the place didn't get visitors every single day. "I'm Echo Charles. I'm here to see Shelley and Rocky Ellison. And before you even ask, no, I'm not a parent. Their father's about to go into surgery and their mother's downstairs handling that. I'm here so they won't be alone. You can call Brandon—I mean Dr. Hall—down in ER. He'll clear it."

A sharp expression flashed across the nurse's round face before she picked up the phone and made the call. She turned her back to Echo as she confirmed Echo's information for herself.

When she placed the phone back in its cradle, she sent Echo down the hall to where a petite nurse with a warm smile was sitting with Shelley and Rocky—little miniatures of their parents. Shelley's birthright included Telia's tall frame and confidence overflowing from her pores.

While Rocky's exhibited an easy laugh, an ever-ready hug, and affection for everyone he met. Both Shelley and Rocky inherited the Ellison blue eyes, which stopped strangers in their tracks as if the kids were a sideshow attraction.

As she entered, Shelley screamed, "Titi Echo. Where's Mom? Where's my dad? What's going on?"

Echo brought Shelley against her body in a hug as Rocky toddled his round little body over to hug her too. Her name became two distinct syllables at the mercy of his young pronunciation. "Ek... hoe." In public, it always caused more than one head to turn, as it sounded more like the baby called her a hoe.

"Your mom's with your dad. She'll be up soon. I haven't seen your Dad, yet. So, we'll have to wait for your mom. I'm here to keep you company for a bit."

Shelley grabbed Rocky's hand. "We're fine. We can go see Dad with you." Shelley gave the nurse the evil eye. "She wouldn't take us."

Rocky cosigned with a loud, "Da."

Echo gazed at the solidarity. "I can't take you anywhere without your mom, Sweetie."

Shelley merely stared at Echo as though trying to hone in on a weakness. Echo had been stared down by this particular six-year-old before. She'd seen many a person get taken in by either Shelley's charm or her grown-woman anger. Echo had sworn years ago that she wasn't going to be manipulated by this little girl, who came out from the womb knowing exactly how to bend people to her will.

So, Echo did what she knew the moment dictated. She stared at Shelley right back and didn't say a word.

Shelley sighed. "Please, Titi Echo. I'm so scared. We'll just stay for a minute. We won't be a problem, I promise. See, Daddy got me this watch and I know how long a minute is." Then she stuck her chest out and pulled her brother close. "Plus, Rocky listens to me."

She tried to hold back a smile before sitting down on a pleather or vinyl rocking chair while Shelley continued to assess her. "You know I can't."

Shelley pouted, and it was an adorable pursing of her lips that had always allowed her to get her way with Dan. Shelley's eyes held the beginnings of a tear. "Yes, you could."

"No, I can't, Sweetie." She patted the empty space beside her. "Come and sit with me. Your mother will be here soon."

Shelley seemed to lose every ounce of fight she had left. She let Rocky's hand go, and crawled into Echo's lap. With round eyes, Shelley whispered, "I'm scared, Titi Echo. My daddy was bleeding. Is he really okay? I just want to see him really quickly." Shelley snuggled deeper into Echo's lap.

Rocky toddled over and gave Echo's leg a few pats. "Go Da?"

Echo exhaled her own frustration. These kids are good.

She stroked Shelley's dark brown curly afro puffs. "Sweetie, we have to wait for your mom."

"You're a grown-up," Shelley explained, as though talking to a child. "You can take us. Or call mom on your cell. Call her and she can let us talk to Dad. Please, Titi Echo—one phone call."

What was Echo going to do? Dan was unconscious and on his way

At the Touch of Love

to surgery. Shelley wasn't going to like that much at all. Dan was her favorite person in the world; truthfully, even more than Telia. Rocky was partial to his mom or any female—especially if they were well-endowed. Lord, they started early these days.

Shelley was a daddy's girl. Her day rose and set with Dan. Echo didn't want to have to be the one to tell Shelley any bad news. Tell the truth, Echo wanted to be at home with her head under the covers pretending that no one else could die on her birthday. Too much loss; too much anguish.

Echo began to play "their" game: nursery rhymes she had taught them whenever she'd been drafted into babysitting, when Dan and Telia chose to strut their respective stuff for a night. "Jack Sprat could eat no fat. His wife could eat no …,"

Shelley studied Echo maybe realizing Echo was as stubborn as she was. They had gone many rounds over the years. Now Shelley understood that Echo was her aunt and not her friend. She'd only get so far. So at the moment, Shelley nestled in Echo's lap with tears falling down her face, sniffling in between efforts to clear her nose. She at least responded to Echo.

"His wife could eat no lean."

Rocky stopped patting Echo's leg and patted Shelley's instead. "Selly?"

Shelley rubbed Rocky's head. "So between the two of them, they licked the platter clean."

Echo started again with, "Old King Cole."

Shelley shook her head, lips in a thin line. "I don't wanna play anymore, Titi."

Echo nodded, completely understanding her niece's sentiments. She didn't want to play anymore, either. But how could she entertain two children who'd just endured something inexplicable? How much had the children seen?

She reached down and pulled Rocky onto her other leg. Rocky tapped Echo and pointed to his sister. "Selly cry?"

"She'll be fine, Rocky," Echo told Rocky, "She's sad."

He tapped Echo and pointed more emphatically. Echo complied by giving Shelley a kiss on the top of her head.

Rocky pointed to himself and said, "Ra kiss." Echo helped Rocky lean over to kiss Shelley. Then, she rocked them both and hummed a song as they waited for news, any news. Echo started tearing up as well. Poor Rocky, barely old enough to walk and now having to deal with two emotional women. Correction, one woman, and one wanna-be-grown woman.

Right now, Shelley would take Titi Echo over a stranger. But she wanted the man that made sunshine out of rain. Hell, right now, Echo wanted her father too. Fathers made the tears go away. Except at times like this, when they were the cause for them.

The months following Echo's parents' death left her wading through the muck of despair.

Her friends would ask her once in a while if she was all right. "Sure," she'd always reply. Stupid question. Really, both parents had died. How could she possibly be all right? But most people want to hear what they wanted to hear.

They would rarely dig any deeper than absolutely necessary. Hell, Echo had been one of them. Barely scratching the surface of emotions, lest it kill her perpetual "I'm a 21-year-old college student buzz."

Freedom was an elixir—minimal bills, minimal responsibility, and no one watching. Echo drank from that often, until her parents' death had caused her to quit cold turkey.

Every evening she crawled into bed with a pillow over her head, whispering part of her nightly prayer—the only part that mattered at the time. "And if I die before I wake, I pray the Lord my soul to take." That was all. The rest was irrelevant. Then Echo would cry herself to sleep.

No, Echo would never slash her wrists. But God was free to do the dirty work. Every night she gave Him permission. Every day she woke up, she gave Him permission again. She knew within the depths of her soul about wanting the security. She understood how hollow it felt, how hopeless, how very badly a girl could want her daddy.

So with this understanding, Echo cried with Shelley, understanding there was indeed a pain that no amount of words could reach. Words were irrelevant at this point. Shelley wanted her dad. Echo couldn't produce him. Really what else was there to say?

Echo hummed and rocked to let the children know they weren't alone. Sadness was an individual emotion. Two people could have the same exact

At the Touch of Love

experience and have depression for two totally different reasons.

Hugs and kisses didn't heal all boo-boos. That was something no one should learn until they were older, much older. In one tragic accident, Shelley had learned that life didn't come with guarantees. And if her father wasn't awake by the time Shelley found someone to take her to him, Shelley's sense of security would fall apart.

Echo hummed and rocked to let Shelley know, she was there as much as she could be. She should've taken those sleeping pills. *Fuck that, I'm going to use my inner strength to get through the day bullshit.* If drugs were ever warranted, today was that day.

She could have passed out and woke up in the morning, and been oblivious to her pain, Telia's pain, Shelley's pain, or getting random lectures by Dr. Brandon—all of it. Yeah, most of it would still be there tomorrow. But instead of being intimately mired in it, she would have been an observer.

She would've been the one to ask, "So, how are you doing?" And when Telia said she was "fine," Echo would have been able to say, "That's nice" and keep going about her day.

Instead, she was left to fight the quicksand of her emotions as they continued to pull her under.

Tonight, they just might suffocate her.

CHAPTER
6

Brandon strode down the hallway. Having completed the most arduous task, getting time off of work, he went to check on Telia. Before turning the corner to the family lounge, he halted and retreated two steps. Bracing himself against the wall, he inhaled a breath deep enough to bring the Crypt Keeper back to life.

He had to prepare himself for any news … good, bad, or anything in between. In his role as an anesthesiologist, he understood that life teetered on a high wire between life and death every day.

Most people didn't realize how precarious that balance was. Right now, Dan leaned too far left. Hopefully, they could still pull him back.

"Brandon."

Brandon cringed and cleared all emotion from his face and raised his head to meet eyes the exact same cobalt hue as Dan's. However, on her, the blue orbs appeared colder than the center of the Antarctic in the middle of a blizzard during the coldest winter on record.

Her eyes could make a man stop in his tracks and back up three paces for good measure. Odd for a mother, much less Dan's mother, to possess such a chilling personality. But this woman, who'd lived on the periphery of Dan's life, did.

Today, she was in her typical uniform of a Chanel suit over a body that wouldn't have the audacity to gain as much as a pound.

As usual, Christoff, Mrs. Ellison's driver-bodyguard-minion, stood a respectful distance away. He always remained within two steps of taking down anyone who posed a threat to Mrs. Ellison.

She didn't go anywhere without the imposing figure, who had to be at least sixty years old, but with thick, muscled arms. If Mrs. Ellison's eyes sent men three steps back, Christoff glared with such intensity that a man might rethink his very presence on earth.

Turning his attention back to Dan's mom, Brandon's lips curved in his most engaging smile. "Mrs. Ellison. I didn't know you made it to the hospital."

Her lips pursed as though she had inhaled or tasted something rotten. "Yes, she called me."

"Oh." Telia was the she in that sentence. Mrs. Ellison referred to her as either she, her, or dear—never her given name as though saying it would validate her very existence in Dan's life.

Mrs. Ellison adjusted the designer purse strap over her narrow shoulder. "I thought that I would be needed to make medical decisions for Dan; but apparently, he gave her that right. Even though she thinks she's too good to marry my son."

Brandon merely nodded. "Oh," was all he could manage. He wouldn't entertain that conversation if Johnny Cochran rose from the grave for the sole purpose of interrogating him.

Mrs. Ellison sniffed at a patient shuffling down the hall with the IV pole and his gown wide open giving anyone behind him a birthday suit view of his backside. "Well, I'm going to get something from their godforsaken cafeteria."

She didn't offer to get Brandon anything, nor had he expected an offer. Their relationship could best be described as tolerance, bordering on acceptance with a side of disdain. Brandon didn't feel too bad, since that was the same way to describe Dan's relationship with her.

With a sharp nod, she strutted toward the elevator bank with Christoff serving as her shadow. Mrs. Ellison's appearance at the hospital changed things—significantly.

Brandon watched as Mrs. Ellison stopped in front of the silver door. He didn't know why the elevators dared not to open the minute she stepped in front of them. Christoff gently placed his hand on Mrs. Ellison's shoulder. Mrs. Ellison leaned to gently rub her cheek against his hand before the steel returned to her spine.

Brandon shook his head trying to fit the rare display of humanity from Mrs. Ellison against the stoic mannequin he'd experienced all these years. Plus, he secretly called Christoff, Mr. Robot.

Mrs. Ellison wasn't a fading flower counting the days until retirement or death. She functioned in a world of power players, and she usually had a few good plays of her own. He'd do well not to forget that.

Brandon turned away from Dan's mother and stalked into the lounge. Telia huddled in a corner, clasping a cup of coffee as though the cup was superglued to her palm. He'd seen vacant eyes like hers several times from family members of patients who were stuck in purgatory between the knowledge of whether their loved one was alive or dead.

Maneuvering past pacing strangers, crying babies, and anxious wives, he removed the cup from her hands and placed it gently on the table.

Brandon knelt in front of Telia until she focused on his face, "Hey Brandon," she whispered, her voice raspy with pain.

Smiling, he replied using his special name for her, "Hey, TeeTee. How's Dan?"

Shrugging, Telia ran her hands up and down her well-toned arms as though a chill had suddenly come over her. "He's in surgery."

The lounge had chairs lined against the wall. They were easily moved to allow clusters of families to collect together. With a computer on either end, families could go online and handle personal or private business while they awaited news.

Brandon refocused his attention on Telia. "So Mrs. Ellison has appeared?"

"Yeah, I called her," she nodded. "But someone had already notified her. She turned up less than five minutes after I hung up the phone."

Of course, she did. Mrs. Ellison probably had this hospital bugged and everyone in the vicinity under surveillance, police stations too. If anything happened to Daniel, she wanted someone to be able to tell the story. Brandon rubbed Telia's hands, which were as cold as Mrs. Ellison's eyes.

At the Touch of Love

While he would have loved to have this conversation in a more private setting, some things couldn't be put off any longer. He understood Dan's need to keep his mother and the love of his life apart as much as possible, but it left Telia in a vulnerable state. "What did Dan tell you about her?"

Telia moved in measured steps toward the window leaving Brandon stooped in front of the chair she once occupied. "Not much."

Brandon approached her and leaned against the window at an angle where his face was fully visible. "Dan didn't have an upbringing like us, not at the beginning anyway."

Telia didn't respond.

Brandon tried again. "Telia!"

Startled, Telia's eyes snapped back to him. "That much he told me, that he isn't close to his mother. But you've been there at holidays, no shocker there."

"True," Brandon conceded. A chill rolled off Mrs. Ellison that was so cold it could freeze a turkey on Thanksgiving. Even Rocky, who loved all females, didn't reach out for Mrs. Ellison.

What would be the best approach to a sensitive subject? How to tell someone who loved Dan so much about the woman who loved him so little. The woman who always had a plan.

"Mrs. Ellison raised Dan until he was ten or at least had a staff to raise him," he explained. "But warming to kids? No, that wasn't her thing."

"So why is she here?" Telia countered, not bothering to move from her position. "She's here for Dan because he needs her. Right?"

Brandon pursed his lips, preparing to deliver the hard truth. "I don't know. Dan loves his mother, but I never got the feeling he trusted her really. Did you?"

Telia moved back over to her seat and he followed, taking the space next to hers. "I don't know," she replied. "I mean she shows up at events. She's never been warm and fuzzy."

"How often has she been left alone with the children?" Brandon inquired. "Never, to my knowledge."

Telia rubbed her arms. "Yeah, none that I know about either."

Brandon reached out and gently held her hands. "All I am saying is be careful. I know you have a lot on your mind, but I just … I'm wary, I guess, is the best way to put it."

Telia nodded absently.

"I don't know the why Dan went to live with his dad, but there had to be something. Judges don't take kids away from their mothers. And, with Dan being in the state he's in right now, she smells blood in the water." Brandon laid his hand on Telia's shoulder. "Dan keeps the two of you apart for a reason. But, Dan's not here now."

Telia whipped her head to him. "He's here! He's just …." She let out a long, slow breath. "He's here."

Brandon was botching this up. He tried to grasp Telia's hands again, but she yanked them away.

"Shit," Telia exclaimed. "She's asked to take the babies for the night, so I can stay at the hospital. She's his mother. What am I supposed to do?"

Brandon pulled her into his embrace. "Echo and I will take the kids."

Raising an eyebrow, Telia challenged. "So now you're volunteering my best friend for child care services, when we both know you could've just offered to babysit by yourself." Telia shook her head.

Brandon countered. "Your children could run three babysitters and two nannies ragged in an hour. I thought having Echo there would make you feel better."

"Not as good as it's going to make you feel," Telia responded, and he could swear there was a little humor in her voice. "But I'll allow it." Telia stared into Brandon's eyes until he averted them. "You may just be what she needs right now."

Brandon's exhale held the hissing quality as if his breathing was a slow leak.

"Just so you know, Echo's my sister," she countered. "You lose your mind, and you'll find out that she's worth me taking a trip to the county jail."

Brandon peered at Telia, shifting so that their eyes could connect. She channeled her inner Mrs. Ellison. But something she mentioned caught his attention. "Why would Echo need me right now?"

At the Touch of Love

CHAPTER
7

The elevator doors opened in front of Rose Ellison. She stayed so deep in thought that she didn't move until Christoff nudged her.

She pressed the ground level, needing fresh air rather than food right now. Christoff didn't even blink about her change in plans.

"I can have food delivered for you, if you wish," he offered, ever the caretaker.

Rose ignored the words and marched out of the elevators, through the lobby and sliding doors. She forced herself to keep walking past a small group of smokers huddled under a heat lamp, until she found herself on the corner of Ashland and Harrison.

Christoff allowed her to pace for a few minutes, scanning the area before attempting to corral her to a less open space. "We can't stay here. It's not safe."

Rose scoffed. "No one is searching for me, Christoff. No one ever does."

Truly, her life contained a smattering of friends with whom she gossiped or brunched, but they'd go for days without having a conversation. Right now, she didn't want to call any of them. They'd feign shock and say the typical supportive words. However, she didn't dare share the level of hollowness in her gut or the fear that she desperately tried to reign in.

Lifting her weary eyes back to the hospital building, she recalled the last time she lost her family. She began taking the same painkillers that kept her own mother in a drug-induced stupor most of her life; lightly tapping at the curtain of life, but never pulling it aside to take her place on center stage.

Rose recalled the time when she allowed emotions to overtake common sense. The mourning period lasted for six months. When it was over, her son, Daniel, had settled in with his father and never came back to her. Not really. Not in the ways that matter.

Now, he may not come back at all.

Rose rotated her shoulders to relieve the knots of stress that settled in the minute she received the call that Daniel had an accident.

"Christoff? Business first. With Dan ...." She blew out a breath. A cab slowed at the curb to gauge her interest in a ride. Christoff glared and waved for the cab to keep moving.

Christoff, as usual, knew best. She shouldn't be hanging on Chicago corners in the middle of the night. She turned on her heel and strode back toward the hospital.

"There is a hotel across the street," she directed as they rounded the corner. "Get the best suite. Reserve it for a week, just in case we need it. Better to be prepared."

Christoff whipped out his cell as she rattled off instructions. "Hire a nanny, call Rachel at the house, and have her make sure two bedrooms are redecorated for the children. Wake up anyone she needs to. I need it done immediately."

The only people qualified to take care of Dobson heirs were Dobsons. Now, she walked with purpose. She had a job to do. "Tell her there are items in the attic that she can use."

Christoff paused. "Ma'am?"

"They're my grandchildren," she bristled at his unspoken question. "I sometimes purchase things for them just in case. Better to always be prepared, right?"

He hesitated before replying. "Yes, Ma'am."

She rarely shopped without Christoff; but she bought most of the items online, in case, the children ever needed to stay. "Money is no object. They are

At the Touch of Love

Dobsons after all. Tutor. We will need a tutor."

Mrs. Ellison stopped suddenly. In the lobby, people moved at every conceivable pace: those shuffling in pain; those with rushed feet, holding balloons clearly going to visit someone; those whose lives had been cut open by some tragedy and their emotions were bleeding out all over the place. At least she wore this latest hiccup in her family well.

Christoff stiffened beside her, eyes constantly scanning for perceived dangers. He didn't interrupt her musings.

"My son could die Christoff," she whispered.

She felt him stiffen even more, though he already carried himself as if he had skin of steel. Yet, he didn't say a word. What could he possibly say? It wasn't a question. No amount of money would solve the issue. They were caught in the clutches of that bitch called time. Time would make a second seem like an hour just for kicks.

Well, Rose was formidable in her own right. She'd lost to time during her "mourning" period. She wouldn't this time. She'd take advantage of every second time offered and squeeze milliseconds more.

"Did you get everything, Christoff?" she inquired. "Everything needs to be right."

"Yes, Ma'am." Christoff set about shifting her life to prepare for the addition of her two grandchildren.

CHAPTER 8

Telia sensed Mrs. Ellison's return before she lifted her eyes from the increased tension that introduced her presence like a master of ceremonies. That intense stare burned into her very being. Placing a smile on her lips, she came to her feet. "Mrs. Ellison, I didn't know you were back."

Mrs. Ellison's eagle eyes searched the room as if trying to decide an appropriate place to perch. Staring at the other family huddled on the other side of the room, she lifted her nose as if she had already tried and convicted them of being inferior.

Christoff stayed by the door, off to the side. Telia prayed he didn't karaticize the next person who walked through it.

Eventually, Mrs. Ellison settled into the chair across from Telia.

"Dear, where should I pick up the children?" Her expression could almost be described as pleasant. Telia's antennas immediately began to go haywire with conflicting signals. Pleasant and Mrs. Ellison were as closely related as chicken and an apple.

Brandon's conversation replayed through her mind. He could be wrong. She was family. Although the kids called her Mother Ellison, but not Grandma or Nana. Shelley slipped up sometimes, but after being icily corrected by Mrs. Ellison she got back on the program.

Telia wanted to bang her head against the window. Why did she say yes? She knew the kids had never warmed to Mrs. Ellison. Matter of fact,

Shelley once asked what was wrong with that woman.

"Well," she began again.

Mrs. Ellison's expression shuttered. "Dear, I really should be going. Where are the children?"

Telia peeked over Mrs. Ellison's shoulder to see Christoff gazing into the distance. He would still hear every word. She put on her big girl panties.

"I forgot that Brandon took days off work to watch them," she explained. "My mind is so muddled right now that when you said you'd take them, I just agreed. I apologize for the mix-up."

Mrs. Ellison leaned back into the chair. Telia squirmed under her scrutiny. She barely had the energy to keep her emotions together. She didn't have the energy to get into a mental battle with Mrs. Ellison.

"So, the fact that I've also adjusted my life for your children is insignificant because Brandon," Mrs. Ellison paused, shaking her head as if trying to loosen the words that had just settled in her mind, "took a vacation day. Is that true?"

Christoff cracked his neck, but stayed by the door.

The door to the family room opened as the other family that shared it with them hustled out the door. What did they think was going to happen? a duel at dawn? Then Telia thought about it. The stupid plan was sitting here talking to Mrs. Ellison with Christoff hovering.

Telia's face warmed, as a sheen of perspiration lined her forehead. "I'm sorry. I don't want to belittle what you've done," she assured her. "I'll reimburse you for any expense that you've put out."

"Well, I've hired a nanny. Right now, I have a designer making two bedrooms in my house appropriate for the children. Depending on the length of Dan's condition, I also have a tutor on standby to ensure the children are educationally challenged throughout the day."

Telia mentally calculated, but couldn't begin to comprehend the cost for a designer, a nanny, and a tutor being on "standby." If Mrs. Ellison mentioned a gallon of paint, Telia's math would be a whole lot better.

Mrs. Ellison's face cracked into a smirk. "Do you have enough to cover that, Dear?"

Telia thought. "Since, I'm a signer on Dan's accounts. He can cover it I'm sure. I'll just …."

Telia paused as Mrs. Ellison held up a perfectly manicured hand.

"As he's told me many times, my son loves you, Dear. He loves you enough to trust you with his life, and the lives of his offspring. But his money?" Mrs. Ellison paused as the smirk turned into a full-fledged smile. "You need to keep counting the pennies in your own account, Dear. In the event that Dan is incapacitated for any reason, like now, control of his accounts and assets reverts temporarily to me."

Mrs. Ellison's blue eyes twinkled, as if she told a joke instead of news that financially crippled Telia. "You can't reimburse me from Dan's accounts. You can't do a damn thing from Dan's accounts."

"News to me," Telia responded. "Regardless, Brandon will be taking care of the children this evening."

Mrs. Ellison stood. "I see. You let me know when my grandchildren gain free time in their schedule. And if you need a bit of cash to tide you over during this most difficult time, call me."

With that, Mrs. Ellison swept out of the room.

Telia leaned back in her chair stunned. Dan didn't just have his money, but he invested some of hers as well. And Telia had no clue about the paperwork for that account.

Her ready cash account didn't have enough for nannies and decorators. She didn't even know the mortgage on the townhome. She'd never be able to afford that, especially not now. She had just quit her job. She didn't even know if the Porsche was paid for. Dan took care of all the major financials.

Dan's coma may have just turned her into a pauper.

She slid to her knees. God, please bring Dan back to me.

CHAPTER 9

Brandon wanted to throttle Echo. Good thing he didn't leave the kids alone with her for the night. They would need uppers to get out of bed in the morning.

Shelley was quiet, which was as rare for her as having cereal without milk. Rocky gave him a wide, drooly smile, but didn't hold up his arms as usual. Shelley's eyes held a question that had plagued her since the paramedics brought him to the hospital. Brandon shrugged the answer.

"You know there's a playroom on this floor, right?" he asked to shift the atmosphere. "It has toys the kids can play with."

Shelley's eyes narrowed to slits. "I don't want to play. I want my daddy!"

Rocky chimed in with, "Yeah."

Rough crowd.

"You may not want to play, Shelley," Echo interceded. "But what about Rocky? I'm sure he wants a toy."

Shelley shook her head so hard her hair kept swimming when her movements stopped. " Rocky wants my daddy, too."

Echo and Brandon glanced at each other. Brandon walked over and scooped Rocky out of Echo's arms. "Rocky, do you want to play?"

Rocky shifted a questioning look at his sister before putting it back on Brandon, "Sel play?"

Shelley was a great sister and would do anything for her little brother. So he added, " We'll tell the nurses where we are so that your mom will come right in the minute her foot steps on this floor. Okay?"

Shelley pondered for a few moments. "I guess." Skepticism dripped from her tone.

Echo took deep breaths, as though she was mentally preparing herself for the trip over to the playroom. Brandon lifted his eyebrows, as if to ask how she was doing. She gave a small smile and trotted toward the exit with Shelley.

The playroom was painted white with colorful numbers and the alphabet on the walls. One side must have been the vehicle section, as trains and cars of all shapes, sizes, and colors held ground. Another corner was dedicated to dolls, tea sets, and little-girl pursuits.

Rocky's eyes lit up when he spotted toys. Shelley let go of Echo's hand to take Rocky over to a train set. Soon, Rocky was crashing trains together and chuckling over the destruction, as Shelley was trying to convince him to allow the trains to go around the track.

Echo sat in a kindergarten chair and leaned her head back against the wall. Brandon sat cross-legged on the floor with his elbows over his knees.

"Was there any other news about Dr. Dan?"

Brandon inquired, "Why do you and Telia call him Dr. Dan instead of Dan?"

Echo gave a sad smile. "Well, the first time Telia met him was when she broke out with adult acne. He was Dr. Ellison at that time. One appointment and she realized she was going to have to find a new dermatologist."

"Wow. That bad?" he questioned. "I don't think he's ever had someone bounce after the first appointment."

"Not even close." Echo shared the story with Brandon of how Telia battled with the thought of asking out her doctor. "If she didn't have me doing laps around the lake, it would have been hilarious to hear about her struggle to get her doc to ask her out. She's always so confident, especially around men. That's how I knew he was different. After that, Dr. Dan sort of became his nickname," she explained. "It was just our thing." Echo's eyes began to water. "So he's unconscious?"

Brandon nodded. "He has a cerebral edema."

At the Touch of Love

"Oh, yes. A cerebral edema." Echo's sarcastic tones made Brandon give a half smile, even as he prepared to give a layman's explanation.

"His brain was swelling." Brandon demonstrated by expanding his hands a little. "They're in surgery right now doing what it takes to relieve the pressure."

Echo's breaths became sporadic, tears welled up, and Brandon leaned in trying to determine if she was in distress before she uttered. "Not good. Not good at all."

Brandon shifted on the floor until he was kneeling in front of Echo. "You cannot keep crying in front of the kids, Sweetheart. What's going on with you?"

Echo focused on the multi-colored carpet and slowed her breathing for a spell. When she raised her head up, her eyes were bright and shiny with unshed tears, but at least she wasn't crying anymore. Brandon watched as Rocky toddled across the floor to grab a little brown bear and held it up to Shelley. "Teddy!"

Echo's soft hand on his shoulder snatched his focus back to the woman's distressed expression. "What else? Is there more? I can … I can take it. Really, I can."

"No, we haven't heard anything else. Telia's in the waiting room with Dan's mom. I came to check on the kids."

Echo snorted. "I'm sure you did."

Giving a knowing smile, Brandon added, "For the record, Mrs. Ellison loves me."

"How would you know?" Echo questioned. "That woman only has one expression: bitter bitch. If you've seen another, I'll need a photograph and DNA proof it wasn't a stunt double."

"Well, she purrs when she says 'Brandon' and she always fingers her pearls." Brandon gave a spot-on demonstration of Mrs. Ellison with hand over her chest and twirling an imaginary strand of pearls.

Echo grinned. "You lie. She clutched her pearls because she didn't want you to steal them."

Brandon's eyebrows winged upward, and he chuckled.

"That woman didn't bit more purr than my imaginary cat."

Brandon winked. "I'm sure I can make your cat purr."

Echo's cheeks turned so red it appeared as if she suntanned on Mars. "I don't have a cat," she mumbled, "I have a kitten and I take great care to make sure it can purr independent of outside influence."

Brandon studied Echo for a moment, even though her focus shifted to the carpet. This could prove to be an interesting evening. "So, you dared to come on the north side of Chicago with White Sox gear on? You know that's blasphemy. Technically, you can be run out of town for that type of infraction."

"It's still a Chicago team. It counts," she insisted.

Smirking, Brandon added, "The Cubs are a Chicago team. They have character. History. Lore. Tradition. Loyalty. We're a real ball club with a real stadium with roots. Y'all kicked Comiskey Park down with your bare feet to build ... what do they call it?" He tapped a finger on his temple as if he was trying to remember, "US Cellular Field?"

This time, Brandon licked his lips and watched Echo scrutinize the way his tongue went from one side of his mouth to the other before shifting to her favorite speck on the carpet.

He placed his hand on her bare leg, Echo jumped so hard she slid off the little chair onto the floor. Across the room, Rocky plopped down on his rear, shouting "Boom" and chuckled at her clumsiness, and Shelley's tinkling laughter accompanied Rocky's.

So Telia's best friend followed baseball, had a little sass, and wasn't immune to his touch. Yes, very interesting indeed.

When this crisis was over and Dan was on the mend, maybe ....

Brandon rose and helped Echo from the carpet, but didn't release her hands. Instead, he rubbed his thumbs along the smooth skin of her palm. "Oh, by the way, you and I are babysitting the kids tonight."

Echo's jaw dropped, her eyes became as wide as the gap in Michael Strahan's teeth, and she quickly searched the room as if searching for an emergency exit. The pulse thrumming through her wrist signaled that she clearly felt something. He was intrigued to find out what it was.

CHAPTER 10

Telia stormed through the door of the playroom. All eyes snapped in her direction as Rocky and Shelley rushed over. She lowered to her knees and ran a hand over their faces, arms, torso, nearly counting all fingers and toes as she had done when they were first born. "Oh my babies," she whispered, crushing them with her body. "I'm so glad you're okay."

Shelley didn't crack a smile. Instead, she wiggled to get down. As Telia complied, Shelley tried to see behind her. "Where's Daddy? I. Want. Daddy."

Echo and Telia locked a speaking glance, using best friend telepathy. No news.

Telia scooped up Rocky and hugged him tightly as he squirmed in her arms. She loosened her grip and focused on her outspoken and impatient daughter.

"He's going to sleep for a while," Telia explained and noticed Echo flinch.

"But I want to talk to him," Shelley demanded, lips trembling as the sign of temper. Let's go wake him up. I want to talk to my daddy. Mommy, why won't you let me talk to my daddy?"

"Baby, you know when daddy is really, really tired, we try and try to wake him up and he just grumbles and rolls over? It's a lot like that."

Shelley sighed as though she had become the adult and Echo and Telia were living a Benjamin Button moment before she continued, "Can we try to wake him? If you take me to him, he'll wake up for me."

Telia blew out a breath. "It's a different kind of sleep, honey. It's asleep so his body can heal." Telia's mind raced with explanations that would work for her five-going-on-fifty daughter, while trying to ignore the fear that cramped her stomach. "Remember when you had the flu last month and you slept all the time? Then you felt better."

Shelley nodded, but the narrow stare told she wasn't feeling a single word.

"Daddy is really sick like that," she explained. "You want him to be all better, right? And when his body is better than he'll wake up. We just have to be patient and let him rest."

"When? In the morning? Will he wake up in the morning? I woke up in the morning." Then Shelley brightened as though the sun had finally seeped into the room. "Let me see him. It'll be like Sleeping Beauty. My kiss can wake him up."

A slow throb began in Telia's temple. The desire to collapse and cry struggled to overpower her calm façade. The children needed strength. Telia needed Dan. Life needed not to suck this much. But with her healthy babies in her arms, Telia couldn't complain.

Every breath from Dan led to the minute, the second, and the moment he would wake and come back to them. So Telia wanted to get through each minute, second by second if she had to, for her beloved. Telia tried to smile. "I don't know, sweetie. We'll have to wait and see. Maybe tomorrow."

Shelley's lips quivered, tears rolled down her cheeks in rapid succession. "I want my daddy."

Telia tried to gather her close, wanting to cling to her baby girl, wanting to draw Shelley's pain out through her skin and absorb it into her own. But Shelley twisted free and dragged her feet back over to the toys piled up in the corner. Rocky laid his head on Telia's shoulder. She rotated her body in half circles to comfort him all while keeping an eye on her daughter across the room.

Echo placed an arm around Telia's shoulder, but Telia didn't slow her rhythm. Brandon gave her awkward pats on her back.

Telia inhaled the stench of helplessness. She remembered the smell of

At the Touch of Love

it well. She's been saturated in it during her parents' divorce.

* * *

"Telia, Baby," her mother, Shaylyn, began on a shaky note. "We need to discuss something with you."

As a high school freshman, Telia knew not to say a peep. If her parent's had caught her in some lie, they were going to have to say it outright. She learned that from Remy, her older brother, who was at college studying economics. Their parents still didn't know half the stuff that he did.

All of her recent transgressions ran through her mind. Some major. Some minor. None did she feel the need to volunteer.

Shaylyn bent down and peered into Telia's eyes.

Drawing back, Telia glanced at her dad who wiped at the sheen of sweat that layered his forehead. The way he shifted in his shoes as if a pebble had lodged inside, reminded Telia of how he acted when they had "the talk." But since they'd already had said talk, this—whatever it was—must be different.

Telia's mother cleared her throat and let out a deep breath of her own. Was someone pregnant? sick? dying? dead? What the hell? She stood as second after second ticked by. Her dad swiped another hand across that forehead. For real, people?

Finally, the word that Telia tried desperately to suppress clawed its way up the back of her throat and jumped out. "What?!" Then recoiled awaiting the smack that would surely follow. But it didn't.

Oh shit. This is bad.

"You know we love you," her mother began.

Maybe they're sending me to boarding school.

"Nothing is more important than you and your brother. But your dad and I haven't been happy for a long time...."

"Wait." Telia frowned, thinking back to last weekend when her father tickled her mother while she tried to wash dishes. "Then what's with all the hugging and kissing that you've been doing. Because none of this is making sense."

Shaylyn turned to her husband. He shook his head indicating that he wasn't going to be any help. Whatever was going on, was all about mom.

"Well, I"—big emphasis on "I"—"haven't been happy for a long time," she confessed. "And there are so many things that I want to do. You know, in addition to being a mother. That's the best job there is, but …"

Telia stepped back. Like tumblers in a lock, everything fell into place. "Did you cheat on Dad?"

The wide-eyed silence confirmed Telia's thought, and she shifted to flicker a glance at her dad's flush face. The expression held for a minute, then it crumbled, but he valiantly pulled it back together. His breath became shaky, and he immediately angled his body to peer out of the window a moment before putting his focus on his daughter again. No matter how he tried to hide it, her mother's betrayal was tearing at him like a lion on a fresh kill.

Telia turned to her mother. "Are you leaving?"

Those words must have been the cue to exit, because her mother packed her things that night. Telia learned that a piece of paper didn't make her mother stay. Telia was different. Every day she had choices. Every day she made decisions. Every day temptation walked by innocently dressed, but dangerous all the same.

Every day, Telia chose her family. She chose her man, Dan. She hoped he realized the fact that she stayed even without that piece of paper meant more than if she stayed with it. Without it, nothing kept her tied to his side except for one thing; she wanted to be there.

She hoped that love, her love was powerful enough to reach into whatever depths he'd sunken and pull him back to them. She hoped, wished, and prayed as she watched her daughter's lackluster play. She sent Rocky over to his sister, hoping that she'd accept comfort from him even while she refused it from her mother.

How could she tell her children that their dad was in a coma and no one really knew what was going on? Everyone was hoping that when the swelling comes down that he'll come back to some semblance of normal.

No one really knew for sure. She couldn't give uncertainty to her children for much longer. She had too much of it in her own life.

At the Touch of Love

"Listen, I don't want the kids to worry," she told Echo and Brandon. "Shelley isn't going to keep taking no for an answer, but I'm not sure she should see Dan. His face is severely bruised and all those tubes are sticking out of him. What am I supposed to do?"

Brandon encouraged her. "I think you explained it well. Shelley will make it through this. You too."

Telia's eyes teared up. She tried to think of fields of clover or flowers or something that would distract her from the pain that gnawed at her insides like a piranha. "She'll be crushed if he doesn't wake up when she kisses him."

Echo's eyes watered with Telia's.

"Cut off the waterworks, ladies," Brandon snapped with a pointed glance towards the children. "You don't have the time to break down. The kids need you."

Echo cleared her throat. "You know, Brandon's really busy. I can handle the kids by myself. Really, it's no problem."

Brandon leaned forward, crooking a finger as though he had some top-secret information to share.

Echo and Telia complied by leaning toward him.

"I've taken some time off. I'm here for as long as I'm needed."

Echo straightened. "Yes, well that's what I was saying. We don't need you. I'll take the kids and you do whatever it is you do at night."

Brandon's eyelids lowered to half-mast. Telia didn't utter a word, but if Brandon turned his charm on high, Echo was toast. Like burnt toast.

"Oh, I'm sure I'll have the resources, if you will," he teased. "to do what I normally do at night."

Telia held in a snorting laugh by the narrowest of margins. The predatory gleam in Brandon's face and the wide naked fear in Echo's made her want to be a fly on the wall in her house. She desired a distraction more than an upside down caramel macchiato extra caramel top and bottom no foam. Yeah, that much.

Brandon graced Echo with a low, unfolding smile before clarifying, "Sleep, of course. What else could I possibly do alone at night?" He pushed himself up to his full height before adding, "That I couldn't do in the morning." He winked at Telia before he sauntered off with a quick explanation tossed over his shoulder. "Going to grab a few things from my locker. Be right back."

Telia watched Echo as Echo paid close attention to Brandon's retreating back. "He's good coming and going, isn't he?"

Echo focused back on Telia. "So, Dan…"

"Nope. Not going to happen." Telia planted her foot firmly on the ground and dared Echo to cross the invisible line of trying to use Dan as a distraction. "I told you all I know about Dan. Now I need you to tell me whether you're going to let Brandon wipe out the cobwebs with one stroke or two."

Echo's lips pursed like they did when trying not to curse. "I can handle the children myself. I've done it before."

Telia rubbed Echo's arm. "I know, but he threw you under the bus and offered both of you. So, I already accepted. It's really for you to keep an eye on him. He needs your help Echo. So do I."

Echo grimaced, and then nodded.

Telia couldn't believe Echo had bought that Swiss cheese excuse. Clearly, Echo's game had left the building, which was a good thing because that woman's defenses against any man getting close to her heart were tighter than her vagina.

CHAPTER 11

Echo sighed as Brandon navigated Telia's car into the garage of the Ellison's four-bedroom townhome in Old Town. They had driven to the north Chicago area in her car since it was already equipped with the proper car seats. The children had cried all over again the minute they realized that their mother was not joining them on the trek home. Gratefully, by the time they exited the parking lot, they had fallen asleep.

She was as exhausted as the kids. What she wouldn't give to curl up in bed and go to sleep. But rules were rules. And the kids bathed every night.

As she unsnapped her seat belt, Brandon said, "Echo?"

She halted but didn't look at him.

"Telia mentioned at the hospital that she knew what day today is. What did she mean by that?"

Echo should've known he had listened a bit too closely. Tension rolled off Echo, but she couldn't ... she didn't have the energy. "Today is Wednesday." She hopped out of the car, managing not to bang the door against the shelf by the passenger door. Using her key, she entered and turned off the alarm. Brandon walked in with Rocky shifting a little in his arms.

Whispering, he explained. "I'll get Shelley out of the car as soon as I put him down."

Echo lifted her eyebrow. Obviously, Brandon was an amateur at this. "You might as well take him up and give him his bath, or you can take a shower with him."

Narrowing his eyebrows, Brandon responded, "He's asleep. He can bathe in the morning."

"Nope. Telia doesn't let anyone in this house go to sleep without a bath especially if they've been to the hospital. She's particular like that."

Brandon mumbled something under his breath.

Echo stifled a laugh. "Yeah, you can grumble all the way up to the shower. I'll grab Shelley. We'll use the guest bath."

The children shared a Jack and Jill bathroom. The guest room had its own complete with all the necessary toiletries. Echo didn't feel the need to let him know that the guest bath came with plush guest robes. She wasn't there to make his life easier. Hopefully, he had packed smart.

"I'll bunk down in the guest room. Are you okay with the office? There's a foldout couch there."

"I guess," Brandon replied.

Shelley slept hard. Echo felt like using a fireman's carry to get her upstairs. Instead, she kept her hand pressed against Shelley's back. Undressing her was such a trial that she finally had no choice but to lean Shelley in the corner while she prepared her bath. Echo was amazed that she slept through the bath. No grumbling. No crying. *Echo* was grumbling by the time she got Shelley dressed and in bed.

Echo took her own hot shower and slipped on the warm terry cloth robe. Each minute drained more of her energy, but she'd need something to wear tomorrow. Telia's form-fitting clothes didn't come close to fitting her. With her eyes at half-mast, she shuffled to the washing machine down the hall only to bump into Brandon holding tight to a towel slung low over his hips.

This time her gaze traveled up those washboard abs, defined pecks, to his smirking, full lips, which appeared soft enough to kiss. She stepped back to take in the muscular arms before traveling back down and settling on the curve of his hips that led to the spot covered by the towel. Her mind was incapable of doing anything besides stare at that V.

Something underneath the towel twitched. She reached out and his abs tightened. Tilting her head, she counted ... 2 ... 4 ... 6 ... 8. The man had an eight pack. And a body chiseled by Michelangelo himself.

She heard a buzzing noise that could have been words. She didn't have the energy or will to lift her head and have a conversation with his face, while marveling at the twitch beneath the towel. Wait, didn't he just call her name? "Hmmm?"

"Echo!"

She snapped her gaze up to a pair of eyes she could get lost in. She'd always thought his eyes were one color, but the combination of brown and green was as mesmerizing as the rest of him.

"Excuse me." He touched her arm to move her to the side.

She shook her head. "Oh, sorry. Gotta wash."

Brandon lifted a questioning eyebrow. "Well, standing here staring at me isn't going to start that load."

Echo heard him and, under normal circumstances, she would've been embarrassed; but she was too tired and he was too fine. If he didn't want her to stare, he shouldn't have come out all greased up and tight.

Brandon used his free hand to pull her in front of the washer and dryer. "I left my clothes in the car."

Echo turned and watched him leave. "Umm hmm." She didn't manage to snap out of her trance until he had practically disappeared down the stairs. Shaking her head again, she gave a mental high five to his parents. Those were some damn good genes.

Minutes later, as she drifted off to sleep, her mind was no longer occupied with her birthday, Telia, Dan, or her parents. No matter how much she tried to summon her earlier depression as a protective cloak, her body was primed and ready to overrule her head and jump that man. Eight-pack abs had a way of working their way into her psyche and producing one hell of a dream.

Wet and naughty.

CHAPTER 12

Brandon trotted down the stairs to the garage and slipped on a pair of Dan's black flip-flops by the door. He grabbed his overnight bag and made his way to the office. He threw on a pair of shorts, thinking Echo could've shared the secret location of the robes.

Her reaction to him proved that those hours at the gym weren't wasted. He'd always found her attractive; but unfortunately, he had been married to Susan when they first met. That was enough to label all women as the devil incarnate. Now that their divorce was final, he'd been holding on to his freedom with a Kung Fu grip.

Echo's eyes radiated a pool of pain that made him want to dive in and pull her out of the other end. Today was a bad day for everyone, but he had a feeling there was more involved where Echo was concerned.

Even though there were definite shadows in Echo's life, she also had a feisty side that he liked to poke at every now and then. One day, they'd been right here in this house and Echo told the story about yet another loser she dated.

He began, believing he should help her out, "Echo, maybe you shouldn't date."

Telia immediately excused herself and scurried to the kitchen, as Echo scanned his body top to bottom like an MRI machine. "You,

… Brandon, … you're giving *me* advice about relationships."

Brandon shrugged, "Or at least date smarter. You seem to pick all the wrong men. That last date you went on, what was his name?"

"Greg." A wiser man would have seen the fire in Echo's eyes and paused. Brandon did not. "He's a police officer."

Brandon confirmed, "That's what I'm saying. He picked you up during a traffic stop."

Echo weighed her words. "Actually, I might have picked him up. He was cute, and employed, and—"

"And a player. I mean come on. You should've been able to tell that a mile away. And the one before him—the stalker, …." Brandon frowned as he tried to remember, "Ummm...."

"Kenny," Echo supplied, folded her arms, and leaned against the wall in the hallway.

"Yeah, him. Showing up at your job and your house uninvited. The only good thing about Greg was that he got rid of Kenny."

Echo stilled.

"I'm just saying that you could do better," Brandon continued.

Echo used her leg to push off the wall. "Are you done yet?"

Brandon peered at her deceptively calm demeanor. He'd known Echo long enough to understand she didn't explode like Susan did. She smoldered. The steam bubbled right beneath the surface. *Oh shit.*

Echo crooked her finger and he leaned forward. From this vantage point, he could see the fire behind those hot chocolate eyes that were narrowed with malicious intent. "Well, at least I don't marry the crazies."

"She was fine when we met," Brandon defended. "When I found out she was crazy, I divorced her. Well, that and the whole cheating thing."

A purely evil chuckle escaped from between Echo's lips. "Nope, she was day-one crazy. You just used your pecker for your picker." Echo gave her Wonder Woman, hands on hips stance. "And from your results, I'd say your pecker was way off."

He didn't know why Echo hid her fire when she dated these broke-ass men. The Echo he knew gave as good as she got. Every time Echo brought some man around it was as if she placed her spine in layaway. He could imagine their surprise when they found that she had her own opinions.

Brandon's hand raised, causing Echo's eyes to narrow. He merely tucked her hair behind her earlobe. Suddenly, crying screamed from the baby monitor in the kitchen. Telia shouted, "Damn," before flying by them on her way up the stairs.

Echo watched Telia bound up the stairs. "You know she eavesdropped from the kitchen."

"Wouldn't expect anything less." Brandon responded, before adding, "Marrying Susan was a mistake."

Echo doubled over in laughter. "So basically, you're admitting the sky is blue and grass is green.

Brandon let her have her moment. Then he stared in her eyes and told her the promise he made to himself, "The next time I walk down the aisle. It won't be with someone I am compatible enough to build a life with. It will be with someone I can't imagine living my life without."

Their eyes connected for a few seconds. Brandon felt something good. He couldn't say what exactly, but he felt a twinge of something before Echo broke the eye contact as she asked, "Right, but how would you or I know that unless we date various people."

"How soon in the dating process do you go from being excited about their possibility to justifying their presence?"

Echo sighed, "First date. Sometimes the second date."

"That's when you cut them loose. Right then. Don't invest in people that waste your time."

"There aren't a lot of Dans and Telias in the world. Sometimes, you have to make do with what you have."

"Maybe. If you were a settling type of person, you probably could have made it work with a few of those guys. But you can't settle, can you?"

"I tried." Echo's shoulders slumped as if the realization that she had standards disappointed her as much as someone cancelling her favorite television show. "Settling fits on me about as well as that glove on O.J."

Brandon dragged Echo into his arms. "Then wait for the lightning."

As Brandon lifted his head to see Telia at the top of the stairs holding

At the Touch of Love

Rocky. She simply stared at him. Her eyes seemed to penetrate his mind. He didn't know if that was a good or bad thing, but it sure as shit felt uncomfortable.

CHAPTER 13

Telia concentrated on Dan's side, holding his near lifeless hand. His mother had left thirty minutes ago. Thank goodness. That woman added a layer of stress just by breathing any part of the Chicago air.

Even Wednesday Adams cracked a smile every now and then. Mrs. Ellison's slowly deepening frown told of her disapproval of the doctors, nurses, Telia, porters, everyone within spitting distance of her only child.

Not one to waste time reading when she could disapprove, Mrs. Ellison didn't even crack open a book. No iPad, iPod. Hell, Telia wanted to purchase her a computer, tablet—hell, a pager, if Mrs. Ellison would use it. Anything to distract from the tension creeping through the room like molten lava on its way to some unsuspecting town.

Telia carefully crawled into Dan's bed. He was the hydrogen to her oxygen, producing a life-sustaining substance that she'd always taken for granted. She always slept better next to him. Any time she lay down in her bed, he would wrap his arm around her torso and pull her close.

Sometimes, in the middle of the night, he would jerk to an upright position after being deep in REM, and still wrap his arm around her, cradling her body in the protection of his arms. She'd merely smile and drift back off into a peaceful sleep.

Now, when she needed his arms the most, they lay limp at his side and steady beeps from one of several monitors were signaling the strength of his

At the Touch of Love

heart. His beat matched hers, beat for beat.

"Hey, Dr. Dan," Telia began, knowing that if she called him Dan or worse Daniel, he would think something was horribly wrong.

No movement at all.

"I guess when I suggested ice cream, I should've added that you come home safe and sound." She choked up, closing her eyes against the pain that stabbed her heart. "I thought that was a given."

Telia's head filled with all the things she could say, probably should say at this point. The television was on in the room, but had been muted.

People were walking in the hallway, but the sounds of heels clicking against the tiles had lightened to an occasional click or clack instead of a staccato march. Night had fallen and only an occasional bout of laughter came from the nurse's stations, as they swapped personal stories about husbands or children who were waiting at home for them to walk through the door. Just yesterday, she had taken this life for granted.

"I'm so …," Telia's voice caught at the thoughts whirling through her mind. "I'm so sorry, Dan. I need you. We need you. Don't leave us. Don't leave … me." Yes, she was supposed to be cheery and upbeat, but she'd have to manage that tomorrow. She had to for the kids. Tonight, those two things were as far from her abilities as they could be.

When she first laid eyes on Dr. Dan, it was at a time in her life that she was feeling neither hot nor sexy. Her face was breaking out all over the place. All through high school, she'd strutted around with a mostly clear complexion. Even her brother Remy had tried everything from Clearasil® to Noxzema to a blow torch. Or he would've tried it, if he thought it would help. One pimple here. One pimple there. Sure. Pimples replacing an enhancing stroke of blush on her cheek. No way.

She found Dr. Dan online and made an appointment. The man was panty-dropper fine. However, the only indication that he even knew she was a female was the way his eyebrows lifted momentarily when he first entered the exam room. After that, he slapped that generic doctor/patient smile on his face and kept it there during the whole appointment.

The broad shoulders, the tapered waist, that full bottom lip kept her thoughts off kilter. Yes, Telia answered all his questions, but crossed her legs delicately, trying to draw his attention to one of her best features. She played with her high heels, slipping her heel out the back and getting more point in her toe. Nothing. She laughed, bringing her hand to play with the pendant on her necklace, hoping the delectable Dr. Dan would notice another fine feature. Nothing.

Finally, she started with safe questions. "So, you have an amazing complexion. What do you do?"

"I drink water." Dr. Dan smiled and tilted his head to the side as if to say, "*Like you should be doing.*"

"That's all," she countered, feeling a little chastised because she was guilty of not consuming enough h2o. "You sure you're not self-medicating over there?"

Dr. Dan laughed. And Telia's eyes widened. That laugh vibrated through the depths of her stomach. The man was fit and handsome. But she dated fit and handsome all the time. There was something about Dr. Dan that made Telia actually want to talk to him, to get to know him. She'd laid her eyes on some great specimens, but none of them stoked the flames of her intellect and her libido.

When Telia tried to figure out if she should ask Dr. Dan out for a date, she invited Echo over for a brisk winter walk on the lake.

"Listen, he's my doctor. Doctors don't date patients. But Echo if you could see him. I mean besides the fact that he kept eye contact and didn't leer once, he has the most beautiful blue eyes you've ever seen."

Echo shifted her eyes to the side. "Okay—beautiful, blue. You do know that this conversation sounds the same in your place as it does outside in the cold."

Telia pushed Echo's shoulder. "I will throw you in Lake Michigan. Right now, I'll do it."

Echo laughed. The foggy breath appeared through the scarf covering her mouth and settled as condensation. She rubbed her hands together as they continued walking. "We could figure this out in the heat of your apartment."

Telia began to pump her arms to power walk, "I think better at the lake. So how do I get the good doctor to ask me out?"

Echo conspired. "Okay. You have two options. You can slut it up on your next appointment. But if he's worth anything, he's not going to fall for slutty Telia. Or at least you don't want him to know this early that you're a slut."

Echo easily navigated around the leg Telia stuck out to trip her. "Not funny."

Echo's body shook with laughter. "Oh, yes it is. The way you tilt your head and lower your eyes and stick your chest and butt out when a cute guy comes within ten feet of you? Come on. You have some good slutty moves."

Clenching her teeth, Telia sent cigar smoke-like rings of breath into the atmosphere. "This isn't about a short-term deal. He's smart. He reads. We were in his office talking about foreign policy. How many men do I discuss foreign policy with?"

Echo searched the sky for an answer before responding, "It may be more if you didn't start with your boobs and butt."

"You're not helping, Echo." Telia stopped and pulled Echo to a halt. They were merely a few feet in front of the bridge that would lead them over Lake Shore Drive towards Telia's studio apartment.

"Fire him," Echo finally demanded.

Telia's eyes bugged. "What? How am I going to see him often if I'm not a patient? That's counterproductive. Give me something else."

Echo stomped her feet as she normally did when her toes edged toward frostbite. "If he's quality, he won't date a patient, no matter what cup size you're sporting. So, you, my dear, will have to fire him and ask him on a date in the same appointment. He's either in or out."

"Wouldn't it be easier if I found out where he hung out, and you and I happened to be there? Then I could bump into him in a more social setting."

Echo strode away with Telia calling after her. "Echo, Echo, come on." She halted suddenly, causing Telia to bump into her back. She blew a full breath. "You see that. That's my breath. I am not going to be rolling all over town in the winter trying to accidentally, on-purpose run into someone that may or may not be interested in you." Echo's arms began to wave like Lake Michigan on a windy day. "We don't know if this man has a wife, girlfriend, boyfriend, or some combination of the three. Not happening."

Telia sighed, "This should be much easier."

"It is." Echo touched her arm. "Put your C cups on the table and ask him out." Then she closed her eyes and thought for a second. "Not literally. Do not literally pull out your breast. But man up. Ask him out. See what he says." Holding up her hand, she added, "'cause what I'm not doing is spending the next month taking laps around your neighborhood until my feet turn blue and fall off."

At their next appointment, Telia did something she never did. She told him straight out. "I'm sorry, Dr. Dan, but I can't be your patient anymore. I need you to recommend someone else."

Raising his eyebrows, he asked. "Is something wrong, Telia? Did I offend you or ...." His face was scrunched as though trying to wrap his mind around any scenario where her words made sense.

Shaking her head, Telia merely stated, "First, give me the recommendation."

"Well, I'll have to have one of the nurses provide you with a recommendation, but no matter what you tell me, I'll make sure you get that name. You have my word."

Dr. Dan appeared truly stressed. She felt bad about putting him through that. Taking a deep breath, Telia started. "I normally don't do this, but I'd like to get to know you better on a personal level." Holding up her hand, she added, "If you're amenable, of course."

Dr. Dan's forehead furrowed with thought. Either he was confused or trying to figure out a way to let her down easily.

Telia pushed on. "You don't seem like the type to date a patient. So, if you say yes, then I can't be your patient. If you say no, I'll need to never see you again. So, I can save myself a shitload of embarrassment." She gave him her best smile, even though her foot was knocking against the chair. "So, what do you think?"

Dr. Dan leaned closer until their breaths entwined. One, two inches and their lips would embrace. One or two inches and her left thigh would be wrapped around his waist as her tongue introduced itself to his tonsils.

He backpedaled until he bumped into the counter. "Telia, while I appreciate your intention, I can't date a patient."

At the Touch of Love

The words slid between Telia's ribs and pierced her heart. Well, she had her answer. Telia stood and began to gather her items. "I'm so sorry. I didn't mean .... Just have someone, not you, but someone in your office call with a referral." She dropped her purse. As she picked it up, her mouth started running, "Yes, you probably have a girlfriend, boyfriend, wife, or all of them."

Dr. Dan whispered. "No, I'm single."

Telia slowly turned. Dr. Dan's eyes captured her. Heat. She felt it as if he branded his name on her body. He held the counter so tightly that his knuckles turned white.

Echo did say put her boobs on the table.

Telia took three steps closer. Dr. Dan transitioned to a corner. He finalized their conversation. "Yes, I'll definitely have a nurse call you."

She arched her back and noticed Dr. Dan's focus lowered as he swallowed. He never said he didn't want to date her.

Telia played with her necklace. "So, if I saw you on the street next month, what would your answer be?"

Dr. Dan shook his head.

Telia smiled. "And if I saw you on the street six months from now?"

His eyes glistened with an intensity that pulled Telia across the narrow space between the two of them. Then he uttered, "Yes."

Telia shivered as she realized she'd need an extra pair of underwear on her—always—if she was blessed to date this man. Telia inhaled his subtle woodsy cologne mixed with his natural masculinity, and it put a spell that shut down all common sense.

"Now is just a bit … premature. But who knows what tomorrow will bring? or that six months you talked about." His husky voice was like the flute of the snake charmer, and she was doing her best not to wrap her body around him like a python ready to inhale its next meal.

"Well, I certainly wouldn't want anything between us to be premature," she said, then clamped down on the words, realizing that they were a little racier than she intended.

Dr. Dan threw his head back and laughed. "Nothing to worry about on that score. But let's go through the basics first."

Telia handed him her cell number. Dr. Dan inquired. "How do you know that you'll still want to go on a date in six months?"

Telia laughed, "A hunch."

Watching him now without the beauty of his spirit, his essence, scared Telia. She was shaking so much that all she wanted was Dr. Dan to assume the position that always made her feel safe. As safe as she'd ever been; even when her father was present, but heartbroken at the sight of her because she resembled her mother.

Lying in a hospital bed with an unconscious person didn't give her the comfort she sought. It gave her the willies.

She carefully extracted herself from the narrow hospital bed and moved camp to the chair. She wrapped a blanket around her, and watched for the slightest movement from her love.

Leaning forward, she whispered, "Where are you? Why won't you come back to me? And why the fuck did you leave my finances at the mercy of your mother?"

She leaned back against the rock-hard vinyl cushion, counting seconds instead of sheep.

CHAPTER 14

Rose walked to the family room situated at the end of the hall. She should go home. There didn't seem any point to her being here. Yet she felt compelled to stay. However, sitting in the same room as Telia proved to be uncomfortable. The way she slouched in a chair as if she didn't have a spine, made Rose want to snap at her to sit up.

However, their peace had always been tenuous. She knew they both tried for Daniel, but the truth was they didn't have anything in common. Telia seemed to fly through life without thought. Literally. Daniel Dobson Ellison could surely provide for his mistress without putting even a small dent in his bank account. For years, she chose to fly the friendly skies, which always led Rose to wonder how "friendly" Telia was to her passengers.

As Rose entered the room, Christoff stood. He didn't like the fact that she relegated him so far away.

His first words were, "The same." It should have been a question, but coming from Christoff it sounded like a statement of fact and it was.

Rose walked over to the window and glanced out before confirming, "The same." Cars drove along the street. People went about their evening, like Dan should be doing this second.

"We should have made him get a driver," Rose muttered.

"He's not accessing Dobson money." Christoff focused on telling Rose the truth she already knew.

Rose whipped her head around. "Did I ever seem to lose my ability to understand the basics of life? Did I suddenly go insane in the past hour? If not, why are you stating the obvious?"

Christoff stood, eyes narrowed, jaw clenched. "Of course not, ma'am."

Rose turned back to the window. Her hands shook with tension that continued to build with every minute that passed.

Christoff didn't move behind her or recommend that they go home; though knowing him for over 20 years, she knew he would prefer it if she wasn't as exposed as she was now. She felt him stiffen when the door to the room opened.

He kept one eye on her while constantly scanning the room. Standing here with Christoff proved more nerve-wracking than sitting with Telia in Dan's room. Christoff knew her too well. He knew how tight her stomach must be with regret over Daniel's condition. He knew, though she didn't show it, that she too would like to curl up in her son's bed.

Christoff missed little. He used to bring up those events. He used to get her to talk, but after her "mourning period" thirty years ago, their relationship changed as well. Guilt is an evil emotion. He considered it his failure. Christoff spent years supplying her mother with neat little pills at her demand.

She never overdosed; Rose had.

That night, his voice cried out for hers through a wavy fog. He heaved her up and tried to force her to walk. Although that voice seemed to swim at her through an ocean of thick, heavy air. That's all she remembered from that night, Christoff's panicked voice.

He later told her that Daniel had almost seen her, but Christoff closed and locked the door. Then, he administered naloxone. Christoff also dropped Daniel off to his father. Christoff thought it would be temporary. Christoff learned the same lesson that Rose learned. Daniel Sr. was a bastard.

That day changed everything for both of them. He pulled his friendship back and buried it deep. He needed to be unbiased. He took orders from Rose still—sort of—as long as they aligned with what he felt should happen. Other than that, he would defy the devil himself.

After the mourning period, Rose didn't pull back her friendships. She just pulled back every emotion and buried them deep. She needed to be

At the Touch of Love

resilient. Funny, she'd thought she had lost Daniel before. He wasn't lost. This, this was losing Daniel. Amazing the way perspectives shift.

"Ma'am?" Christoff inquired.

"Yes," Rose nodded, "let's go home."

Christoff opened the door to the hallway. His hand skimmed Rose's arms. Shocked, Rose stood back and turned to Christoff. Public touching wasn't allowed. He seemed to forget his place twice now. However, he didn't even meet her eyes, since he was too busy scanning the hallway. He would do well to remember propriety.

CHAPTER 15

Echo shuffled into the kitchen focused on her mission. The Keurig commanded the top of the list of man's best inventions. A pod. A cup. A short wait. And she double fisted a mug of coffee. Blessed. Hot. Elixir of the Gods. A deep inhale proved to her mind that it wasn't a mirage. She indeed held tight to her liquid savior—caffeine. She'd bow later. Now she needs a mere sip, a taste.

Echo's senses tingled, signaling the presence of Brandon whose proximity interrupted her coffee bean love affair. She couldn't deal with that until at least the fifth sip.

Through her peripheral, she saw his shoulders shake as he tried to hold back his laughter. Echo didn't care. She had coffee. Brandon could suck her big toe. Oh hell. Her body tightened at the thought. Wrong image.

"Morning, Echo," Brandon ventured, his voice gravelly with the remnants of sleep.

Holding up her hand, she laid down the morning law. "We do not speak in the morning."

Echo should've closed her eyes. That would have been the smartest move, but she hadn't. His smile assaulted her brain in the worst way, penetrating her morning fog. Though her brain still hadn't awakened, his gaze dipped her body into a pool of need. His lips curved like they knew the thoughts running through her head. Or worse yet, if he knew her thoughts from the previous night.

At the Touch of Love

He turned and leaned against the counter and tried again. "Did you sleep well last night?"

Echo glared at him and mumbled, "Fine." Her mind erected no barriers this early, and the very thought of the memory of her dream last night could singe her clothing and his, since he wasn't too far away.

Even when she blinked, snapshots of the dream lived behind her eyelids: their bodies glistening with sweat as she lay in front of him; his lips trailing along the curve of her shoulder; his hand lifting her thigh as he eased into her; her body tightening to feel every inch of his length slowly slide until his hips connected with her ass.

She catapulted awake at 3 a.m. and dared not to go back to sleep. Of all the emotions she should be feeling at this time—fear, depression, loss—the one that percolated to the top was horny. Damn, Brandon.

She hid in the room as long as she could; but in addition to sex, her body also demanded it's morning cup of Joe. Echo happily obliged. Hell, if she could stay up forever, she would.

Dreams like those were an ever-present danger to her peace of mind. And right about now, she needed to be focused on Dr. Dan's condition and the kids and not on Brandon's penis.

Brandon's hand on her forehead jolted Echo. How did he get that close?

His touch held an electric charge making her jump. He held up his hands in surrender. "You seem a bit flushed and you're a bit warm. I was just checking to see if you were coming down with a fever."

Echo inched away. Her downcast eyes allowing a good view of the slight bulge below his waist instead of the floor like a good girl would. No, the bulge called to her at a frequency that only she, and maybe the neighborhood dogs, could hear.

Retreat. She must retreat. "Nope. Fine. Coffee is just hot. Making me warm. I'm good. I'm going to call Telia and check up on Dan."

Brandon smirked and leaned against the quartz counter in one smooth motion. "When did Dr. Dan become Dan?"

"I don't know. When his mother put it on his birth certificate? Be right back." With that, she all but ran out of the room.

Echo sprinted up the stairs to the kids and guest room floor. Shelley's voice sounded off in Rocky's room. "Come on now, Rock, we have to get dressed."

Echo pushed the door open. Amazingly, the six-year-old was completely dressed in a pink legging set with a Doc McStuffin's t-shirt. Even Shelley's wrist was adorned with the watch her dad gave her. Though the shirt could've used a quick hit with an iron, it was on and she matched. Echo wasn't going to push her luck.

Shelley stared up at the crib with her hands on her hips and head tilted to the side, as if figuring out the complex problem of releasing Rocky from his wooden prison. Rocky, ever the good soldier, awaited her instructions.

Echo rushed into the room and put her cup down on the changing table, before Shelley figured out how to teach Rocky to do something that would drive their parents up the wall—again, When she attempted to teach him to slide on his butt down the stairs, his feet caught underneath him and Rocky ended up launching himself down the last three stairs. Telia said keeping up with Rocky tired her out, but keeping up with Shelley trying to "big sister" Rocky gave her gray hairs.

"Good morning, Shelley and Rocky."

Shelley gave Echo a once-over so filled with disdain that she had to take a step back. "How's my daddy?"

"Good morning, Shelley."

"Good morning, Auntie Echo. Where's my daddy?"

Rocky chimed in, "Titi!"

Reaching into the crib, Echo liberated Rocky the proper way—with no little accomplice leading the charge. "I was just about to call the hospital. But let me get Rocky situated first. Did you brush your teeth?"

"You know," Shelley replied as though an adult hadn't posed a question. "Rocky, used to be able to climb out on his own, but they've moved all the furniture to a different wall. He doesn't know how now."

"But did you brush your teeth?" Echo repeated.

Shelley grimaced, then shuffled into the bathroom and yanked down the tube and the toothbrush and slapped it on before turning on the sink. "Wait

At the Touch of Love

a minute. Okay," Shelley mumbled around a mouthful of toothpaste. "You can put it on speaker because I want to talk too. I'll be quick. See? I'm brushing."

Echo laid Rocky on the changing table and prepared for morning poop. Which was more like days-old adult shit. "Dude, you need a vegetarian diet," she scrunched her nose, trying not to inhale.

Rocky laughed as though even he knew he'd created something of horrific proportions.

After getting Rocky and Shelley presentable, Echo headed down to the kitchen, dialed Telia's cell phone, and put the call on speaker. Everyone, including Brandon, surrounded the cell phone.

At Telia's hello, Echo quickly explained, "Hey, girl, you're on speaker."

"Hi, Mommy," Shelley chimed in with Rocky giving a ten-decibel "Mooooomm."

Brandon nodded even though Telia couldn't see him. "Hey, Telia."

"Hey, my babies," Telia responded with a strained voice. "How did you sleep, baby bug?"

"Fine, Mom," Shelley responded, almost rolling her little eyes at all the pleasantries that were keeping her from asking the questions. "Rocky slept well too. Did Dad sleep well?"

Echo heard Telia's breath hitch. "Like a baby. He's actually still sleeping."

Shelley sighed, "Well, when is he going to wake up?"

There was a slight smile in Telia's voice when she answered, "I don't know, honey. But we must be patient. We want him to be all well when he does."

Shelley's lips tightened in a grim line before she conceded with, "Okay."

"Shelley, baby, I need to ask you a question."

Shelley's eyes widened as she answered, "Yes, Mommy."

"Baby, do you remember what happened last night? when your daddy was driving?"

Echo lifted Shelley into her arms as Shelley began to cry.

Echo rocked her back and forth, as Telia made soothing sounds over the phone and Brandon rubbed her back.

"Shhhh, Baby. I'm going to have Auntie Echo and Uncle Brandon bring you to the hospital. Rocky can't see him, but I'll let you talk to him for a while."

Shelley stopped crying and sniffed, "Okay, mommy."

"Love you, bug. Love you, Rocky." Rocky blew a kiss to the phone. "Go on up to your room. Let me talk to Echo and Brandon now."

"Okay, Mommy. Come on Rocky," Shelley instructed. Rocky climbed the stairs at a slower pace, but soon the footsteps signaled they'd be in the room in a few seconds.

Echo watched them, noting the pep in Shelley's step. All it took was even the hope of talking to Dan. For a moment, Echo tried to remember if she'd ever favored one parent over another. With them both gone, in her mind, she'd always loved them as equally as she missed them. As the little troublemakers made it to the top stair, Echo whispered, "They're gone."

"Go into the office," Telia recommended, causing Brandon's attention to pull away from the youngsters to focus on her. "That girl's hearing is like Superman."

Brandon snorted and nodded as if he was well aware of the superpowers held by their little miss.

Brandon closed the door behind them and perched on the heavy steel desktop next to Echo, who asked, "So how is it really going?"

"It's hard," she replied, and both Brandon and Echo shared a sorrowful glance. All the cheeriness had shifted from her voice and an exhausted whisper was left, creating a heaviness that wouldn't leave anytime soon. "I mean, he's sitting there getting poked, prodded, and all, and he's not responding." Telia's voice cracked, breaking down her everything-is-ok masquerade.

"Telia, it's been less than twenty-four hours," Brandon reminded in a soft tone. "Give him time. He's a plotter. He doesn't make quick decisions. And right now, his brain is trying to redirect some things so he can get it straight."

"The police came today." Echo and Brandon shared a look. "They said Dan, with our kids in the car, ran off the road by himself. Possibly a medical event. Possibly this that or the other thing."

Brandon merely sighed, "Telia."

At the Touch of Love

"We have a hospital full of brilliant minds who can't figure out when or if Daniel will wake up." Telia's voice became shrill. "Then we have police who don't have a clue why Daniel ran off the road. Shrugging. No answers."

"Telia," Brandon tried again.

"How inept is this world? Doesn't anyone need to do their work? It's like the pilot needs to land the plane, but instead, he just shrugs." Telia continued, "Whatever."

"Telia!" Brandon shouted.

"What!" she replied.

In his deep timber, he just uttered, "Breath."

Telia blew out a shaky breath. "I just want to know what happened. I just want Daniel to come back to me."

Brandon sat on the edge of the desk that appeared to be built out of an airplane wing, with an easy smile. "Remember how long it took for Daniel to ask you to move in."

"Yeah," Echo cosigned, loving the direction that Brandon had taken in trying to lighten the mood. When he smiled, Echo could swear she felt a drip in her drawers, even after Telia's tirade. Something was truly wrong with her. "Didn't he carry the key around for like a month?"

"Waking up shouldn't be a decision he has to make," she shot back.

Evidently, Telia Arthur wasn't giving free passes tonight.

"He knows I need him here. We need him. He's the one that …. I just need him."

Echo felt the stirring of those unwanted waterworks again, but looked up in time to see Brandon give her that "straighten it up" glare. "Are you sure you want Shelley to see him?" she asked, swallowing her own sadness to be strong for her friend.

Brandon's lips twitched and he nodded a thank you.

Telia paused for a few moments. "I don't know. But he needs to hear more than my voice. That woman is coming today."

Brandon grimaced. No need to have a name for who Telia meant. Telia reserved those two words for one person alone.

"I just can't handle being in the room all day, all alone with her," Telia seethed with an edge creeping into her voice that said that things wouldn't bode well if Mrs. Ellison tried her today. "Anyway, I'd rather hear Shelley break down the plot to each and every Disney movie, before I hear about the gossip of what happened at some country club way out in Bumble Hell Egypt."

"It'll be like your own version of the "Real Housewives," Echo teased, knowing there wasn't a damn thing funny about Mrs. Ellison.

"Was that the pro argument or the con argument?" Telia inquired.

Brandon tamped down on a laugh, mouthing the words, at least she still has her sense of humor.

"Hey, I want to get back," Telia sighed. "I don't want to leave him for too long. See you guys later."

Echo disconnected the phone, took a moment to process things before looking up at Brandon, and forming her lips around a lie. "She sounds good."

Brandon narrowed his eyes on her, and the heat from his eyes caused her abs to clench. "Really?"

Echo glided the phone along the smooth planes of the desk. "No, she doesn't have the Telia energy." She rubbed her hands together as if she was trying to warm them. "She's losing her spirit. And we have to help her get it back."

CHAPTER 16

Telia wandered back into the room. Mrs. Ellison would be there at 9 a.m. sharp. Since it was only 7:30 a.m., she had some time alone with Dan, to just exist with her man.

A short nurse ambled into the room, smiling at Telia. Dang, these people didn't quit. According to the dry erase board, this should be Kayla. Telia acknowledged her presence and then just rested her eyes until Kayla left. Rude, yes. But she needed to conserve her mental energy.

Sitting hour after hour was harder than watching a worm inch its way down the sidewalk. Talking to someone who may or may not hear what was being said, someone who normally would have had a witty response made her feel alone. Yesterday had been a long day, and the lack of response was giving her a consistent cramp in her stomach. A beeping monitor does not a husband make.

They'd spent time apart before. Almost every week she had at least one overnight trip, but those trips were planned for well in advance. Often, the night she landed in another town, she would go out drinking with the girls. No matter what she did, or how much fun she had, she was more than ready for her flight the next day to come on home to Dan and their children.

Even then, she would talk to Dan several times a day. They'd text. They'd share what was going on with the children, the flight attendants, or the pilots. In some cases, she'd share what was going on between the flight attendants and the pilots. They'd laugh at things going on in his office or with other people they knew.

The ease of their conversations were things that she'd heard so many married women wish they had; not to mention the touches that still made her skin tingle; the hugs that she sank into; and the kisses that served as foreplay every time their lips met. Why had she waited to give him what he wanted? All he desired was for her to be his wife. He loved her enough to wait, and kept on waiting and now ….

The last thing he said to her was, "Go show Echo how a birthday is supposed to be done."

She replied, "I would need you, whipped cream, and blindfolds for that."

Dan lowered his voice, giving her a saucy wink. "Hmmmm. We'll save that for later."

She laughed and went out the door. She didn't tell him she loved him or how he made her feel. She didn't tell him that she didn't know how she got so blessed. She should have told him every single day that he was the spark that lit her life.

And now his mother lurked around with who knows how many hidden agendas. Well, one was already fulfilled. She now managed the Dobson fortune and, in that, managed the future for her children and quite possibly her future as well.

One day in and she was an entire hot mess. She didn't know what to say to her children. It was one thing to shuttle them off overnight with Echo and Brandon. They could manage the children for that long. But what if Dan didn't wake up today? tomorrow? What would she do then? Would she spend all her time at the hospital and ignore her two angels at home? They needed one parent to be there with them; and even more than that, she needed them with her.

She had a hard enough time trying to figure out what to say to this man lying in the bed. But she needed to talk, to do something. He needed to know she was here, pulling for him, fighting for him, fighting for their time together.

"Dan, do you remember our first date?" Telia chuckled to herself. "I'm

At the Touch of Love

surprised we made it to date number two."

Dan and Telia's first date consisted of a cooking class. They pulled up in front of the Calphalon Cooking Center. As Telia began to open her door, Dan touched her arm, "Hold on, Speedy."

He hustled around to the passenger side of the truck and opened her door. She was feeling so warm and fuzzy from the manners that she missed the foot rail and basically fell into Dan's strong arms. In her heels, they weren't eye to eye, given his six-foot-one height. However, even through his coat, she could feel the strength of his chest.

He chuckled a bit. "Falling for me already, huh?"

Telia clamped her lips shut to keep the "YES! YES! YES!" that was pushing through her mind from escaping. Once she controlled her mind, she replied, "That's a big step you have there."

"Well, it makes it easier to get you in my arms that way."

Then, they went to the cooking class. She's in white, and they are learning how to cook paella. She stood off to the side most of the evening, making Dan—dressed in black— cook while she sipped her white wine.

Occasionally, she would chop an onion. The instructor would come by and check on their progress. Dan kept her entertained, made her laugh, and made her think. Then, he brought over the spoon to let her taste. Even though she was wearing an apron and he held his hand underneath the spoon and she slurped as neatly as she could, it dribbled on her collar.

She immediately grabbed the wet wipes that she kept in her purse to try to minimize the damage, but that was merely the first volley.

As they sat down to eat, she placed a napkin under her chin and on her lap.

Telia lifted her eyebrows playfully. "When you were a kid playing doctor, were you always the dermatologist?"

"No, I was the OB-GYN."

Telia snorted laughter. "Yeah, right. That's what all men say."

Dan chuckled. "No, seriously," Dan's brows furrowed. "Wait a minute. You're too far away." He got up and pulled Telia's chair next to his while she was still in it.

"Ohh," Telia exclaimed, surprised by his plan. He rearranged the plates.

He smiled, "Better. No, I was planning on being a doctor. I settled on dermatology my senior year in high school when I had to go to one for acne." Lifting the left side of his mouth in a self-deprecating smile. "And by go to one, I mean my dad, who was a dermatologist."

Dan reached over with his fork. "Here, let me help you with that." He placed one arm around her chair and began feeding her. What are you supposed to do when your man starts feeding you? You eat. That's pretty much it. However, he was doing it with one hand; and she was getting more nervous by his closeness, intoxicated by his smell, and then the arm that was around her chair was placed on her shoulders and he began rubbing her arm.

The minute he touched her an electric shock blasted up her arm, causing her to knock the portion of food on his fork down her shirt, making her hit the plate, and flip it into her lap.

Telia felt exposed like a nudist at the Mormon Church, and a mess. This was more than wet wipes could clean up. She wanted to cry. She wanted to throw a tantrum first and then cry. No … curse, throw a tantrum, and then cry. She noticed Dr. Dan's jaw clenching unnaturally tight. His eyes were glistening with tears.

She eyeballed him hard. "Are you laughing? Are you really laughing at me and my ruined outfit? No sympathy. No concern. Just mirth."

The minute she said mirth, Dan exploded in laughter. While the instructor was trying to come to her aid and guide her to the bathroom, Dan was still bent over at the waist, cracking up laughing. By the time she got back to the table, Dan's laughter was under control and the table was cleaned off. Her outfit was, of course, ruined.

She was starving, but refused to stand there one more minute. Dan helped her with her coat and held the door while she walked outside. When he opened the passenger door, he stopped her.

Dan grazed her arm. "Just so you know. I felt it, too."

Telia scanned his body like the airport security machine and scowled, "What?"

"The jolt. There was something there wasn't it."

Did they turn up the heat? Outside? "I guess." Telia wanted to fan

At the Touch of Love

herself, but she seemed to be the only person whose temp shot up like she'd been dropped at the equator.

"I'm sorry for laughing, but your expression. And then, who says 'mirth.' It was too much, I couldn't."

Dr. Dan stopped her movement with a finger trailing down her arm. "You know I am a doctor. I have a perfect prescription to help this out."

Shit. But in for a penny in for a pound. "Fine."

"If we have a jolt of electricity when we touch, I say we touch more often." Dan leaned in and gingerly placed his lips against Telia's. Again a jolt, but softer, more subtle this time.

He pulled back. "See, better already."

Telia closed her eyes as he leaned in again. This time he whispered a poem that she later found out was E.E. Cummings.

By the time Dan got to the second stanza, Telia barely breathed. Her body fed off the energy of Dan's. Who needed oxygen?

There is no woman in this world who has a defense against a fine man regaling them with poetry. He could have thrown her over the hood of his car at noon on North Michigan and peeled back her top, and she would have done nothing to stop him.

Telia leaned in, gently introducing her tongue to the kiss. He began to aggressively claim her mouth. He pulled her close until their bodies were completely touching.

They pulled apart and just stared at each other. Snowflakes began to fall. Telia smiled and gently brushed a flake from his eyelash. "Okay, that was worth this whole outfit."

Dan gave her another gentle kiss before helping her into the truck. "And that's only the beginning."

CHAPTER 17

Brandon smiled as he watched Echo run up the stairs. He'd pay cash money to learn what thoughts were rolling around in her head. He'd also give up cash money to be that coffee cup. The way her hands wrapped around the base while her pursed lips made contact with the rim definitely perked up his morning. His touch came as much from her flush face as it did the yearning to caress her skin.

He stood to straighten up the kitchen, not that it needed much. But he needed to keep his hands busy and off Echo. As he swept the two crumbs from his toast, his phone buzzed. Brandon didn't recognize the number, but considering how many people at the hospital had his cell number, he always just answered, "Dr. Hall."

"Hey, baby." Brandon slammed his body in the chair as his head dropped down to the table. Apparently, divorce wasn't enough to get Susan out of his life. Neither was blocking her number, since she kept calling from different phone numbers.

"Don't you have a new man to harass now? What happened to Dr. Phillips?" Susan giggled, which meant she needed something. She only called for two reasons, to curse him out just because she remembered some imagined slight or to ask him for something.

Susan purred, "Don't be like that. I wanted to see how you were doing.

I heard about Dan's accident. I'm sorry."

Susan had always liked Dan. It's possible she liked him a bit too much. One day, Susan laughed at something Dan said and placed her arm on Dan's sleeve. Telia plucked Susan's hand up by the tip of her fingers saying, "Sweetie, don't touch my man."

Susan always searched for the come up, which is why Telia didn't like or trust her. They circled each other like sumo wrestlers. One day, he knew Telia would have jumped Susan, slammed her to the ground, and stood on her back, if Susan hadn't disappeared from Telia's life when Brandon divorced her.

Even Mrs. Ellison held a high level of disdain for Susan. She pulled him to the side one day. "I hope you had that one sign a prenup. With her type, it's a necessity."

The best thing Susan did was cheat on him with the neurosurgeon, Dr. Phillips. Once the hospital grapevine got a hold of that tidbit, Brandon hired a private detective, got hard evidence, and filed divorce papers before Susan could blink twice. And yet, she's still on the other side of the phone.

Brandon responded, "Dan's fine. Thanks for checking."

"Tsk," Susan continued. "Being in a coma isn't fine. It must be hard for you. I heard Telia spent the night at the hospital. I can come over to console you if you'd like."

He snorted. Brandon knew Dr. Phillips, the neurosurgeon who was unfortunate enough to be Susan's current man, loved women. He might even say he loved Susan, but no woman had ever called the 54-year-old man husband. Susan's come up turned from an easy hike up a well-worn mountain path to a slow hike up a steep hill.

Brandon declined the consolation. "No, thank you. I'm at Dan and Telia's house with the children."

She isn't crazy enough to show up at Telia's house. To this day, Telia glares at her like she's looking for an excuse to shove her Manolos up Susan's ass.

Susan dropped her voice, "Well, I can always stop by your place later."

Brandon tapped his forehead lightly against the table. "What do you want, Susan?"

He could hear the smile in her voice as she answered, "Baby, you know what I want?"

In less than a minute, his life had become a bad porn movie. All he needed was a flat bass guitar in the background and the scene would be complete. "I'm hanging up."

"Wait. Wait." Susan's voice laced with irritation. "I can't even joke with you anymore."

Brandon couldn't do this. "Hanging up."

"Fine," Susan huffed. "I need a few extra dollars this month."

Brandon met the request with silence. This wasn't the first time that Susan asked him for money. His fault really. He compared it to paying for peace. If he wrote her a check, she'd disappear for a couple of months.

Dan had once asked him if keeping Susan in his life, even in a financial capacity, was peaceful. He still hadn't gotten back to Dan regarding that; but since he had just banged his head against the table, odds are the answer was no.

He lifted his head from the table and leaned back in the chair, rubbing his eyes in pure exhaustion, which he felt every time he heard Susan's voice. "You get alimony. That is supposed to sustain you."

He could hear the motor in Susan's mind rotating from one scenario to another. He guessed she settled on anger. "You know my alimony is bullshit. How am I supposed to pay my rent, my bills, and shop with the little bit of money you give me?"

And because Brandon couldn't help himself, he uttered, "Try budgeting. As for shopping, there's always Goodwill."

The tirade began: how he didn't care about her, how he never cared about her, how he left her alone all the time, how he didn't love her, how he never loved her. After a while, Brandon pulled the phone away from his ear and just stared at it, but he heard a change in her tone. Anger led to something worse. He could feel it like a needle pushing its way into a spine.

"You act like you're all high and mighty now. Won't act like this when your family finds out that your G-Ma committed suicide, instead of the accidental medical overdose like everyone thought. The question is, what else did the good doctor do for his dear demented grandmother? Question is, did

At the Touch of Love

she administer a lethal dose of her medication, or did you?"

Suddenly, he heard a shuffle behind him. Turning, his gaze met with Echo holding Rocky on her hip and with Shelley's hand in hers. Echo asked, "Is that Susan?"

He heard a screech from the phone right before he just hung up.

CHAPTER 18

The consistent beeping of the monitor broke through Telia's reminiscing. Beep. Quiet. Beep. Quiet. The same rhythm of their relationship. She wanted fun, excitement, and jolts of chemistry; while he wanted trust, faith, and permanency. The fact is they had both, though not in the way they wanted. That unsolved expectation stood between them like a chasm of quicksand.

Telia smiled at Dan. "You know what, Dr. Dan. I don't think that I've told you that sometimes I still feel that jolt when you touch me or when you kiss me. Seven years later and you affect me the same way you did on that first date."

At that exact moment, Mrs. Ellison made her entrance into Dan's hospital room, followed by a tech to take Dan's stats. Telia couldn't help closing her eyes for a few moments before opening them and smiling her welcome to Dan's mother.

Mrs. Ellison met Telia's smile with those infamous lemon lips, pursed and disapproving. Mrs. Ellison brought a tote bag of stress everywhere she went. She was like Oprah in reverse, giving away migraines—a headache for you, a headache for you, and three headaches a day for you.

Telia needed to call Dan's financial planner. Why would he give his mother control of his money? He might as well have made her a reservation at the nearest homeless shelter. Friends and family described Mrs. Ellison in different ways. Generous wasn't among them.

Mrs. Ellison actually used air quotes when she asked about Telia's 'job.' Which she considered pedestrian. You would think that due to Mrs. Ellison's low opinion of Telia that the old bat would think that Telia had found the perfect career. No, Dobson women didn't need to work. Telia wasn't a Dobson or an Ellison. She could do whatever she damn well pleased.

And Mrs. Ellison always called her dear in such a dismissive fashion. Telia wanted to slap that woman into next Tuesday and leave her there. "What are you working on now, Dear? How was your day, Dear? Oh, that's nice, Dear, is Dan around?" However, Dan wouldn't appreciate Telia slapping his mother. At least she thought he'd have issues with it. She probably should have asked him directly.

The only benefit to their nonexistent relationship was that Mrs. Ellison kept her distance from Telia, which was fine with her. The last thing she wanted to contend with on a daily basis was a meddling mother-in-law. The major part of Dan's job was to appease his mother. Telia handled running interference from her overprotective father and brother, who were both gracious enough to live in Wisconsin and only made a guest appearance for holidays and special occasions.

That woman's lips were puckered once again, as though she'd been sucking on lemons for a living. "Did he wake up?"

Clearly, she could see the man was still comatose in the bed. Why was she asking stupid questions? *Patience.*

Telia bit down on her reply and shook her head.

"Oh. Well, how are you holding up, dear?" Mrs. Ellison asked as she placed an Hermes purse on the bedside table, pushing aside Telia's Michael Kors in the process.

"I'm doing okay. I guess."

Mrs. Ellison eyed Telia's form-fitting burgundy dress, which was perfect for spending a night out with Echo, but not so much for a visit at the bedside of an unresponsive husband. "Well, I see you haven't quite made it home to, umm, freshen up. Have you, dear?"

Telia worked her jaw back and forth, fighting the immediate urge to scream, "No, not yet."

"Well, dear, I'm sure you're doing your best." Mrs. Ellison folded her manicured hands into her lap.

Thou shall not kill. Thou shall not kill. Not even the mother-in-law? No. No. Thou shall not kill.

Nodding, Telia answered, "I'm trying."

"So ..." Mrs. Ellison started before she scanned the room, as if searching for someone to help break the awkwardness that had settled in for a long stay. "What were you saying when I entered?"

Telia gave Dan's hand a little pinch, so he'd do that thing he normally did—be a buffer between this woman's passive aggressiveness and Telia's temper. *Now would be a good time to join in the conversation.* "Talking about our first date."

Mrs. Ellison brightened. "Well, don't let me stop you, dear." She nodded her approval and moved a few feet to the right and perched on the edge of the seat by the door. "Go ahead."

Really? As if Telia needed *her* permission to talk to Dan about anything.

"Oh, I'm done now," she said, eyeing the exit.

Telia inhaled a deep breath. "If Dan just had an accident yesterday, how could you possibly have access to his money today? It's not like the bank knows he's in a coma. So I can reimburse you after all."

Mrs. Ellison chuckled. "Of course they know. I called his financial planner, Mr. Grimm, last night. I took care of the paperwork this morning before I came here. So no need to worry your pretty little head." And then Mrs. Ellison continued, "Shelley and Rocky's money is safe and sound."

Telia needed a scalpel, just one slide, one simple slide.

"So yesterday I could have reimbursed you for everything. But you told me I couldn't. Today, you signed papers to ensure it. That's our money, mine and Dan's."

Mrs. Ellison chuckled. "No, dear, actually that money belongs to my family—a long line of Dobsons—unless I'm underestimating how much you make, dear."

"I think I'm going to check in on Echo, Brandon, and the kids. Give you some time alone with Dan."

Telia unfolded her body from the vinyl chair and walked toward the door. "Just to let you know, I'm going to let Shelley spend some time with Dan today."

Mrs. Ellison's glare locked on Telia. "Do you think that's wise, dear?"

"Well, you know Shelley," she said with a pointed look at the woman who was becoming more irritating than ten mosquito bites in the center of her back. "I can't keep them apart for long. And it might help for him to hear her voice."

"She's so young, though, d—"

"I think we just have to reassure her that he's fine," Telia snapped before another of those godforsaken "dears" rolled off the woman's lips. "He's sleeping, but he'd love to hear her voice so he can dream about her." She opened the door to exit. "That's the best I have right now. Plus, she really wants to see her father."

Mrs. Ellison pressed her lips together in that all too familiar position. "I'm sure she does; and since you spoil her, you just caved, as usual. You shouldn't spoil the children, dear. Makes them impossible when they get older."

"And you would know that because you were mother of the year?" Telia retorted before she could keep the words from tripping over her lips. Shaking at her own cruelty, she immediately followed it with, "I'm sorry, that was uncalled for."

"Yes, it was," Mrs. Ellison's eyes narrowed as she dug into her purse. "You must be hungry. Would you like a few dollars to get yourself something to eat, dear?"

Telia stomped out of the door before she tried to do a tracheotomy on Mrs. Ellison with a straw, like she saw on television. Telia would love to see Mrs. Ellison try to talk with a straw sticking out of her esophagus.

Telia leaned against the wall outside Dan's door. She just needed one minute to get her thoughts together.

As much as she hated to admit it, Mrs. Ellison was right. She did need some new clothes, but she didn't want to leave Dan. Granted, his mother could handle a few hours, but who could understand how much damage that woman could do in a short amount of time. Should she stay or should she go?

A pair of arms encircled her body and she tensed at the fact that those arms were familiar, but they weren't Dan's. She glanced upward to find a pair of sympathy-filled eyes shining back at her. Telia returned her friend's embrace. "Hey, you. I was just about to give you a call." She lay her head on Echo's shoulders, asking, "Where are the kids?"

Echo wiggled her eyebrows like a comedian. "Temporarily diverted by Brandon. He's quick, alright. We saw you when we turned the corner, but the kids hadn't laid eyes on you yet. I think he's lost somewhere on this floor. Shelley won't be put off for long. That girl is on a mission."

Telia stood up to her full high-heel-aided six feet and two inches. "I guess I'd better prepare myself to prepare her for seeing her father."

Echo held up a bag. "You'll be happy to know I brought over a ton of stuff you didn't ask for. Actually, I just grabbed your flight toiletry bag and some clothes from your closet."

Telia snatched the bag from Echo, relieved that her earlier decision was now a moot point. "You're the greatest." Lowering her voice," she added, "Mrs. Ellison is already staring at me, like I spent last night mud wrestling in a little hole in the wall and showed up here today."

Echo glanced around. "I've never spent the night as a guest of a hospital. You sure there's no mud wrestling. With the money from gambling, everyone would have free healthcare."

Shelley's angry voice rang out loud and clear, "How can you get lost at your own hospital?!"

Telia grimaced, "He will *never* live that one down."

"Mommy." Shelley ran up as Telia scooped her for a hug.

"Ahh, I missed you, baby bug."

Shelley smiled. "I missed you, too. Mommy." Then that smile disappeared as quickly as it had come. "How's Daddy?"

"He's still asleep, but the doctors say he's doing okay."

"If he's okay, Why's he still asleep?" Innocence laced Shelley's voice, but that little girl didn't fool anyone. Sharp was not the word.

"Well, I told you his body needs sleep to recover. The doctors did what they needed to do. He's sleeping, which is what he needs to do. He'll wake up

At the Touch of Love

when he's better," Telia explained. "Until that time, we're going to be patient."

Brandon handed Rocky over as soon as Telia put Shelley down. Rocky gave her a big kiss on the cheek. "Mommy." And then he was off talking in that one-year-old language that only Shelley and possibly his stuffed animals truly understood.

Telia nodded at what seemed to be the appropriate spots, but she only understood a few words interspersed with the others. There was apparently something going on with his shoes and the sky or ceiling maybe.

After Rocky slowed down, Telia merely said, "Well, you don't say." That seemed to satisfy her son that his issues had been addressed.

Bending down to her daughter, Telia began a conversation that she'd rather cut off her left pinkie than to have. "Shelley, I need your help. Although your dad is asleep, it helps when he hears voices of the people he loves. Now his face may be a bit shocking. It's," she shifted a look toward Brandon and Echo, who nodded for her to continue, "scraped up a bit. But he's strong. The doctors said that we need to talk to him, to keep him company while he's sleeping. He can't respond, but hearing our voices helps. Would you like to spend some time talking to Daddy? If you'd rather not, I understand. I don't want you to be scared."

"I won't be scared, Mommy," Shelley said with all the certainty of a child who believed in magic and rainbows. "I can talk to Daddy."

This should not be a conversation to have with a six-year-old. But this was today's reality. "Well, Mother Ellison is visiting too."

Shelley folded her arms. "Mother Ellison isn't my friend."

The adults glanced around at each other, shocked. Taking her friendship away meant Shelley was truly ticked about something.

"Why isn't she your friend, baby bug?" Telia inquired bending to see Shelley's eyes.

"Mother Ellison was mean to Daddy—and Mommy," Shelley whispered with a comforting pat on her shoulder. "I don't think she likes you."

Brandon and Echo tried to silence their chuckles by clamping their hands over their mouths, but Telia wasn't fooled.

"Why do you say that, baby?" Telia probed.

"I know I wasn't supposed to listen, but Rachel wanted to make us a snack and I had to ask Daddy if we could have one and I heard them talking and Mother Ellison wasn't very nice."

Telia ran back through her mental Rolodex and came up empty. "When was this?"

Shelley traced the floor with her shoe. "The night Daddy had the accident."

"You were at Mother Ellison's?"

Shelley nodded. "Before we went for ice cream, Daddy drove to Mother Ellison's house."

Brandon and Echo exchanged looks, but didn't utter a word. "Shelley, baby, do you want to visit when Mother Ellison leaves?"

"No, Mommy," Shelley verified. "Daddy needs me. Let's go."

Echo took hold of Rocky and pulled a piece of candy out of her purse. She never had any problems bribing kids. To be honest, that was how she earned her favorite-aunt title. That, and since, technically, there wasn't any other competition.

Rocky's eyes widened like the door opening on a refrigerator, as he recognized his favorite food group. And yes, candy was a food group that rated right up there with chocolate. His eyes stayed on Echo unwrapping the candy, as Telia quickly ushered Shelley into the room.

Shelley jumped onto Dan's bed, practically ignoring her grandmother, who was scowling so hard at Dan that the heat from her should have given him a tan.

Mrs. Ellison repeated, "I'm going to state again that she shouldn't be here."

"I'm gonna talk to him," Shelley whispered, studying that familiar figure in the bed. "Mommy said it's important, even though he's asleep."

Mrs. Ellison tightened her fists in her lap, but nodded.

Shelley piped up, "Mommy, what should I talk to him about?"

"Have you told him all about Chrissy's birthday party, yet?" Telia prompted, inwardly grateful that Mrs. Ellison didn't press the issue any further.

Shelley pondered for a minute. "No, I forgot."

As Shelley launched into her story, Telia rushed out of the room. Brandon walked her to the staff locker room to take a quick shower. Echo stood in the corner of the room as a surrogate devil for Mrs. Ellison to glare at until Telia rushed through the door twenty minutes later.

"Okay, Shelley, babe," Telia said when she returned, a bit refreshed and a little more prepared for mental sparring. "I'm going to go grab something in the cafeteria. You want to come with me?"

"I want to stay with Dad."

Telia blinked twice. Will wonders never cease? Somebody besides Christoff wanted to be in the same room as Mrs. Ellison, "Okay, babe."

As Telia walked outside the door, Rocky was doing the I'm-happy-I'm-eating-food rock in Echo's arms. "You spoil that little boy. Doesn't she, baby?" Telia reached in and tickled his stomach.

Rocky giggled. "Candy!"

Telia gave Echo a fake "mean stare." "Yes, I see that Titi CoCo gave you candy. Even though she won't be paying for one dentist appointment."

Echo lowered her gaze, but only a little; and Telia could swear that the woman was smiling.

Brandon nodded towards the door. "How's Shelley?"

Telia shrugged. "I think she's okay. She's telling stories."

"Brandon, would you mind keeping them company while Echo and I grab something to eat?"

Brandon smiled. "No problem." He straightened his collar and winked at Echo.

Echo cut her eyes over to Brandon. "Brown nose."

Telia watched the exchange and grinned. "Interesting. What's going on with that?"

CHAPTER 19

Echo placed Rocky on the floor and grabbed his hand before he had the option of running away. The boy's need for speed sent him careening into his highest gear the minute his body felt unencumbered.

Telia pushed Echo with her shoulder. "Spent the night with Dr. Hall, huh?"

Echo's eyes double in size before settling back in their sockets. "I slept in the guest room. He camped out in the office. That doesn't count as spending the night."

"Girl, please," she replied with a sly smile. "You mean, you didn't imagine him naked in the shower."

"No, absolutely not." She bit her lip, as if contemplating her next words. "But the dream I had last night. Girl. *Gurl!*"

"Was he naked in the dream?"

"Head to freaking toe."

Telia covered a hand over her bosom and squealed. Rocky squealed and laughed, clapping at whatever had made his mom happy. Nurse and patients alike were turning to check out the commotion.

"Inside voice," Echo warned.

"Okay. Okay," Telia agreed, sighing with pleasure. "I need something to be happy about. "He hasn't dated anyone seriously since," she crooked her fingers as quotes, "The Crazy One."

Echo shuddered. "Would you? If I'd been married to that shrew, I would've put my genitals in a safety deposit box somewhere."

"Mental picture," Telia said, screwing up her face for comic effect. "But you might be the one to ease his aching heart." Telia reached over and slid Rocky along her leg until he settled into her arms. "Isn't that right Rock Rock? You want Titi CoCo to give Uncle Brandon big kisses, don't you?" Telia placed a few loud kisses on his face. Rocky laughed.

"Kiss. Kiss," Rocky chanted.

"See," Telia said smugly, "even Rocky approves."

"That doesn't count. He's a baby. He doesn't know anything about relationships—other than the fact that he tends to love women who are a little over-endowed."

Telia gave Echo's bosom a quick glance and said, "So how does that explain you?"

"I … have candy."

"My baby is brilliant." Telia nuzzled Rocky. "Don't listen to Titi CoCo. She's been sitting in a tree K-I-S-S-I-N-G."

"It wasn't a tree. It was a truck. Thank you," Echo amended as Rocky reached a hand out to touch her face. "And I don't think we actually kissed in my dream."

Telia lifted her left brow. "So just straight action. Interesting?" She let it go for now. At least Echo was much better than she was yesterday. Maybe dream sex could do that.

Telia ordered a fruit smoothie and a boiled egg. Echo ordered a coffee. They sat down in a booth that gave them a view of the distant Chicago skyline. Telia grabbed the diaper bag from Echo and slid out one of the over-sized crayons and a piece of paper to keep him occupied.

Rocky pointed at her clear plastic container. "Juice?" Telia grinned and opened the lid to tilt it towards his lips. Not a drop missed, as he sipped and then smiled before putting his attention on his masterpiece.

Although the cafeteria was bustling with people talking and laughing, their table was suspiciously quiet. Rocky started humming to himself, evidently feeling the need to fill the unusual void.

Echo reached over and touched Telia's arm. "Talk to me."

Telia tried to come up with the right words to describe how she felt. Everything was jumbled in her head. "You haven't seen him yet. It's … It's him. But it's not. It's his body, but not his soul. It's so weird."

Echo nodded. "I understand."

"And I have to talk to him. About whatever. But he doesn't respond," Telia sighed. "Last night, I crawled into bed with him. It was all wrong. Normally, he pulls me to him. He cradles my rear with," Telia glanced over to make sure Rocky was engaged. "with his special place."

Echo jumped and the coffee cup tilted. She barely managed to right it before it spilled.

"Echo. What the hell?"

Her hands shook slightly, as she presented the coffee and saucer for inspection. "We're fine. See, cat-like reflexes."

Telia hitched her head. "Why are you so red?"

Echo opened her eyes wide, as though the action could return her normal shade of cinnamon skin. "Hmmm.

Telia squinted long enough to pierce Echo's attempt at being nonchalant until Echo was squirming. "That dream you had last night. He was behind you, wasn't he?"

Echo didn't respond.

"Wow. You have it bad."

Rocky gestured toward the diaper bag.

"We were talking about you and Dr. Dan," Echo tried to redirect the conversation away from herself.

"That's how he made me feel the first month we dated." Telia extracted another crayon from the package and handed it to Rocky. "I was a nervous wreck and a complete klutz. I was forever stumbling, tripping, spilling, and dropping. He would just give me this knowing, confident smirk. He knew exactly what he was doing to me. And he loved it."

Echo clenched her teeth, not appreciating the parallels that her friend

At the Touch of Love

was trying to draw between two totally different relationships. "I didn't spill anything. I almost spilled something. Not the same. Brandon and I aren't dating. We are co-babysitting your kids. Brandon has never shown interest in me."

Telia raised one eyebrow and then concentrated on her egg like it had been laid by the Golden Goose. "Of course, he hasn't."

Echo glared at the blandness of her friend's tone. "What do you know?"

"Nothing," she shrugged. "It doesn't matter. You aren't dating, remember. But he is going to drive you home for fresh clothes. Unless …," Telia's eyes opened wide in a portrayal of fake innocence. "You want Mrs. Ellison to drive you?"

"The hell you say," Echo snarled. "I'd order an Uber from the depths of Hell with Satan smiling at me from the app before Mrs. Ellison."

Telia held out her fist for a pound and Echo obliged. "That's my girl."

CHAPTER 20

Echo paused, deciding between hurling herself into oncoming traffic or at Brandon. Just being in his car, smelling his essence turned her insides into leaky plumbing.

She wished her shorts were longer and the leather wasn't caressing her skin quite so softly. She kept her eyes forward, focusing on the eclectic array of storefronts as they drove to her one-bedroom apartment in the South Loop area.

It would be just her luck he'd want to come inside for some reason. Since no one of the male gender besides the cable guy, the maintenance man, or the Peapod delivery guy had seen the inside of the place since she'd moved in. She never concerned herself with trying to make it presentable to anyone but herself. She followed her mother's ten-minute rule. If she couldn't make her public spaces company ready in ten minutes, then she had work to do.

Brandon lip-synced along with Maxwell's *Something, Something,* playing on the R&B station he tuned into.

Even though she pays me no attention ...

She witnessed the words as they formed on his lips, although no sound escaped.

All I wanna show is my affection ...

If he could sing as well, the only way she would keep from straddling him would be choosing to jump into traffic.

Lose myself inside her ebony ...

The good old tuck and roll should work.

But she ain't even checking me ...

What the hell was wrong with her? And was he sending out subliminal messages? Why was he singing along with this particular song, but he had skipped over Donnell Jones *Where I Wanna Be*, BlackStreet's *No Diggity* and Tupac's *I Get Around,* but this song somehow received that added touch of his sexy voice?

"So Echo, tell me a bit about yourself. Like what do you do for a living?" Brandon's shift from singing to speaking caused her to readjust her position in her seat. This was ridiculous. *He's only a man.*

Yes, but he was a man with that kind of swagger that made great-grandmothers bat their eyelashes. And for some reason, the vibe between them generated enough electricity to power a small village.

"Well, I was a data analyst. But I was recently downsized, along with half the workforce at Corgan Financial Management. But thanks for bringing that up."

Brandon grimaced an apology, and put one to voice. "I'm sorry. Would yesterday have been your work anniversary?"

Echo examined Brandon through lowered lashes. "You're determined to find out what yesterday was." Echo knew how to shut this particular line of questioning down. "Yesterday was the anniversary of my parents' death."

Brandon did a double take and stared at Echo.

"Hey, eyes on the road," she warned, glaring over at him. "They died in a car crash. I would prefer if history did not repeat itself."

Brandon snatched his gaze from her and quickly focused on the road. "Sorry."

"Yeah." Echo closed her eyes and leaned her head against the back of the seat.

After riding a few minutes in silence, Brandon asked, "What were they like, your parents?"

"Excuse me?" Her eyes popped open. No one with the exception of

Telia ever talked about her parents. Telia would reference them all the time, trying to keep the best parts of them alive for Echo. Most of her friends mumbled their apologies, then avoided the topic—and her—like the plague. Sometimes, even Echo believed the stork dropped her off full grown at college. But it was softer moments with Telia that made the loss bearable ... at times.

"You remember the time when your mother threatened to come to the homecoming dance with us?" Telia giggled as she poked Echo in the ribs. "And I thought she was joking and told her she could come?"

Echo cringed at that memory that started when they were putting the finishing touches on their gowns.

Echo's mother hopped in the family car and followed their limo for a mile before she turned around. All the while, a panic-stricken Telia had her eyesight glued to the back window, and Echo tried to calm her down.

Echo always tried to keep a straight face, but she always dissolved into giggles. "She scared the bejeebies out of you."

"You know I wasn't allowed to date," Telia responded, all smiles wiped from her face. "And I didn't know how I was going to explain Jerry meeting me at the door with a corsage."

Echo giggled. "Yeah, you had him mesmerized by your senior-year boobs."

"Indeed." Telia ran her hand down her curves. "Funny, the more I developed, the crazier your mom got."

"I think she felt responsible for both of our virtues." Echo would lean her head on Telia's shoulder.

Telia leaned her cheek against Echo's hair. "Well, she had to get in line behind my crazy family."

"Yeah, but she was determined nothing was happening on *her* watch."

Echo's mother became the James Bond of parents, when it came to ensuring both her daughter and her other daughter made it through to college with no babies and no baggage.

When Telia and Echo left for college, Echo's mother gave them both a wrapped gift that she made them promise not to open until they reached college. Condoms.

"Well, it worked." Telia gently bumped her head against Echo's.

At the Touch of Love

And now, Brandon was asking her to talk about the people who had been snatched away so quickly that she felt the Grim Reaper had to have needed them to meet a quota. "Well, they were from the East Coast, so we buried them in Philadelphia," she explained, fast forwarding to the end of what she could say about her parents. "It was supposed to be easier for their family to visit them."

"I don't want to know about their death," Brandon's voice softened. "Tell me your best memory of them."

Echo remained silent for a minute. The best memory? The. Best. Memory. "As a high school graduation surprise, we went to this revolving restaurant my mother was always talking about. Swirl had a fabulous view of Chicago that kept changing," Echo laughed. "They told us to stay away from the windows, but Mom was kind of crazy. I took this photo of her leaning like she was going to fall through the window and Dad grabbing onto her suit coat as if he was holding her back."

Brandon snickered as Echo tried to picture her parents through a stranger's eyes. For some reason, she wanted him to like them.

"They were seriously crazy at times, like when they walked barefoot in the rainforest in Puerto Rico on a day that was overly wet even for a rainforest, or danced on Michigan Avenue to a panhandler's music." Echo reminisced. "We had fun together, and they had fun with each other." The image of the petite woman with an audacious attitude and quick wit and the dashing, energetic man that was her father came to view. "In a way, I'm glad they died together. I can't picture them separately. You know. They came as a team."

Brandon took his hand off the steering wheel and placed it on her knee. She jerked and his hand slammed into the bottom of the glove compartment.

"Son of a —" Brandon bit off a curse.

Echo grabbed his hand and stroked that smooth skin, trying to take the pain away. "I'm so sorry."

Brandon sneered. "I think kissing it actually makes it feel better."

Echo dropped his hand, as though its temp shot up 210 degrees and stared out of the window. "I hadn't heard that."

Was that a laugh she heard from him?

"What I was going to say before you damn near crushed my hand was that you were lucky." Brandon gingerly laid his hand back on her knee. "It sounds like you had great parents."

Echo closed her eyes and visualized the madhouse that she grew up in. "I was … lucky. I always wanted that special kind of love. You know, to marry my best friend and have it to be fun and fulfilling." She sighed, forcing the melancholy to make a quick exit. "So what made you marry someone like Susan?"

Brandon removed his hand from her knee and put it back on the steering wheel. "She didn't start out crazy."

Echo drew her lips to the side and gave him that "Whatcha' talkin' bout Willis" look made famous by the precocious child actor on *Different Strokes*. "I think that secretly men love crazy women. They love the drama. I know a ton of sane single women. But the true nutcases always have a man."

"She didn't start out with me as crazy. She was pleasant to be around. She took care of me. And for someone who was truly focused on our relationship and my career, that's what I thought was important." Brandon tapped an unfamiliar beat on the steering wheel.

"Every man I know who's currently hitched to some crazy broad says they started out nice. They act like there weren't any indications that crazy was waiting to jump out like 'hee-ya.'". Echo accompanied the yell with her best karate chop. Brandon took in that weak attempt and roared with laughter.

"No, I'm serious," he added. "Everything was great until it wasn't."

Sort of like her life. Sort of like Dan, right.

"The first time I met Susan I knew something was off," Echo admitted.

"Your crazy-lady radar must be better than mine," Brandon confessed.

Echo didn't let it go. "Did you ever talk to her? Like *really* talk to her before you all got together."

"Yes, but afterwards I figured out that we were never friends in that sense. We didn't tell each other secrets. We didn't talk about the things that mattered. On the surface, we were great." Brandon tilted his head in thought. "I don't think she even knew my middle name when we got married."

Echo burst out laughing. "Even I know your middle name."

Tightening his hand around the steering wheel. "It's a family name."

"It's a letter," she clarified. "Brandon W Hall. Who slides through with just a letter?"

"All of the first-born men in my family have a W as their middle name."

"Well, there should be a declaration at the next family reunion to stop the madness. Echo crowed, giving him a playful tap on the arm. No more alphabet names."

Brandon paused, giving her a side eye while trying to keep his focus on the road. "Wait a minute. Your name is Echo."

"That counts," she shot back. "It's four letters."

"Maybe, but you're not your own person. You're a reflection, a repeat."

Snorting, she responded, "Whatever. But I'll take Echo over Dubya any day. And you still didn't answer the question."

Brandon compressed his lips before proceeding. "Susan wanted a husband, and I was ready to get married," he acknowledged. "I don't know if she really wanted me the person. Me, the doctor absolutely. Brandon Dubya Hall?" he admitted with a glance at Echo. "I'm not sure."

Echo tried to resolve what he said with his ex. "Why do you say that?"

"Everything was about image: What she could say to her friends, what I did, what I did for her. It was all pushed outward. It wasn't concentrated on our marriage, but what everyone thought of our marriage."

"Yow." Echo grimaced. "That sounds like a lot of work."

"It wasn't easy," he added.

There was a world of pain in those three words. Wanting to lighten the mood in the car, Echo's eyes twinkled. "Telia and I used to sit in the corner at parties and figure out ways to torture her. She was such an easy mark."

Glancing over, Brandon asked. "Like what?"

Echo raised her eyes to the ceiling of the truck as she flickered through her memory banks. "Oh. The easy one would be as she was walking by, I'd make some type of remark about how cute you were. She never turned, but she shot daggers at me for the rest of the evening." Echo gleefully rubbed her hands together at the memory. "I gave you both a hug when you were leaving, which I think pissed her off even more."

Echo bent over in her seat laughing, trying to catch her breath. "We thought she was going to beat you on the way home."

"So you think I'm cute, huh?"

Echo froze in the middle of her merriment, holding her breath. "This is my street. You need to take a right coming up."

Brandon smoothly executed a right. Echo's breathing accelerated. She actually inhaled and blew out a breath to calm down. He pulled up to the address she gave him and unbuckled her seat belt, as though she'd suddenly reverted back to Shelley's age.

When she tried to hop out of the car, he placed a steadying hand on her arm. The tension coursed through her body like oil gushing through a geyser. Smiling, he got out and jogged around to the passenger side. He opened the door, gave a slight bow, and offered her his hand, "My lady."

She nodded and jumped down to the pavement without touching him. Quickly, she trotted to the apartment, but not quick enough to keep him from following. The tension-filled air in the elevator threatened to suffocate her. Brandon merely leaned against the wall as if he didn't feel a thing. However, his lips stayed locked in a half smile that threatened Echo's sanity.

She unlocked the apartment and walked in, and the image that she'd conjured earlier of a tidy place as its normal state was swept aside as memories of how the previous night ushered in a new reality.

A bowl of soup camped on the table in front of the couch with tissues surrounding it. Several changes of clothes were draped over the armchair, and to the right a crumpled blanket lay on top. The living room, in all its disarray, appeared as if she was recovering from some major illness or a minor tornado.

Brandon slowly circled 180 degrees, taking everything in, including the birthday balloons. "Echo, when was your birthday?"

Echo cursed.

Telia and her flipping birthday balloons.

CHAPTER 21

Mrs. Ellison strode into the room. The confident clack of her heels opposed the soft soles of Christoff's. "You know I was thinking that I could take the children today. Is that okay, dear?"

Telia spent the morning doing two things: She called Dan's financial planner and, sure as shit, her personal account held all the money to which she had direct access. Any account with Dan's name remained locked tighter than Prince's pants, and Mrs. Ellison held the key. Damn Dobson money. She might as well get her tin cup now and beg on the street. That held more allure than asking Mrs. Ellison for anything.

The next step she took included babysitting. She refused to allow the witch to have her money and her kids. Damn that.

After she contacted the nurse, who babysat sometimes in the evening, she called her brother, Remy. "Bro, I need your help."

Remy, true to fashion, replied, "Anything. Dad told me about Dan. I've been trying to reach you."

Telia cut to the chase. "Can you be in Chicago tomorrow?"

"Of course, but—"

"Great. Text me your travel information. I'll need you here in the morning."

Remy responded, as she knew he would, "No problem. But we need to talk—"

Dragging her hand through her head, she added, "Not now. Tomorrow, maybe. I can't now."

"But Telia."

Telia couldn't handle one more item on her plate. "Tomorrow, please."

Remy spent several quiet seconds before he agreed, "Okay."

Sighing relief, Telia nodded. "Great. Fantastic. See you then, brother of mine."

She heard the smile in his voice, "Of course, sister of mine."

Now she had "Mrs.-Ellison-proofed" the babysitting operation.

Not only did she question Mrs. Ellison's motivation, but also Rocky became a magician when unsupervised. Breakable objects appeared in his hand, as if they flew through the air and landed in those pudgy digits. Then they'd just as quickly hit the floor. It wouldn't do for Telia to have to ask Mrs. Ellison for money to replace some pricey artifact that Rocky destroyed.

Telia refused to be stressed about breakable items at a time like this. Plus, Brandon's warning rang in her eardrums like an orchestra cymbal. Her last thought before going to bed the previous night consisted of her children holding the iron gates that led to Mrs. Ellison's house like they were bars in a jail cell.

No, Telia refused to be in a position for that to happen—refused. Mrs. Ellison would not get the children alone; not while Dan was in a coma, and maybe not ever.

"One of the nurses, who babysits for us sometimes, took them out for lunch," Telia responded. "And Brandon already took off work to help out with everything. So I think we're squared away."

Mrs. Ellison's eyes narrowed to slits. Then she lifted her chin and gave Telia a once-over. "Well, I guess you have all of your avenues covered."

Telia's heart raced like the winner of the Kentucky Derby. "I definitely appreciate your offer, but I think we're all set for now. By the way, what happened last night? What did you say to upset Dan when he came over?"

Both Mrs. Ellison and Christoff paused before locking eyes. "We discussed family business, dear; nothing for you to worry about."

"Christoff is clearly aware. He's not family," Telia retorted.

At the Touch of Love

Mrs. Ellison turned to open the door. "I'm more than willing to put you on the Dobson payroll, especially since you quit your job without another one to manage your expenses. Which job would you like? I know you're accustomed to being a working girl."

Did Mrs. Ellison call her a hoe? Telia wasn't sure, and did not dare to ask for clarification, because at that point, she would have to punch Dan's mother. "Well, you might not consider me family; but my daughter, your granddaughter, said you were mean and that you didn't like me. Where would she get that impression?" Telia demanded.

"Oh, I'm so sorry … if I ever gave you the impression that I did like you, dear?" Mrs. Ellison responded.

Before Telia could retort, Mrs. Ellison swept out of the door followed by Christoff.

With the close of the door, Telia's breath went from DEFCON 5 to DEFCON 1.

"Dan, something is definitely off about Mrs. Ellison." Telia paced the room.

Telia's attention shifted towards the open door, thinking Mrs. Ellison forgot something, but another nurse made her way into the room to check on them.

"How are you holding up, Miss Arthur?" the strawberry blonde inquired.

"How do you think?" Telia wanted to scream. Her husband was in a coma. That meant every time they asked that question, the answer was, "I'm in hell."

Telia knew that wasn't the answer the nurse wanted. And she needed them to take good care of Dan. She just nodded or shrugged or gave a vacant smile whenever the hospital staff inquired about her well-being. If she said she wanted to jump on top of the bed, straddle her husband, grasp the front of his gown, and shake him until he woke up; that might get her kicked out of the hospital at the very least or a permanent stay in the psych ward.

But over the last twenty-four hours, that's exactly how she felt. She probably needed more sleep than she could get at the hospital. Every time she would drift off someone was drawing his blood or checking his pressure; and for a moment she watched him, hoping that something they did would bring him back from wherever he happened to be.

As the nurse left, Telia stroked his hand said, "Dr. Dan, this is Day One and I'm not doing well at all. She lightly tapped his cheek. "Sweetie?"

When he didn't respond, she blew out a breath, slammed her body into the chair by his bed, folded her arms, and glared at him.

"You know I hate waiting," she seethed. "You know I do. And I know I'm a flight attendant, and we wait at gates on the tarmac all the time. I can handle that. I'm used to that. I'll watch a movie or read a book or deal with impatient passengers. I can't even concentrate on a book." She pointed at the television. "Do you have any idea how bad daytime television is? It's making me miss the Disney channel."

Telia paused in her diatribe, as WGN News came on: more murder and mayhem and selling medicinal marijuana. Way to go, Chi Town. She snatched up the remote attached to the bed, switched off the television, and rested her head against the back of the chair.

Talk to him. He can hear you. Don't let him hear how defeated you feel.

"So I don't think I ever told you," she started, "but after our first date, Echo and I had this big argument about whether or not a dermatologist qualified as a doctor. She said it didn't. I took up for you though, sweetie. I gave it that old one-two punch."

Back then, Echo sat across from Telia eating a stack of Bursting with Blueberry pancakes from Sweet Maple Café—one of their favorite spots on Taylor Street. Telia snuck some pancakes off Echo's plate, as retribution for her laughter over the previous evening's events.

Sweet Maple Café had some of the best pancakes in Chicago. On the weekend, the place got packed in a hurry. Patrons barely fit into the vestibule. It was worth it, though. Telia had always thought about getting one of those Sweet Maple Café t-shirts that adorned the wall.

"Echo, I killed it in that outfit last night," she explained. "That's the outfit I would trot out and people would wonder what movie set I walked off of. I was all"—she waved her hand in an elegant flourish—"Diana Ross in Mahogany."

"Well, maybe you need a bit of color. Nothing says I'm a hot momma like residue from spilled paella on the front of a winter white outfit." Snickering, Echo added, "Maybe you can say it's the latest fashion from Paris."

Telia took another bite of pancake as retribution. "Anyway, so he's helping me in the car and he leans in to kiss me."

Echo's lips curved upward. "The first kiss. Do tell, do tell."

"Perfection." Telia's lips started as a small smile, but the memory of how powerful and sensual that touch of his lips to hers had been soon had her showing every molar in her mouth.

"Wow. You're flashing a lot of teeth over there," Echo teased. "So you're telling me lip texture, technique, and taste were all aligned."

"Lips soft like butter, but not wimpy—soft and forceful." Telia pulled at her shirt, using it to fan herself. "Like he knew what he was doing. Technique. Yes, I'd follow his lips wherever they want to take me. And he must've had a mint while I was in the bathroom trying to save my outfit." Telia leaned forward and rested her chin in her hands. "So like I said, perfection."

"Go on with your bad self, Dr. Dan." Echo's forehead scrunched. "Are dermatologists really doctors?"

"Come on, Echo, don't go there," Telia glared.

Echo held up her hands in surrender. "No, I'm serious. Are dermatologists actually doctors? How much schooling does it take to identify acne?"

Giving Echo a disdainful once-over, "Years and years. Just like any other medical profession. There's more to skin, nails, and hands than acne."

Echo stared at Telia then cocked her head. "Right, Google or Bing?"

Telia snapped back to the present. "She was right, Dan. The minute you dropped me off, I went online and found out everything I could about dermatologists, in general, and you, in particular." Telia held up her arms as though her love could see it. "Sue me. When you generate the kind of electricity that we did, it was necessary to make sure you weren't a serial killer."

Telia closed her eyes, taking in the sounds in the hallway. A set of heels clicked past the door as well as the shuffle of one of the staff member's feet. There was a bout of sudden laughter from somewhere, and the happy sounds didn't lift her mood. "Sounds like they're having a party."

The number of prayers that had to come from this wing alone

probably outweighed the ones offering up from all of the megachurches in the surrounding area. ICU. Intensive Care Unit.

Did God see her? Really? Did He understand how much she needed that man lying on the bed appearing more like a scientific experiment than her beloved?

"I guess if you don't wake up today,"—Telia gave Dan a pointed stare—"I'm going to have to call some of your friends to come visit you. I'm thinking any minute you're going to open your eyes." She stroked the fingertips that had swelled with all the fluid they were pumping into him. "But I can't have Shelley giving her Disney revival every day. Our little girl didn't seem too fazed by seeing you this way. She's so strong; she's so much like you, love." Telia's heart hurt. "Remy is coming tomorrow. That will save you from hearing another Frozen revival."

She leaned forward and plucked at the fuzzy balls on the top layers of the thin blanket.

As another bout of crying filtered in from the hallway, Telia took in the depressing pall over this area of the hospital, the stench of disinfectant, and the sudden onset of color codes that spelled death.

"Maybe instead of this, you need to be in the middle of a party," she whispered. "Remember that party you took me to for our second date."

Dan had a book launch party to attend on the following Saturday night after their first date. Although they had remained in contact, their schedules hadn't allowed them to get together any sooner. This time Telia dressed in all black. She wasn't taking any chances.

Chicago had accumulated three feet of snow that week. Flights she was supposed to work had been delayed twice. But nothing could squelch her excitement at seeing Dan again. When he came to the door, she gave him a big hug.

Dan bent back to lift her feet off the ground. "Hey, stranger."

She gave him a big peck on the lips. "Hey, you."

As she gathered her black coat and purse, they chatted about random things. Dan was cool, collected, unruffled; while Telia's mouth had a sudden case of diarrhea, and her hands couldn't stop fidgeting with her purse strap. When she talked, they took on a mind of their own, moving to emphasize each and every point. When they were driving to M Lounge in the South Loop, she had to clasp her hands in her lap to keep them under control.

She held a glass of wine with both hands and eased into a space at the bar that gave her a good angle to see everything. If one more person muttered, "Excuse me," as they tried to squeeze into the invisible space in front of her to try to flag down the bartender, she didn't know if she could keep her heel from digging into their toes.

A jazz band played in the background, as a singer soulfully poured every broken promise and dream into her microphone. Telia watched as Dan made his rounds, talking to various people around the room. She took a gander at his backside, as he talked to the author, who had signed over fifty copies of his new release.

The man must have squats on his gym circuit because a butt that round and firm was a rarity among men. Her fingers were itching to give it a little pinch, or swat, or full-on grab.

Suddenly, Telia's view was blocked by some random guy who leaned in so close she sneezed at the assault of his cologne. "Hey, gorgeous."

Telia's eyes adjusted so that she could inspect the well-lined haircut and pullover shirt sporting the familiar man on a horse. His shirt strained over defined pecks, and he also wore expensive jeans and fancy shoes. She used to date a shoe horse, so she knew expensive kicks when she saw them.

She tried to keep the amusement out of her voice, when she responded with a simple and un-encouraging, "Hello."

"My name is Spencer," he whispered in a voice that held a false ring, as though he had deliberately lowered it for her sake. "What's yours?"

"You're kidding, right?" she countered.

He frowned, and the confidence he displayed found somewhere else to be. "What … kidding about wanting to know your name?"

Telia bit her bottom lip and glanced up through her lashes. "I'm Gorgeous."

He leaned closer and showed a set of teeth that could use a visit to every dental specialist known to man. "I know what you are, but what's your name?"

Telia gave a smirk. "Gorgeous. My mom was optimistic."

Spencer threw his head back and laughed. Telia glanced over his shoulder and saw Dan watching them.

"Well, maybe she called you into existence." Spencer winked.

"Ah, maybe she did," Telia responded as she glanced over Spencer's shoulder to take in more of the club.

"So why are you standing at the bar all alone, Miss Gorgeous?"

Telia's attention made its way back to him. Again, Spencer smiled and she wished fervently that he wouldn't.

In addition to overpowering cologne, he could use a bit of mouthwash in his life. Telia responded, hoping it would speed up the end of their conversation, "Waiting for my date."

Spencer turned around and spotted Dan staring in their direction. "I take it the man whose eyes are boring a hole in my back is your date."

Peering over Spencer's shoulder, she answered, "Yeah."

"Silly man, to leave you alone." Spencer's eyes dropped as he perused her body.

Telia glanced around the room at the various groups talking. Normally, yes, it would've been a stupid move. She'd managed on many occasions to get numbers from men at events such as this, even when her date was standing right by her side.

The level of noise always made it difficult to hold any real conversation. So she'd drink and sometimes catch the eye of someone interesting. Today, that's not what she wanted to do. Today, she only wanted to catch the eye of one man. And he was already looking.

Telia replied, "Maybe he's just confident."

Spencer reached for her hand.

She snatched away, wagging her finger at him. "No touching, Spencer."

"So he has the right to be confident?" Spencer stepped back and turned his head to gaze at Dan and then back at her.

Meeting Dan's eyes, she answered, "Yes, yes, he does."

"That's because you've never had me," he maintained.

Telia kept her eyes locked onto Dan's. "I've never had him, either. But the possibility of him absolutely trumps the promise of you." She shifted her gaze to Spencer. "It's like that sometimes."

At the Touch of Love

"Wow. Guess it is." Spencer glanced over his shoulder again, a little slip in his swagger. "Lucky man."

Telia raised her glass to Dan. "I have a feeling it's going to go both ways."

Dan raised his drink in response, and then made his way over to reclaim the space that Spencer quickly vacated.

Telia stroked a hand over the right side of Dan's face, the monitor still beeping out the signs of his life.

"I always thought it weird that you'd let some other hard leg push up on me. Even then, you were so sure, so secure. I don't know if I could've been." She never thought about losing Dan to another woman. But evidently, death was a mistress who was trying to make Telia well aware of who called the shots.

Telia walked over to the window and stared down on Lincoln Avenue as a CTA bus stopped at the corner. The passengers, dressed in light jackets, lined up to get on the bus, trying to get out of the rain. A guy dashed across the street to make it to the bus and almost got taken out by a cab. The bus driver closed the doors and pulled away from the curb.

Telia was about to shake her head, knowing that it could be another hour before the next one arrived. The bus stopped a few feet away, and the man moved forward and hopped on board.

Telia smiled. She loved a happy ending.

"I was watching you work the room; and I must say, if some chick sidled up and started talking to you, I would've been all up in the mix, but not you. You were always in the cut, watching."

Throwing her head back and laughing, "For a while, I thought you were just a freaky little something, waiting to see if I could get a threesome going. But that wasn't you, either. You're a ready, steady family man. One woman, just one woman for you. And she … And I—" She stopped talking. This couldn't be the end of them.

She walked over, sat on the edge of the bed, and ran the back of her hand down the side of his face. "Yeah, it was that spark. I had never felt it either … with anyone. You believed in the spark even more than I did."

Telia put her forehead on Dan's chest. "Come back to me, Dan. We don't have this kind of time."

CHAPTER 22

"Echo? Echo! When was your birthday?" he repeated, then narrowed his gaze on the items strewn about the place. "It was yesterday, wasn't it?"

His gaze swept over the bright pink and yellow balloons, filled with helium which had them doing a slow bobbing dance close to her couch. That's what Telia was talking about. "Why did you need the tissues and soup? WTF?"

However, there were only tissues, no bucket.

Brandon strolled over to the iPod and turned it on. The first song he came to was *Love Takes Time* by Mariah Carey. He clicked the arrow on the docking station to the next song and the next. Each one mimicked the last with their slow, soulful notes.

Echo's eyes penetrated his consciousness, following him and yet not uttering a word. He settled on a Luther Vandross.

He went to the kitchen, opened a few cabinets, and grabbed a plastic garbage bag. Soon he was in the living room, plucking the tissues off the coffee table, the sofa, the end table, the floor, and dropping them in the garbage. Then he removed the dishes and made a few trips to put them all in the dishwasher.

Echo stood mesmerized, as he, with every motion, was putting away all signs of depression that had hung in the apartment earlier like a cloak on a cold winter day.

Brandon threw the window open, and a fresh breeze of air swept in.

Turning, he scrutinized Echo, who hadn't left her spot by the door. "So on your birthday you focus on the death of your parents, to the point where you're immobilized on your couch?"

"Slow down, Sherlock." Echo glanced around her condo. "I'm fine, healthy as a horse. Yes, yesterday I had a few issues that I refuse to discuss with you; but I'm fine now."

"What's wrong with me? I'm trustworthy. I'm a doctor. I know how to keep a confidence."

Something clicked in Brandon's memory. Dan, Telia, and Brandon sat around the dinner table in their Lincoln Park home discussing Echo.

Telia told him, "With Echo, timing is everything. And this next month is not the time to spring any news—good, bad or indifferent—on her."

"What, is she on a month-long menstrual cycle?" Brandon asked.

Telia's gaze narrowed with a focus that indicated she was thinking of five-hundred ways to end his life, "You sexist mother—"

A bout of laughter erupted, and Brandon couldn't contain himself. His side hurt something fierce, and the pain had him inhaling short breaths.

This was it. This was the reason. He couldn't imagine the kind of pain brought on by the death of both parents. Or the strength needed to rise out of bed on the day that it happened, especially since it happened to be her birthday.

Obviously, Echo read something in his expression, because her feet shuffled backward. "What? What are you doing?"

Brandon took Echo by the hand before nervousness sent her running for the door and guided her over to the couch. He tossed a blanket over her, sat down, and propped her feet up on his legs.

He eased off her shoes and she mumbled, "Oh, brother." Then in a louder voice, she added, "I'm really ticklish."

"I'm sure you'll survive." Brandon peeled off her socks and began to dig his fingers into her instep, stroking any remnants of tension. At first, Echo was stiff and unrelenting.

Her arms stayed folded on her chest, as she tolerated his touch. Then the music and the massage started working their magic. He could feel her relax, little by little. First, her legs lost their tension, and her feet naturally turned to first position then her arms fell by her side. She was no longer glaring at him; her head now rested back on the arm of the couch.

Then she groaned an, "Mmmm, brother," and blew out a slow, even breath.

Brandon smirked as he kept working his hands over the points that he knew would make her melt like butter in a hot skillet. His hands itched to stroke higher on Echo's thighs, but he was trying to be a good boy. But hell, sometimes bad was just as effective. Instinct told him that if hands left her feet, she'd stiffen up again.

These two days must've been like walking through hot coals, carrying ten shopping bags in the depths of hell. Yet, she was doing it. She was doing it. She didn't have to. She could have begged off.

Remembering her expression when she came into the hospital yesterday, he understood her less attentive fog. Yet, she stayed by Telia's side, actively talked and took care of the kids. She had blocked away her own pain to do that.

The more he thought about it and his eyes caressed those gorgeous legs, he shifted her foot away from his crotch. If any part of the body rubbed against his crotch, he'd be rock hard in a minute, and a quickie with Echo wasn't what he had in mind. He planned on enjoying her for much longer than that, for however long it took for his lips to follow his hands, as they explored the soft curves and crevices of her body.

Now with her eyes closed and her mouth slightly open, his lips yearned to connect with hers.

However, sunk into the depths of her own pain, she had found the strength to swim to someone else's aid. That kind of person doesn't come around often.

Even now, as he was massaging her feet, he noticed a lone tear making its way down the side of her face. He didn't even know if she realized that her emotions had come to the surface again.

Suddenly, a truck horn blared from outside. Echo jerked up like the horn was a cattle prod stuck into her back. She yanked her feet from Brandon's hands and put them on the floor. "I need to change and pack a bag. We have to get back to the hospital."

As she scuttled off, he closed his eyes and adjusted his pants. Dan had warned him to tread slowly with Echo because any sudden moves would send her scurrying for her protective wall faster than Mario Andretti on an empty track. This was the first opportunity he's had to tread at all. The timing was the suckiest in the world.

They were both worried about Dan. She had her birthday, the death of her parents, and she didn't even know the extent of the issues with Telia's health. But all he wanted to do was wrap her in his arms and let them draw comfort from each other—soon.

Now he better think about baseball, the Bulls' chances to win an NBA championship, maybe the Cubs starting line-up—something, anything that would soften his staff, or Echo would have another reason to run.

When they arrived at the hospital, Telia and Echo disappeared, to get the kids down for a nap, leaving Brandon alone with Dan.

Brandon sat on the chair next to the door, listened to the television with half an ear, as thoughts of Echo eased their way in and around the pathways of his brain.

"Dan, I tell you, man, Echo is driving me crazy," he confessed. "And she has no clue."

He leaned all the way back in the chair and rubbed his whole face. "Dude, you could've told me some shit, you know. Like, her parents died on her birthday. That would've been a useful piece of information. Now you get into an accident … on her birthday. Really? Everyone associated with her should go to an underground bunker on April 27, because this woman is going to have a breakdown."

He leaned over resting his forearms on his thighs. "But she's handling it. She is. You'd be proud," he admitted. "But how are you handling it? I would say fight to get back to us, but I know you're fighting. You wouldn't want to leave Shelley and Rocky. And you definitely wouldn't leave Telia."

Listening to a distant cheer on the television, he added, "Well, I think I'm going to take her out tonight. Not just her, it'll be us and the kids; because I know Telia will be here again tonight. I'll figure it out, something that'll work for all of us, I'm sure."

Brandon burst out laughing. "If this is your way of getting the people

At the Touch of Love

you love together, then it's working." Then he sobered. "But you're leaving Telia alone with Mrs. Ellison. I see Telia cringe a little every time Mrs. Ellison calls her "dear." If you hadn't told me about that, I would've missed it."

Shifting in his seat, he continued, "Shelley is so adorable. But you know that already. She's smart and such a trooper." Brandon babbled, "It's a good thing that Echo is here with me. I do believe that your daughter may be smarter than I am. She'd turn those eyes my way, and I'd do her bidding, for real. That little girl is dangerous."

Footsteps made their way to the door and then passed on by.

"I thought that was the fam coming back," he mused, after the sound outside the door lowered to its regular near-silent level. "Anyway, Rocky's a bit fussy at times, but in general, he's the same happy kid. He does ask about you, but Telia told him you went on a plane like Mommy. Now he wants to call you."

Brandon turned as another cheer erupted from the television, and this time it was because the Cubs hit a home run. "Echo keeps distracting him with candy, but I don't know how long that's going to last. So tonight we'll go out. It'll be my first almost date since the battle axe and I parted ways. I wish you were here to tell me where to take them."

Tapping his heel on the floor, he pondered. "You were all cooking lessons and book signings when you were dating Telia. I don't think Echo's that kind of woman."

Brandon sighed. "You come back to us soon, you hear. We need you, Dan. You've been with me through all that bullshit with Susan; helped me to survive G-Ma's death. Don't you flake out on me now."

Brandon sent up a prayer for all of them. Dan was the glue that held so many together. Even Mrs. Ellison didn't know the true extent of his influence. She now held the purse strings. If she examined the books, her head would do a 360 on her neck.

So few were aware of how Dan spent his money, lately. Mrs. Ellison would release the hounds of hell if she ever found out.

He leaned back and watched the television a bit, until the television was watching him.

Brandon added soft snores to the machines keeping steady watch over

Dan Ellison.

CHAPTER 23

Back in a family room in the pediatric ward, Telia and Echo watched Shelley and Rocky, who were taking blessed naps. Rocky was so off-schedule that he was delirious; and Shelley was trying so hard to entertain a man, who still didn't wake up, despite her best efforts, that she passed out as soon as her head hit the pillow.

Telia caressed Shelley's head as she slept. Shelley didn't so much as twitch. Rocky was curled up with his thumb in his mouth. Even though he was too young to talk about everything going on around him, the thumb itself was an indication that he knew something was off in his world. He had never been a major thumb sucker, only when he was truly upset.

Echo eased next to Telia, who gave her a small smile before turning her attention back to the steady breathing of her sleeping children.

"Isn't Rocky Dan's twin?" she inquired. Out of the corner of her eye, Echo nodded. Rocky had those impossibly long lashes, as well as the strong jawline that was all Daniel Ellison. He wasn't predisposed to tantrums or manipulation like Shelley. But there were days when that jaw would jut out, and he would refuse to be swayed from whatever position he held.

"It's better up here," Telia stated. As Echo searched the room and a confused expression drew deep lines in her face, Telia felt compelled to explain. "The beeping of that damn monitor drives me crazy," Telia growled, "plus, all the nurses, technicians, doctors, lions, tigers and bears coming in and out of that room. Why call it a private room, when it appears the whole world rolls through at one time or another. It would be different if they were helping, if five more visits from them would mean he would wake up."

"That's not how it works," Echo whispered, as though Telia didn't already know that. "They're doing everything that they can."

"I know how it works," Telia snapped. "I'm living how it works."

Letting out a deep breath, Echo tried to hold Telia's hand. Instead of finding comfort in that, Telia glared and snatched her hand back.

Echo inclined her head towards the chairs, silently pleading with Telia.

Telia flattened her lips and glanced at her children.

Echo grabbed Telia's hand again. This time Telia let herself be pulled from in front of the children over to the seating area. Echo inquired, "How are you holding up? Really."

Telia whispered, "Girl, I want to shake him."

Echo snorted and clamped her hand over her mouth to hold in her laugh. That was such a Telia statement.

Most women at this time would be crying and wailing. Telia probably wanted to. She probably had. However, she hated crying in public. So, of course, she wanted to shake him.

"I wouldn't recommend it. Someone would call security on your crazy tail," Echo warned.

"I know. That's the only thing that's saving him." Telia continued to keep her focus on the kids. "I'm so scared." Echo pulled her over until Telia's head was on Echo's shoulder. "What am I going to do if he doesn't wake up?"

Echo stroked a comforting hand on Telia's arm. "Come on. Dr. Dan would never leave you all."

"Voluntarily, hell no. But he might not have a choice this time. And I honestly don't know what I'd do without him." Telia wiped her cheek, trying to stem the tide of tears that were tripping over each other to make it down her face first.

Abruptly, she changed the subject, "So Echo, Brandon's a bit of yummy deliciousness today. He's like a Werther's butterscotch sweet brown."

Echo's hand stilled as her eyes darted back and forth in panic. Echo

At the Touch of Love

happened to be a terrible liar. She'd manage, if she prepared, but off-the-cuff questions get the truthful answer. "Brandon? Sure."

"You guys were in your condo, alone, together. Come on, I need something else to think about. It's your role as my best friend to provide it." Telia poked her. "You can't tell me that nothing happened."

Echo paused for what seemed like two minutes. Yeah, something happened alright.

"You do know we left my place in a mess." She started.

Telia held up her hand to stop Echo. "It was a mess when I arrived. That mess didn't have anything to do with me."

Echo glared at Telia, giving her just short of the evil eye. "Those damn birthday balloons."

Telia nodded. "Ahh. So you told him about your birthday?"

"What choice did I have, with all that latex slapping the man in the face?"

Telia raised one eyebrow. "Did you tell him everything?'

"Well, how could I not?" Echo huffed. "And now, he wants to take me and the kids out tonight to celebrate my birthday."

Inwardly, Telia laughed. This was just what Echo needed. Someone she couldn't manage or avoid. The situation forced Echo to be in Brandon's presence. It wasn't that Echo didn't date.

She just didn't date people who had a hope in hell of touching her heart. Telia had a sneaky suspicion that Brandon was the type of guy who Echo wouldn't be able to block.

Telia studied Echo's facial expression closely. There was no way Echo was immune to Brandon.

"Stop staring at me," Echo demanded.

Putting her fingers to her lips and glancing over at the sleeping children, Telia asked, "Should I try to find a babysitter tonight?"

Crossing her arms, Echo grumbled, "No, he wants to take the kids too."

Oh, Echo was in deep trouble. Telia wondered if Echo even knew. She leaned back with a self-satisfied smirk.

Echo leaned forward and grabbed Telia's hands. "What are you going to do? I mean if he doesn't wake up today or tomorrow. What are you going to do long term?"

Long term, she might be locked in Mrs. Ellison's house like that book *Flowers in the Attic*. Telia ran down everything she found out. "Well, with Dan in a coma, all of the money decisions revert to Mrs. Ellison."

Echo hissed.

"Right," Telia responded.

Echo offered, "You know I can always …."

Telia knew Echo would empty her bank account for her. Echo shouldn't have to. One: Dan should be awake. Two: This wasn't just Dan's money. It was her money too. She should at least have access to the joint accounts.

Telia patted Echo's hand. "Thank you, but let me at least try to get this straightened out."

She bit her lip. That was just money. Not just money. But in addition to money, what would she do if Dan needed long-term care. Sure, Echo would be around, and even Brandon; but her kids needed a parent. They couldn't spend all day, every day at the hospital.

They needed to run and play and see their friends. She wouldn't even think about Mrs. Ellison and the number of lawyers on her payroll, who could make Telia's life very difficult, at a time they should all be focusing on Dan's well-being. Money. It always came down to money with Mrs. Ellison, never about her child. And because Telia hadn't sealed her place in Dan's life, the woman had an edge that Telia never considered would be a thing. Now, every time she turned, she feared that someone would snatch up the kids; and her depleting energy level left her unequipped to handle everyday situations. This wasn't every day.

Telia closed her eyes as if shielding herself to the reality of her situation. "I don't know. I don't know what I'm going to do. But it's been a day. It seems like forever, but it's only been one day. I know that reality has to set in soon. Actually, it starts tomorrow."

Echo's eyes shifted in thought. "Tomorrow's Friday. What's so special about that day?"

Telia weighed how much she should tell Echo. In the end, she stuck with her original plan. She didn't know if she had the mental wherewithal to outsmart Echo. Not today. "Something that can't be rescheduled. It's a gift to Dr. Dan. You're coming, of course."

Telia continued as if she didn't notice Echo's eyes boring into hers. "The kids have a play date with my brother, Remy, who's coming in town specifically to hang with them. Dan's friends can visit while we're gone, and Brandon will get a break."

"Wait, what in the world are we doing tomorrow?" Echo demanded.

Telia lifted her eyebrows up and down rapidly. "Wouldn't you like to know?" Shelley began to stretch on the bed, indicating she'd be getting up soon. "Oh, and find some time to shave your legs?"

Echo gaped, but gave a quick glance down at her jeans-clad legs. "Why the hell would I need to shave my legs?"

Telia gave a full-watt smile, "Well, you should be shaving anyway for your date tonight. But just in case you pull that *if-I-don't-shave-I-won't-have-sex* logic, I'm letting you know that tomorrow your legs will be exposed. You can mirror a sasquatch if you want to, but might I suggest that you don't." Telia paused and gave a side glance to Echo's shoulder. "Matter of fact, clean all that shit up. Someone could probably braid your underarm hair by now."

Shelley cuddled in Telia's lap, forcing an end to the conversation and the smart retort that Echo had dancing on the tip of her tongue. Telia kissed her on the top of her head.

"Hey, Baby Bug. Did you sleep well?"

Shelley nodded. Telia rocked her baby girl from side to side, humming. Although Shelley didn't think she needed naps, these minutes afterward were so precious to Telia: when the world was quiet, or at least quiet-ish; and Shelley was in her lap, and they were just loving on each other. Telia could just inhale her baby's scent and breathe; no worries about anything.

If God wouldn't give people anything they couldn't handle, every psychiatrist in the world would be out of business.

Echo's eyes widened as she pointed to her cheek. Telia ran her finger down her face and realized it glistened with an unchecked tear. Could she do this? Could she manage telling her children it was okay, when it wasn't? Could she tell them that she'd be in a better place, when there was no better place than by their side? Would she be able to tell them any of this, if she wasn't even able to leave them with Dan?

Telia handed Shelley to Echo and hurried out of the door. She didn't have a choice. She wondered how people managed to push back the darkness, the depression that now stayed on the periphery of her psyche 24/7.

At the Touch of Love

CHAPTER 24

Thanks to a streaming music service, Shelley and Rocky entertained Brandon and Echo by singing Disney songs as they left the hospital. Rocky didn't actually know the words, but he was game to add his voice in anyway. Shelley was the breakout star of that duo, hitting nearly every note, high or low, whether or not her voice complied.

Brandon and Echo shared a smile.

A feeling, warm and fuzzy. She snatched her eyes away from Brandon's and focused on counting each building they passed. In his truck, she didn't need to look at him. The spicy smell of his cologne wafted over, tickling her senses and her memories.

She was ambushed by flashes of her dreams: his smile, his lips; the trail of his fingers along her smooth skin. No body hair in her dreams for some reason. *Focus. Echo, Disney is playing for God's sake. No one can think about sex when Disney is playing.* No one, except her freaky "a-dick-ted" ass.

"So Brandon, you know if you're tired or something, we can do this another time." Echo offered, "There's so much going on that it's bad timing."

Brandon laughed. "You're not getting out of this."

Echo turned at the lights flashing in her periphery and realized they were outside of Dave and Buster's. Echo turned. "Really? Dave and Buster's?" Dave and Buster's was an upscale video arcade. Well, maybe medium-scale video arcade: food, drinks, televisions, games.

Brandon opened the car door for Echo and extracted the kids from their mini-seat prisons. As they all clamored out of the car, Brandon led them into the front door. Echo picked up Rocky as they slid onto the escalator. Rocky's eyes widened, as he chortled and clapped his hands; loving the movement.

Pointing at Rocky's reaction, Brandon huffed. "At least someone appreciates the effort I put into planning a birthday that everyone can enjoy."

If he thought she was going to get all mushy for Dave and Buster's, he was mistaken. She just wasn't the video game type.

When they reached the top of the escalator, Shelley did a quick scan of the place and bounced up and down. "Do we get to play games? Can we play games?"

Brandon tweaked Shelley's nose. "Food first."

The dark wood, coupled with the high walls of the booth, gave the area a dungeon ambiance. However, the bright lights overcompensated for the lack of natural sunlight, making the place a little more inviting.

The area buzzed with the murmur of conversation from both families and couples. A couple at the next table over leaned into each other. The electricity bouncing between the couple stopped Echo in her tracks. She licked her own lips in anticipation of their touching.

Echo inhaled the scent of Brandon's cologne, the same cologne that had cloaked her in a promise-filled cocoon all the way to Dave and Buster's. That scent had ignited a fire in her core, spreading sensual heat causing her nipples to tighten against the cup of her bra.

Brandon's body lined her back, but didn't touch hers; his breath whispered against her cheek. Even so, his presence alone felt like a massage of her senses.

"One word," he murmured. "Give me one word … just one and I promise you—"

"Do they have a ball pit?" Shelley inquired.

She felt Brandon's smile before she heard the humor in his voice. However, he didn't bother to put one centimeter between them before responding, "Whose birthday is it, Shelley?"

Shelley gave her signature pout.

At the Touch of Love

"You know it's all about Auntie Echo."

Echo literally shivered. He was talking to the baby, and she couldn't look at a table without thinking of being on her back on top of it.

"Fine," Shelley grumbled with a quick glance at Echo as she perked up. "I think Auntie Echo would like a ball pit. Wouldn't you like a ball pit?"

Oil pit? Maybe?

Brandon stepped back, but his cologne continued to be a naughty muse guiding her imagination in all types of inappropriate directions.

"Yes, Echo," Brandon's gaze intensely locked on her. "*Exactly* what would you like to do?"

Oh, fuck.

"Well, isn't this the cute little family," a shrill, familiar voice commented.

All heads snapped around to find Susan's triumphant smile.

Shelley spoke first. "Hello, Auntie Susan. How are you today?"

Echo clenched her teeth to keep from smiling. Those were Shelley's company manners. Clearly, Auntie Susan wasn't a fan favorite.

Then Echo drew back. It seemed unlikely, but was Dave and Buster's Brandon and Susan's spot?

Dryly, Brandon inquired with a voice so devoid of emotion that he could do robot voiceovers. "What are you doing here?"

"Well," Susan started. "I saw the cozy quartet at the hospital parking garage. And since we didn't finish our conversation earlier, I decided to see if there would be an opportunity to talk."

If the depth of inhalation was an indicator of anger, Brandon reached DEFCON 25.

"Of course," Susan continued. "We could talk about your poor G-Ma later."

Tensing now, Brandon turned. "Why don't you all go ahead and order while I talk to Susan?"

Echo ushered the kids away from Brandon and Susan, but not before she heard Susan's triumphant, "If you had written me a check this morning, we could have avoided this little scene...."

Had Brandon forgotten to pay his alimony? What did that have to do with his grandmother? If he had forgotten to pay alimony, why would Susan follow them to Dave and Buster's instead of calling her lawyer?

Echo followed the hostess, who sat them at a booth. She sat on the side that allowed her to watch the angry hands of Brandon and Susan flying through the air. He turned and saw them staring.

Susan said one more line and his head dropped. He said something, and Susan's face beamed like she'd swallowed an LED light.

Brandon slid into the booth and tickled Rocky. He hummed a *Frozen* song and then sang the wrong lyrics until he had Shelley laughing. However, at no time did he explain Susan's presence or departure. He kept going through the evening as if his ex hadn't shown up out of the blue.

One time while the children were stomping on a dance machine that they both were too young to play, but insisted on trying, she broached the topic. "So what's going on with the Susan?"

He paused before responding, "The same stuff."

Echo contemplated throwing Brandon under the feet of the stomping kids. But she elected for the high road. "And that stuff is?"

Brandon put his arm around her in a tight half hug. "Let's not let Susan ruin your birthday."

Echo rolled out of his hug. Based on what she saw of their conversation, Susan was doing more than just ruining her birthday "celebration." But if Brandon wanted to pretend, fine. Whatever, even though Susan's comment about his grandmother still nagged at her brain.

CHAPTER
25

Echo plopped down on a couch in Dr. Dan's room.

Telia gently placed the bright pink journal on the edge of the bed, and hurriedly wiped the tears from her eyes. She glanced at Echo to see if she noticed, but the way her eyes narrowed as she focused on the hospital's drop ceiling and the way she gnawed at her bottom lip told of her preoccupation.

Although her exhaustion wore her down to the nub, to the point where shifting in a chair seemed too much trouble, curiosity piqued her stamina— that and the befuddled expression on Echo's face. "Problems in paradise?

Echo snarled, "Yes. For one, Susan sucks donkey balls."

Well, isn't this interesting. Telia schooled her expression, hoping for nonchalance instead of the glee that was pushing the overwhelming sadness aside and demanding attention. "Is that new information?"

"We're at Dave and Buster's for my birthday." Echo drug her hand through her hair and twirled a lock between her fingers. "He does this thing when he leans in and whispers into your ear, and the heat it generates causes enough friction to start an explosion. And then your girl shows up."

Telia's mind couldn't comprehend the logic. She probed, "He told her where you all were going?"

Echo threw her hands up. "No, the trick followed us from the hospital.

Shocked him as well as me."

Telia nodded in understanding. They weren't running from the law. Who keeps an eye on their rearview? "She doused that fire real quick, didn't she?"

"Like Niagara Falls on a weenie roast." Echo leaned in and stared at Telia. "Girl, you look rough."

Telia's finger combed her hair. "Well, shit, tell me how you really feel?"

"No, I mean, you need to sleep for about 24 hours straight with a cheeseburger IV drip."

Telia held up her hands in surrender. "I get it. I get it. Distract me, what happened with Susan?"

"Girl, I can come back." The concern in Echo's eyes signified how rough Telia obviously appeared.

Telia grabbed a straw out of a pitcher of water. "If you don't finish, I will stab you."

Echo yawned, "With a straw? And what, suck my blood for nourishment?"

Telia brandished the straw more emphatically.

Echo conceded. "Fine. Susan. I don't know what's going on, but it starts with money."

Telia snorted. "Of course, it does. That woman can run through money like a Kenyan running the marathon."

Echo smirked. "But she gets alimony. Isn't that enough?"

Telia smiled. "So innocent, you are? It's never going to be enough. It's about control, not cash. Right now, she's in limbo. She didn't file for divorce. Brandon did. Probably messed up her plans to leap from one bank account to a larger one. Being a gold digger doesn't really come with unemployment insurance. She might have had to budget. Gasp."

Echo's smirk grew to a full smile. "She mentioned something about Brandon's grandmother."

Telia thought back. "Yeah. G-Ma's death. Why would Susan mention her? Maybe she left a will? Surely, she wouldn't try to profit from Brandon's …. Wait, who am I kidding? Of course, she would. If there is a remote possibility that she can get one more dime out of Brandon, nothing would stop her."

Echo peered at the floor. "Telia, my heart pounds whenever he's within five feet. My spirit lightens. But Dan's in a coma, and Susan is following us, and the timing is the absolute worst."

Telia grasped Echo's hand. "Do you want him?"

Echo stood up, yanked her hand free and paced the small room. "I don't know. I want him. Like, my underwear feels like my vagina has sprung a leak. But it's all so intermingled. The accident, the kids, my parents, you, Brandon. I can't think clearly. I don't know."

Telia grabbed her and forced Echo to stand still. "And how do you feel?"

"It's just," Echo started. Her mouth opened and closed a few times.

"Yes?"

"Well—" Echo tried again.

"Waiting."

Echo's slumped shoulders told the tale of defeat, even if her mouth didn't own up to it. "How's Dan doing today?"

"Wimp." Telia laughed, and then turned her adoring eyes to her husband. "Well, it would be better if he was awake and at home, but he's not worse. We'll take what we can get at this point."

Telia played with Dr. Dan's ring finger. "You remember when Dan proposed to me?"

"You mean, when you tried to send the ring back."

Telia glared. "Why do you always start the story with the fact that I tried to send the ring back? That's not the important part."

Shaking her head, Echo sighed. "Think of all the planning Dan had put into that evening."

"I know," Telia responded. "I mean, it was pretty darn perfect."

"All the planning I put into it," Echo reminded Telia.

Telia's left eye twitched. "You won't let me forget. You tell me that part of the story at every opportunity. Like going jewelry shopping was as boring as plucking thorns out of a cactus."

After a year of dating, Dan popped the question. Echo even went with him to pick out the ring. Dan had gone to the family jeweler to select something that was as unique as his Telia.

The minute they walked into the door of a multilevel cream building on Oak Street, Echo knew they had taken a step up. The interior had a few strategically placed display cases.

A saleswoman handed them flutes of champagne, as she led them to a dark wood table. A guy introduced himself as Darius, which may have been a salesperson, a jewelry designer, or the store muscle, given the cut and fit of his suit. As he opened a smaller case with a case of rings flawlessly displayed, Echo felt she needed to shield her eyes from the sparkle, but she didn't want to give herself away as being new to this kind of opulence.

Dr. Dan spent the first few minutes sweating, and he was wiping his hands against his pants leg.

Echo put a hand on his shoulder. "You're a doctor. Shouldn't you have a better poker face? If this is how you look when you're about to give someone some news, I'm surprised more of your patients haven't jumped out of the window."

Dan picked up one ring and put it down. Then he rubbed his hands against his pants again. "She isn't the easiest to shop for."

Echo scoffed. "It doesn't have to be huge, just distinctive.

"She needs flash, but …"

Finally, Echo provided guidance. "No diamonds."

"It's an *engagement* ring."

Patting his shoulder, Echo explained. "It's Telia's engagement ring. She's fire. Go for a ruby with a gold setting."

Hesitating, Dr. Dan picked up another white diamond and platinum ring, which was no different than so many other white diamond and platinum rings the place had on display.

Echo put her hand on his shoulder. "She's going to say yes. Just turn the yes into a hell yes."

Darius smiled, rose, and returned with a brilliant ruby setting resembling a flame.

"She'd do you for that one," Echo mumbled.

Dr. Dan threw his head back laughing. "Well, hell. That's all the input

I need." He nodded to Darius. "Wrap it up."

Glancing between the jeweler and Dan, Echo quipped. "Shit, you got it like that."

"Like what?" Dan asked as he handed over his credit card.

"You didn't check the price," Echo whispered.

"It's Telia. Why would price matter?" Dan questioned.

"Damn it. You *do* have it like that," Echo confirmed.

Telia felt her eyes soften. "Yeah, he does have it like that. That's part of the issue with Mrs. Ellison, apparently: the fact that he's not acting like a Dobson, but an Ellison, the fact that he's decided to be a dermatologist like his father.

"However," Telia continued. "It's not my fault that he tried to propose at a restaurant. The waiter kept trying to force a strawberry desert down my throat when I didn't ask for one. You don't maintain this body scarfing down desserts every five seconds."

"But you cursed the waiter out," Echo reminded her.

"The waiter," Telia explained, "got on my nerves."

"He was trying to do his job. And Dan's proposal was so romantic." Echo's eyes crinkled with amusement, and then they chorused the line that brought that evening to a head.

"Would you let the damn waiter give you the damn desert, so you can put on the damn ring and spend the rest of your stubborn-ass life as my damn wife?"

Echo and Telia squealed with laughter. "It wasn't our finest moment."

"And your reply, 'Oh, yeah, okay. I can do that.'" Echo added, still giggling.

"Dr. Dan was appalled that he'd gone there. He wanted a do-over, didn't you, baby." Telia tweaked Dr. Dan under the chin. "But that was us, and it was right. And I did put on the damn ring."

Telia felt the thoughts whipping around Echo's mind like a Kansas tornado. "But you still haven't married him." As if Telia needed a reminder of that.

CHAPTER 26

The next day Brandon made his way past the nurses coming on duty. They gave him the usual greetings, and he trudged the rest of the way to Dan's bed.

Even with the heart rate monitor beeping, he still put his hand on Dan's wrist. He needed to feel the pulse for himself; feel the life coursing through Dan's veins, when there was barely movement in the body itself to indicate his friend remained among the living.

He settled in the chair by the door. Though Telia's presence had left the room, somehow the chair closest to the bed seemed to have her imprint all over it. Rubbing his hand along the prickly skin of his beard's shadow, he realized he probably should have shaved this morning.

"Dude, you picked a damned bad time to take a break." Watching closely for any reaction from Dan, but there wasn't even so much as a twitch and as a doctor, this tended to be the case. But now, like so many families, he too held out for any little sign of hope.

"While I know Telia could've used the company last night, I really wish someone would've sent Echo home." Brandon ran his hand over his thick natural hair. He could use a trip to his stylist too.

But this, being here for Dan, being at the house with the kids was way more important than his vanity. Of course, Shelley took about ten years off his life when she woke him up this morning.

Shelley poked him in the arm. "Auntie Echo didn't come home."

He might as well have been awakened by machine gun fire, as it was the same as Shelley telling him that damning piece of information. Yes, he managed to keep it together for Shelley and Rocky, but all the possible scenarios were scurrying in his head like mice sniffing for the last morsel of cheese.

"Uncle Brandon?" He felt another poke as well as the hesitation in Shelley's voice. But when he opened his eyes to peer at her, he instantly knew something was wrong. The boundless energy, the staunch determination was held in check. She felt more like the little girl she was. Even when he was carrying Shelley's baby form around on his forearm, she had a larger than life presence; like an old woman's soul stuffed into that pint-sized package.

"Auntie Echo didn't come home."

Brandon mumbled a curse under his breath. *Dammit, Echo.* "Come on, Shelley. Hop up here." Reaching for his phone, he prayed she was safe at the same time as he cursed her lack of communication. She could've told him she was leaving; left a note or something, rather than disappearing like a damn cat burglar.

Once he heard a hello, the war between worried and pissed tipped all the way to the pissed-off fuck side of the scale.

"Echo, sweetie, your niece is asking about you," he announced. "She was worried because you didn't come home." He didn't add that it might have turned at least two strands of his hair gray.

Echo paused. "I'm sorry. I thought I'd be home by now, but Telia—"

"Don't tell me. Tell her." He handed the phone to Shelley.

Hell, he was ill-equipped to handle emergencies, even pseudo emergencies, without his morning cup of tea to balance his day.

Of course, he may need to start mainlining caffeine, because those two kids could wear a man out—even the tiny kids, even though they have a nap time. It seems like someone always needed to be picked up or put down, or they were trying to run somewhere or needed something.

What happened to the good old days of playing quietly in a bedroom?

He was starting to believe he was born "UncleBrandon." No space between the Uncle and Brandon. Just all rushed together, as if Shelley didn't want to waste the second it was going to take to get his name out.

Brandon made his way through hallway and into the bathroom. Sighing, as he finished his morning rituals, he sat on the edge of the bathtub.

"Auntie Echo didn't come home."

God, he could do with about five shots of whiskey, but he didn't have the time for that. He still needed to get Rocky, since apparently, the "co-babysitter" dipped out on him. He ran over the last night in his mind.

He'd seen the way Echo responded to his voice at Dave and Buster's until Susan made her entrance. Yeah, she needed money, but not this bad. He wouldn't doubt the need to follow him came when she heard the female voice over the line earlier the day before.

Whether she knew the voice belonged to Echo didn't matter. She knew it now. And she'd never let him forget the betrayal.

Shelley banged on the bathroom door. "UncleBrandon? Mommy wants to speak to you. She said to tell you there's no hiding in the bathroom."

Brandon watched in wonder as the bathroom doorknob rattled, as if Shelley was trying to break into his private reprieve. "UncleBrandon?" she yelled, between pounds on the door. "He locked the door, Mommy."

Brandon leapt to the door, before baby girl learned how to pick a lock just to fulfill her mother's request. "I'm here. I'm here."

Grabbing the phone away from Shelley, as she did what could loosely be described as cartwheels in the hall, he whispered a growl into the receiver, "Telia, I think your daughter tried to get into the bathroom. I could have been naked." Telia's amused chuckle on the other end only frustrated him more.

"Yeah, those parents who use the bathroom as a getaway clearly have not met my kids. Good thing you locked it." Amusement continued to lace her voice. She wasn't nearly upset enough.

"What possessed you to have your lovely daughter get me?" He glanced down at Shelley, who had finished her bid to become an Olympian and was now listening aptly to the conversation. Clearly, privacy wasn't a word she had learned yet.

"I need you to go to my closet and pull out the pink bag and bring it

At the Touch of Love

to the hospital. The kids are going to spend some time with Remy. And I'm kidnapping Echo; so you'll get a free day."

"Telia, don't you think it's time that you told Echo about—"

"Okay. I have to go. Thanks, bye."

She disconnected the call before he could take her to task about leaving Echo in the dark about her medical condition.

Now he was in the ICU, talking to the one person who would absolutely understand, even if he couldn't respond.

"Dan, Telia wasn't herself today. I mean … Telia will always stop traffic, but you know she's fighting, fighting for you. She's keeping it together, but we both know that with your mother being an absolute 'beyotch,' time isn't on her side. You have to wake up, man. You … your family needs you."

Brandon remembered when Dan first met Telia. Dan tried his best to keep his interest appropriately doctor/patient, but something, in the amount of time Telia's acne made its way into the conversation, made Brandon curious.

"So, you're saying that this hideous wildebeest came into the office today."

At the time, they were playing pool at a pub around the corner from the hospital. Dan shot and accidentally hit the eight ball that teetered miraculously close to the pocket, but didn't drop in. Lucky Dan.

"You know, if this patient has this impact on your game, I may start paying for her visits myself."

The possessive glint in Dan's eyes paused him in his tracks. *Interesting.* Dan narrowed his eyes, glaring at Brandon, who smoothly cleared the rest of his balls on the table before tapping in the eight ball.

Brandon placed his pool cue on the table. "So you are aware that you really can't date your patient right."

Dan gave up the pretense of shooting pool and plopped down on the high top. Sipping his PBR, he admitted, "It's not just that she's beautiful. I have beautiful patients."

Nodding, Brandon had seen quite a few women in Dan's waiting room, but there were enough women to date in Chicago without having to troll his patient list. That could get messy, and it wouldn't do to jeopardize either one of their practices for a date. They had a hard-and-fast rule about work and dating.

The fact that Dan entertained the idea indicated either he needed a reminder course on ethics, or this woman was unique in a way that didn't come by too often.

Dan paused and let the sounds of drunken laughter and clinking glass fill in the gap. After a while, he continued, "It's like the air had a current that pushed us closer together. It's hard to explain."

"Are you sure your pants didn't have the current?" Brandon joked.

"Really? I'm trying to be serious and you're talking about physical attraction. Physical attraction's easy." Dan tried to explain, "Have you ever felt like you knew you could be with someone after a five-minute conversation? And I'm not talking about sex. I'm talking about something about her just fits for me."

Brandon inhaled deeply and scanned the activity happening in the pub. Women were practically inhaling the idea of having both him and Dan over their beer mugs. One of them even winked when their eyes caught. He nodded at her. Beautiful women were all around. Normally, Dan would've noticed and struck up at least a mild flirtation across the room. Now, Dan was more focused on his drink and his patient.

"Do you guys need anything else?" the waitress said, interrupting his musing.

Both he and Dan declined.

Needing to probe the story behind the mystery woman, Brandon inquired, "So the question of the hour Dan is, what are you going to do about it?"

Back then, he had no clue what Dan was talking about. Even with Susan, Brandon had liked her. They had good conversation. They *seemed* compatible. But that combustible energy, he never felt that until he bumped into Echo in the hallway of Dan's house. His eyes traveled down to her lips, and he wanted nothing more than to pull her forward until she felt the reaction she gave him.

"Auntie Echo didn't come home."

Brandon suspected that overnight hospital visit was an effort to create some distance between them. She didn't know that tonight, while the kids were with their uncle, his plan was to close a bit of this distance. Based on his conversation with Telia that morning, she agreed.

But right now, he needed to focus on his best friend.

"So Dan, Telia needs you awake and healthy. What are you going to do about it?" Brandon challenged.

CHAPTER 27

A strong knock rattled the theater door. "Come in," shouted Telia as she played fifty-two-card pickup with her kids. Rocky found endless amusement in throwing the cards up in the air and letting them fall around him.

A tall, chocolate man strolled in with the face that caused women on the street to swoon and a cocky quirk of his lips.

Telia wanted to roll her eyes every time she saw him, but she couldn't hate. Brothers are like that sometimes.

Shelley ran in first, yelling, "UncleRemy. UncleRemy. UncleRemy's here."

Rocky turned in circles laughing. Apparently, Uncle Remy maintained his star appeal even with children.

Remy swept Shelley into his arms, lifting her over his head. Rocky held his hands up waiting for his turn. Remy obliged.

Telia rose from the carpet and soon enveloped Remy in a hug. Running her hand over his bald head, she inhaled deeply. She missed him.

As they rocked together, giving and receiving comfort, Telia realized that it had been way too long since they had seen each other. She ended the hug with a light punch on the arm.

Remy pretended as if it hurt. As if they both didn't know that a chiseled body held up that charming face. "Owww." Remy acted hurt. "What was that for, sis?"

"You need to visit more often."

Remy brought his hand up to her face, gently cupping her chin before rubbing her hair. "Brat. Maybe if you didn't abuse me when I was around I would come more often."

Telia waved him off. "You've survived worse. Remember, I met a few of your exes."

Remy laughed. "Ahh, but their packaging was always delightful."

Telia handed Remy a large bag that held clothes for the children. He took the bag with the tips of his fingers. "You expect me to believe you didn't have one black sedate overnight bag," he stated as he twirled the screaming pink bag covered by cartoon character straps. She laughed. "Of course, I did. This just seemed more fun."

"Brat." Remy grinned. "I'm sure it reminded you of your bedroom growing up. Of course, if I remember correctly that leaned more towards a Pepto-Bismol pink."

Telia stuck her tongue out at Remy and collapsed in a chair.

"So why exactly are we meeting at a theater instead of the hospital?" he inquired.

Telia shrugged. "Things to do."

A commanding knock shook the door on its hinges. Before Telia could even utter, "Enter," Zephyre, the buxom makeup artist marched in and announced, "A lot to do and too little time."

She stopped when she saw Remy. "Oh, that smile and those eyes." Then she shivered. "Boy, the things I would have done to you back in my day."

Remy's voice dropped, "The day is still—"

"Children!" Telia nodded towards Shelley, who was noticeably quiet as she absorbed every word. "Behave yourselves."

Remy winked at Zephyre before turning to Telia. "So, sis, do you think I can get a moment?"

The makeup artist unloaded her brushes. "No time. So behind."

Telia shrugged.

Remy added, "It's important, very important."

Telia waved. "Tomorrow. I promise. We will chat. Take care of my babies."

Remy paused as if he wanted to say more, but merely added, "I always do," before gathering the kids up and ushering them out of the door.

Minutes later, as Zephyre worked her magic, Telia peered at her reflection. She tilted her head to the side, trying to surmise how much she had changed. The bags, of course, were new; not new necessarily, but definitely more pronounced. Her complexion lost its natural vitality. The makeup artist adjusted Telia's face back to where she wanted it.

"Sorry to make your job hard."

The makeup artist assessed the work she'd completed thus far.

"Please, girl, your cheekbones and eyebrows are everything."

Telia attempted to smile, but her mind wasn't behind the effort. Her cheekbones were nothing. Her insides are what counted. That's what she always told Shelley. It's what's inside that counted, and her insides were eating her alive.

She fingered the notebook in her lap. She planned to cover the pink journal with purple glitter. Shelley would love it now, and the good thing is that girls never outgrew their glitter. Even now, Telia enjoyed the spark of rubies, mesmerized by the way they sparkled in the light.

Telia hoped Shelley would be mesmerized by this gift. As time sucked her strength like a leech letting her blood, she wanted to document thoughts, feelings. Love.

The makeup artist pulled out the eyeshadow, and Telia closed her eyes, forcing her to focus less on her face and more on the man she left at the hospital. The decision to leave him tore at her like a shredder … but she had to leave him.

She felt her face being pulled to the right as she complied.

Echo's thoughts from the night before reverberated through her mind. Even the nurses at the hospital gave her the droopy dog eyes when they came into the room. Zephyre would give her back her color.

Donna burst through the door. Zephyre glared. "You almost made me poke a hole in her eyeball."

"Telia, maybe you should have given your best friend more rehearsal

At the Touch of Love

time."

While the books were gifts for the children, this was one of the many gifts for Dan. She decided to reenact one of Beyonce's videos. She planned this before the illness, before the accident. As she lay holding Dan's hand, she thought about canceling. If she didn't do it today, she might never have the chance.

Plus, it wasn't like she was getting her deposit back, and the rest of the production costs would wipe out her savings. Dan's ass had left her with two choices: beg his mother, not an option; ask Echo, who would help. Even her brother, who was now playing Uncle Remy at a corporate apartment he'd rented for a week, would happily assist.

But shit, part of that money was hers. She could give less than the hair on the back of a rat's ass about the estate money. She'd be damned if that withered crypt keeper would take her money. Time to do what the rich people obviously did, get a lawyer.

Mrs. Ellison may know all about finances and estates; but Telia, at her core, knew how to fight.

She knew she wasn't winning the battle against cancer. Dan's condition required way more patience than she'd been born with. But maybe she could win the battle against Mrs. Ellison.

Donna stared at her. "You seem like you're ready to cut slow and steady."

Telia opened her mouth. "Well—"

Donna held up her hand. "Don't want to know. Plausible deniability. That's how murderers get caught today. Can't keep their big mouth shut."

"Point taken," Telia conceded. "Let's say I'm ready to kick ass in this video."

"I don't know who you decided to shank, but thank goodness. Two seconds ago I thought you were going to take a nap, which isn't Beyoncé-like at all. Let's go kick some ass. Figuratively, of course.

Telia winked. "Of course."

CHAPTER 28

The morning started off with a call from Brandon, who was clearly displeased that she hadn't shown up at the townhouse. Then he passed the phone to Shelley. She knew she messed up when Shelley got to lecturing. She apologized to a six-year-old, while Telia barely contained her laughter.

"Shelley, you were asleep when I left," she explained, giving Telia the evil eye. "I didn't want to wake you."

The little girl didn't even take a breath before launching into, "When Mommy goes on flights, she always wakes me up and says goodbye and gives me kisses."

Telia confirmed with a nod and an air of superiority that forced Echo to take Shelley off the speaker, so there weren't any witnesses to being dressed down by a tyke.

"Shelley, baby, next time, I'll wake you and give you kisses. And I'll tickle you until you squeal." Echo continued in a soft whisper, "And just when you close your eyes and drift off to sleep," Echo shouted, "I'll tickle you again."

Shelley squealed with glee, which made Echo feel slightly better.

Telia gestured for the phone. Echo handed it over and listened to Telia exchange greetings with her daughter and ask Brandon to bring a bag to the

At the Touch of Love

hospital and collect a few items from her work closet.

Now Echo knew why Telia had gone all Columbo on her. Echo felt as if she was two breaths from meeting her maker. She could barely breathe, strapped in five-inch heels and a purple velvet corset that turned her manageable B cups into XXXs, which obscured the fact that she actually had a decent neck.

The makeup on her face was so heavy that it felt as if it was a mask she could chisel off and sit on the chair next to her. Inhale. Exhale. Deep breaths were more like shallow pants.

As she sat in a chair behind the curtain on stage right, with a water bottle in her hand, she vowed she'd catch her breath. She couldn't die yet, not until she killed Telia. Only Telia would pay people to help her reenact a music video for Dr. Dan, set to Beyonce's song Partition.

Only Telia would hire professional backup dancers. And only Telia would drag her unsuspecting best friend to the theater to participate. Brilliant and fucking insane. Telia expected Echo to keep up with trained dancers. As if. This wasn't a two-step. Hell, at this point, she'd be ecstatic if her thighs held up to dance the Tootsie Roll.

How Telia thought Echo could manage even the minute and a half of low grinding choreography and hair whipping was beyond her. Echo hurt both physically and emotionally.

Before this break, Donna, the choreographer, told her she danced like a virgin. And not like a virgin in the singer Madonna non-virgin way; like Mary in the manger, a never been touched, white wedding dress virgin. Maybe that's why she didn't have a man.

Echo knew she only had one more attempt in her to get this music video right, before her legs completely gave way and gave her the finger.

As Telia strutted across the stage as if her heels were house shoes, Echo considered throwing her water bottle at her, but that took a lot of energy. She'd need every ounce when Donna, the choreographer/director/sadist, ended the break.

When Telia gestured for the phone and talked to Brandon, Echo should have escaped, but no. Echo handed it over and listened to Telia exchange greetings with her daughter and ask Brandon to bring a bag to the hospital.

"Telia, did I miss something in your bag?"

Telia responded, "No," and mumbled something unintelligible. Echo should have known then something was off. She should have sensed treachery in the making. She hadn't, and now she's paying the price.

If Telia wanted to keep the spice alive in her marriage, fine; but did Echo have to play along? Half her butt cheek hung out of the minuscule piece of fabric doubling as shorts. Dr. Dan seeing her butt cheek didn't seem like something friends should share, but apparently, Telia didn't care.

As Telia finished the last few steps, Echo wondered the likelihood of a banana peel falling out of the sky and causing Telia to slip, just a little slip to make Telia seem as clumsy as Echo currently felt.

Telia inquired, "Echo, are you sure you are going to be okay? "Echo merely glared a response. It would have been better if Telia had inquired about her feelings before she handed her a purple velvet bustier, insisting this was going to be fun.

Ok. Enough was enough. Echo had to figure out a way to keep up.

The choreographer clapped her hands. "Okay, come on guys, we have time for one more take." Echo pushed her knees and pulled herself up to full height. She could do this. She could do this.

The choreographer turned to Echo. "Okay. There has to be someone in your life that you want to dance for."

Telia's eyes twinkled. "Yeah, Echo. There has to be someone." Telia struck her pose in the center with Echo to her left. Echo closed her eyes. She felt the house lights dim. And as she heard Beyoncé implore her driver to roll up the partition, Brandon's image materialized before her, clad in a towel, six-pack, and a smile.

She opened her eyes half-mast and danced the way she should have that night. She dipped lower in her body roll. She smirked at the camera, imagining it was Brandon. She danced as if this dance was the only thing standing between her getting him in her bed for one night. Her back arched harder. Her leg kicked higher. Her eye glinted with a level of seductive knowledge that she didn't know she had.

If she was going to do it, Brandon was going to love it. Even if he never, Ever, EVER saw one single second of this video.

She strutted across the stage, flipped the endless tracks of weave the hairstylist had put on her head just that morning, dipped lower than she thought her knees could handle, and popped back up in her end pose. After Donna yelled cut, the other dancers surrounded Echo, congratulating her and giving her high fives. She laughed and enjoyed the camaraderie. She knew she had slayed it. And thank God she wouldn't have to do that damn dance one more time.

In the distance, though, she heard another set of hands clapping. The public wasn't allowed on set. Who could that be?

As the form walked from the shadows and she recognized Brandon's gate, she stiffed and pierced a mental arrow through Telia's forehead. She'd invited Brandon, no doubt. Telia crossed the line. Oh, yeah. Her best friend was going to die today.

CHAPTER
29

Echo huddled in Brandon's front seat, not quite sure how she became his passenger. One minute, the dancers surrounded and congratulated her. The next, Donna ushered everyone out of the theater, almost throwing their bags out behind them.

When Echo mentioned that Telia was her ride, Donna merely said Telia had arranged for another ride and nodded toward Brandon. Echo quickly donned her jacket, as the theater door slammed in her face.

The casual way Brandon leaned against his car indicated he knew that he was her ride. She felt like she'd been dropped in the middle of a story that everybody knew, and she didn't have so much as a cheat sheet.

Where was Telia? Who the hell knew? In the commotion, she hightailed it backstage.

Echo should call a cab just to mess with them. It would serve both Brandon and Telia right. She's hogtied into an outfit that any burlesque dancer would be proud to own, heading to Brandon's car.

As they rode, Brandon actually made the initial attempt at conversation, "Telia suggested we head to your place so you could get some clothes."

Echo grunted and focused her view out of the window. God, the temperature had to be two-hundred degrees inside his truck. Air. Echo needed air. She made an attempt to unzip her jacket, until she met the boobs that were two sizes bigger than normal and realized she would be damn near naked in front of Brandon.

Wait a minute. Why was she cowering in the corner of the passenger seat? She'd been victimized, bamboozled, run amuck, set up, trussed up in high-class call girl clothing. Now she was headed to her house with a man whom Telia knew that she wanted to ride like a freaking pony.

Telia had removed herself from the situation, probably congratulating herself on her own ingenuity in getting her and Brandon together. Brandon would pay for playing Telia's game. No matter what Telia or Brandon had planned, Echo would rather swim through a Louisiana swamp in July than allow them to dictate a second more of her life.

Plan "Like a Virgin" was in full effect. Echo slid out of her jacket, making sure she arched her back as she freed herself from the restraint. "Wow, I'm boiling. I'm surprised you can take it." She pulled her hand off her neck to fan a bit.

Brandon did a double take and tightened his hands on the wheel. "You know I could just turn on the air. I wouldn't want you to melt."

Echo giggled, bringing her hand to her chest, and ran her fingers along the edge of the top of the bustier. Brandon glanced out of the side of his eye, and then shifted in his seat.

"I'm good," Echo purred. "Phenomenal."

Interesting. Funny, his biceps bunched as if he could rip the wheel out from the column. Echo lifted her leg and broke the cardinal rule for wearing uncomfortable heels. She took them off. Her aching toes sighed their thanks. She propped her foot on the dashboard and massaged her calf.

"You don't want the car next to us to get into a crash staring at your thighs. You should probably lower them."

Echo turned, giving him a knowing smile. Making a show of looking out of all the windows, to confirm that no one was even within twenty feet of them, she inquired, "What car?"

Brandon sighed his frustration. "Never mind."

Echo turned up the radio and began to dance to the beat, making sure there was plenty of body rolling and gyrating. Every song was "her song" or "her jam" or "the shit." Tension rolled off Brandon thicker than San Francisco fog in the morning.

By the time they pulled up to her apartment, Echo swore she witnessed a certain member of Brandon's anatomy saluting the gearshift. But there was one way to be sure. "Brandon, would you mind helping me down? The truck is soooooo high."

Grumbling, Brandon trotted to the passenger seat and opened the door. As Brandon held out his hand, Echo jumped into his arms forcing him to hold her tightly. Internally, Echo grinned like a Cheshire cat with a plate full of tuna, as she felt the brick encased in his pants. As she slid down his body, she realized all she had to do was lean in, and she'd have access to those full lips. Without further thought, she gently touched her lips to his. He palmed the back of her head, pulling her tighter, arching over as her feet touched the ground.

Delectable.

Smiling against his lips, Echo ended the kiss. "Pick me back up in the morning."

Brandon blinked twice. "What?"

Echo inched back, her heels clicking on the pavement. "Tomorrow. Pick me up tomorrow." Although inside she danced a Charleston, the tides were turning.

Brandon reached for her hand, but she scooted out of reach. "Well, the children are with Remy. We don't need to hang out tonight."

Brandon recovered enough to lower his eyelids and the timber of his voice. "Oh, I can think of a few things for us to do."

Crap. Echo only had about one move a day, and she had already used it with the slide down Brandon's body and the kiss. Her body liquefied at the invitation. Unconsciously, she leaned in. This time she was the one shaking her head to clear it.

"The morning then. I'll see you in the morning." She scurried to her door before she did something crazy like jump into his arms, wrap her legs around his waist, and stick her tongue so far down his throat that she would French kiss his esophagus.

At the Touch of Love

CHAPTER 30

So little Echo had some gumption after all. The way her body moved on stage, and the way her lips moved off stage before she scurried into the relative safety of her apartment, added a little spice to her sugar.

Now she needed convincing to sprinkle some of both on him.

He leaned against the door watching Echo run away from him or at least attempt to run, given the height of the heels.

Brandon's phone buzzed, bringing him back to the reality that he was basically daydreaming, as he stood in the middle of a Chicago street with his car running and the keys in the ignition. It would take less than a minute for someone to hop in and drive off. Trotting around to the driver side, he continued to watch Echo as she entered her building safely. Brandon debated following her and taking her up on the gift promised in that kiss.

His phone buzzed again. He read the message. Shit. The hospital was calling all hands on deck. Within five minutes, he'd get the official call to see if he could come in from vacation. Luckily, his co-workers continued to keep him abreast of what happened, so that he could answer or avoid as needed. Hell, this was his leave. Considering all the hours he put in while he was there, someone else needed the opportunity to play hero. That's the bad part of being the go-to guy. Even when he wasn't available, they kept trying to go to him. These days had to be about Dan. He'd go to the hospital, but he'd be in Dan's room.

Nothing was more important than that.

As he entered the locker room and waved to a few other doctors before sitting on a bench in front of his locker, he gripped the wood as memories of conversations he had with Dan in this exact room whirled around his psyche.

Brandon recalled one night when Telia found out that she was pregnant with Shelley. She'd been so pissed that she kicked Dan out of the house. He found Dan sitting on one of the hospital cots, totally dejected.

Brandon sat beside him. "I thought they only let real doctors in here."

Clearly, Dan didn't take the bait. Brandon tried again. "What's going on, man?"

Dan blew out a breath so dejected that Brandon thought something was seriously wrong, but then Dan came out with, "Telia's pregnant."

Brandon paused. Two adults having a baby didn't warrant the slumped shoulders, long face, and general negative countenance of Dan.

"And?"

Dan shrugged. "That's it."

Brandon wanted to jump up and slap him on the back, light up a cigar or two, shout it from the rafters—not mourn. The reaction seemed oddly inappropriate. He remained quiet while Dan continued.

"Well, see, I'm in charge of birth control basically; and so I have options—condom, rhythm, whatever. And I chose to let nature take its course a couple of times during her fertile period."

"You set her up?" Brandon could feel his jaw drop, but for the life of him, he couldn't lift it back up.

They automatically quieted as a page for a doctor came over the loudspeaker. Both of them almost shifted into gear, before realizing they were both off the clock. They continued the conversation.

"Well, the first time she was pissed, but she didn't get pregnant; so I was fine. So she kind of rolled with it; but as I suspected it would, it caught up with us."

"Yeah," Brandon responded, trying to match Dan's somber expression.

"And she's pissed." Dan's shoulders slumped.

"Okay." Brandon furrowed his eyebrows, trying to come to terms with

At the Touch of Love

the fact that Dan thought Telia would be okay with a surprise pregnancy.

Dan's head hung lower. "And she kicked me out of the house."

Brandon didn't know what Dan expected. "Well, you did set her up."

"Here's the thing, Brandon. She was never going to be 'ready.' Come on. She lives to flit around the world."

Another doctor walked in, and they gave him a friendly nod as he walked over to a locker and gathered his things. Brandon thought about filling the silence with inane talk, but he was too interested in their present conversation to give attention to anything else.

"So how long is your exile going to last?" Brandon inquired, after their co-worker cleared the room.

Dan crossed his arms and shrugged. "I don't know."

Brandon couldn't hold his excitement in much longer. "So are you like 'country song, slit your wrist, my baby done left me' depressed, or can I congratulate you on the impending birth of my niece or nephew?"

Dan's eyes gleamed with pride. "That's going to be one kick-ass baby."

Brandon threw up his hands in relief. "Finally."

They embraced, slapping each other on the back. "She might not have been mad enough to kick me out if she didn't have morning sickness on a flight, threw up on herself, had to change clothes in an airplane bathroom, grab a pregnancy test in a different state, and then had hours to plot my demise on the return flight."

"Wow." Now Brandon got it.

"I know," Dan replied.

Brandon hesitated a second before asking, "Did anyone—"

"Yeah, full flight. From what I could ascertain from the shrieking when she got home, she was doing first-class food service. Something in the meal didn't agree with the baby.

She managed to drop the food on the passenger's tray, which of course splattered. She covered her mouth, tried to run, but was caught in the aisle, and kinda spewed it everywhere."

They observed a moment of quiet before they both roared with laughter.

"It was all I could do not to laugh in her face," Dan exclaimed, "but if you had seen her face, you would've understood why I decided laughter was a horrendously bad idea."

They glanced at each other and broke into another round of laughter. "You can't tell her I told you. You can't."

Brandon grabbed his side. "But this one is too good to keep under wraps. Please. One joke. Just let me have one."

Dan's eyes were so huge they could have doubled as globes. "No, you can't. She'll freak."

"Who'll freak and over what?" Laughter came to a complete halt as Telia stood at the door. She glared at Dan. Her hand shaking as she pointed. "You ... you."

"Hey. You told Echo. I know you told Echo. So you can't get mad at me for telling Brandon."

Telia pointed her fingers and put roots on Dan like Celie in "The Color Purple" "Until you do right by me...." Only Telia was saying "I swore you to secrecy."

"Yeah, but I didn't agree to go along with it."

Telia turned to flounce.

Brandon couldn't help himself. "You better watch those sudden moves, Upchuck."

Telia launched herself across the room, but Dan anticipated the move and grabbed her before she managed to choke Brandon.

Telia stood stiffly in Dan's arm as he whispered in her ear. Her lips twitched, and twitched again. Dan continued to rub her arm as he whispered. Finally, she broke out into a full-fledged smile. "I'm still pissed."

Dan's face held no expression. "As I expect you to be."

Telia pointed again. "And you owe me."

Dan nodded sagely. "I absolutely do."

Then she melted in his arm. "And we're going to be parents."

"Yeah, yeah we are."

As they rocked each other, Brandon eased out of the room. He was going to be an uncle. How early was too early to break out the cigars?

Now as another doctor left the locker room, he wondered, would Dan's condition and Telia's move him from uncle to parent?

He hoped to hell not.

CHAPTER
31

As Telia eased her weary limbs into her new home in the chair by the window in Dan's hospital room, she perused the sterile setting. Extra chairs created a maze for anyone who walked through the door; and the television was tuned to some sports station, of course.

"Did you enjoy spending time today with the fellas?" Telia inquired. The ambient noise of the television and monitors were her only replies.

"So I made a surprise for you today, Dan. I can't wait for you to see it. I'd tell you about it, but then"—Telia let the sentence trail off without stating the rest of her commonly used sentence—"I'd have to kill you."

It's surprising how often people bandied about death, with little regard for the severity of what they were saying, until reality came and drop-kicked them in the face. One common expression, "I'd tell you, but then I'd have to kill you" meant nothing a few months ago. Hell, she would've uttered it with a fake accent, without blinking. She had sent him out there with the children without people-sized bubble wrap, and without letting him know how much she truly, truly loved him. She had waited too long, and now ….

Now with Dan in a coma and her insides turning against her, she didn't play with death. Yet death toyed with her like a marionette—dance, bitch, dance.

And she was dancing like Debbie Allen held a stick in one hand and music in the other; dancing around Mrs. Ellison, who seemed a bit too excited about the thought of Telia needing her for money; dancing around the children, and a child who has figured that something is extremely wrong, and the adults are bullshitting; dancing around the fact that her life was not coming to the kind of end that she was prepared for.

Now she officially ran out of good excuses. How, when, and where would she tell Echo that one more person in her life was going to leave her? Couldn't someone just tell Echo when they gave her directions to the funeral? Telia was dying. Wasn't that enough?

Telia let out the reclining chair and sighed. "One thing I will say is that we are definitely getting a recliner in the house," she whispered to her husband's non-responsive form. "Mentally, I always associated them with a bachelor pad, but I've been wrong before. Hopefully, out of all the things you remember, me being wrong isn't one of them." Smiling, Telia snuggled deeper into the chair, preparing for a short nap before she launched into yet another memory to share with her husband, hoping that he was somehow hearing her on a subconscious level.

Telia shot up, clutching her heart as the door was whipped open by clench-jawed Mrs. Ellison, followed closely by Christoff. Christoff leaned nonchalantly against the door frame as Mrs. Ellison attacked.

CHAPTER 32

"You. You called a lawyer on me." The tight lid Mrs. Ellison kept on her emotions blew, the minute her lawyer notified her that he had been contacted by Telia's lawyer.

Telia rose to her full height, as Mrs. Ellison walked directly up to her. Telia stood, and Rose's hands itched to knock her back down in her seat. Dobsons didn't lose control. Dobsons didn't get violent—they get even.

Mrs. Ellison scanned down, taking in the bustier and boy shorts, nostrils flaring. "Well, at least you're now embracing your chosen profession. The oldest one in the book."

Mrs. Ellison pushed a manila envelope onto Telia's chest. Telia stepped back to place air between them before asking, "What the hell is this?"

Laughing, Mrs. Ellison folded her arms. "Why, your medical records, dear?" Rose could now clearly see where Dan spent the money. Medicine became a significant expenditure of late.

Telia tossed the envelope on Dan's food tray. "Those are private."

"My gosh, you have such a poor people's mentality—always obstacles. Money makes solutions. Tell me, do you really think when the judge finds out how sick you are that you are really going to keep the children from me?" Peering closely at Telia, Rose could now see the dry skin, the circles under her eyes. She attributed that to stress over Dan's condition. Rose had been wrong.

Telia's condition slowly sucked away at her vitality. The stress of Daniel in the hospital bed didn't help.

Telia survived off meds and moxie. Respectable, but now more than ever, Rose needed to ensure the Dobson children were raised as Dobsons—not Ellisons, and surely not Arthurs.

If she learned anything from Dan's father, it was to strike while the iron is hot. Now, the iron was blistering.

Telia ground out. "It's irrelevant."

"Maybe, but by the time this rolls through court, you won't see a dime of my son's money."

"It's my money too," Telia responded.

Chuckling, Mrs. Ellison drew a check out of her purse and held it towards Telia. "Would you like me to write you a check now for your little drop in the bucket, and then this will all be over?"

Telia's body shook and she swore, "You have no right."

Mrs. Ellison smiled as she folded her arms. "No, legally, I have every right."

Telia took a deep breath and closed her eyes. When she opened them again, she appeared calmer. Rose laughed to herself. All she had to do was prick the right place and Telia's temper would erupt again.

"What are you going to do, dear?" Mrs. Ellison edged closer. "Going to ask your dear friend Echo for a loan? My bank account doesn't have a bottom. She'll be living in your basement before you manage to get one court proceeding."

Telia spoke through clenched teeth, "I want my money."

Mrs. Ellison smirked. "All you ever had to do was ask. How much, dear?"

"NO!" Telia tried another breath. "I can handle the family finances. Transfer the money to me."

She'd have a better chance of convincing the devil to play hopscotch than Mrs. Ellison to give up, evidenced by Mrs. Ellison's response. "What are you going to do? Put it between your mattress for a rainy day? You have no idea what to do with the Dobson money."

Taking another step back, Telia held up her hands. "I guess that's it. We will see each other in court."

Rose unfolded her arms, Silly girl. Telia truly believed she had a chance. "You're stubborn, and you'll lose. But it may be a good lesson for you."

Telia stared her down, as if they were on equal footing.

As Rose turned to leave, she added, "But just so we are clear, I want my grandchildren at my house first thing in the morning."

Time for Dobsons to get their shit together and conquer the world like their bank account dictated.

Straightening her spine and adding her hands on her hips, Telia responded, "My children are a commodity that you don't control."

Rose merely reiterated, "Have my grandchildren at my house first thing in the morning."

Telia erupted. "Your own son didn't want to be raised by you. What makes you think our children want to lose themselves in the mausoleum you call a house?"

That one fine razor sliced her every time. You'd think she would have a defense to it all these years, but it was as raw as the day the judge declared that Daniel would live with his father full time. That's a wound that doesn't heel. That always leaves you vulnerable.

Even Christoff, who knew to allow the scene to play out, stiffened and stepped forward. This wasn't a crazy person on the street. This was Telia. She could handle Telia. She would.

Mrs. Ellison's calm demeanor returned, and she held up one hand to hold off Christoff.

"You should read those notes. I was surprised at some of the meds you're taking, considering no doctor in the United States would prescribe them. Even if my son wakes up, those documents will have him answering some interesting questions. My son risked his reputation and medical license for you," Mrs. Ellison spewed. Telia started the war. She'd better be prepared to see it to the end.

"What the hell are you talking about?" Her mind automatically rejected the possibility that Dan lied to her. "All I have are meds to control the pain."

"Are they really?" Mrs. Ellison waved at the file. "If you follow the

At the Touch of Love

money, even you will notice something fishy about some of those payments."

"I trust Dan." Telia stood firm.

"Stand by your man. Admirable. Just like so many other silly women." Mrs. Ellison sneered. "Read the file, and have my grandchildren at my house first thing tomorrow morning." She flounced out of the room.

CHAPTER 33

Later that night, the creak of the hospital door opening made Telia stir. Normally, she never even bothered to lift her head after 10 p.m., since the only person making moves into the room was hospital staff.

Normally, she was on the pullout bed that made her dream of a better time when mattresses had names like Posturepedic. Tonight, she had curled into Dan's bed, which meant she needed to scoot off so the nurses could work their magic.

Mrs. Ellison did a number on her today. The file that she placed on the bedside table called to her. What good would it do for Mrs. Ellison to lie? Easy enough to find the truth. All she'd have to do was make sure the pills she took were the pills she thought she was taking.

However, if she went down that rabbit hole and proved Mrs. Ellison right. Would she be able to protect Dan? Would he spend their last days in jail? Would her family be able to fight Mrs. Ellison for custody? If Mrs. Ellison held their inheritance, would the judge side with her as the best place for the children.

Cracking one eye against the onslaught from the light from the hallway to make sure Mrs. Ellison hadn't snuck back in, she immediately sat straight up. "What the hell are you doing here?"

Oh shit. Squeezing into a bed that could only accommodate one butt cheek meant when Telia sat up, the other butt check hit nothing but air. As she tumbled to the cold, hard hospital floor, she swore vengeance upon Brandon.

Brandon came around to help her and stopped suddenly. *See it's situations like this when I need those eyes like Cyclops from the X-Men to burn a hole through someone's skull.* Hell, if Brandon had been using his brain, he wouldn't be in the hospital.

As she righted herself, the night nurse peeked in. Taking a deep breath to resist snapping at her, too, Telia merely stated, "I need a few minutes alone with Dr. Hall."

She enunciated every word so that his small, feeble male brain could understand. "Why aren't you with Echo?"

Brandon didn't move, didn't flinch. But he responded, "She told me to come back and get her in the morning."

"Good Lord." Telia raised her hands in prayer. "I know I'm wearing you out with prayers these days, but please help me to not lay hands on this man. He's trying me, Lord. He. Is. Trying. Me."

She took a step towards Brandon. "I trussed up my best girlfriend in some hot-assed Moulin Rouge-type clothing." Telia took another step. "Got her all hot and bothered and ready for you by taking her to a place where she could learn to loosen up."

She continued a slow, deliberate pace, punctuating each sentence. "All you had to do was have a thimbleful of game, and you would've had a chance to stop dancing around this thing you feel for her and show her what you were working with—brains being part of the deal."

Brandon's fool ass opened his mouth as if he was going to respond. There wasn't a response to this. None. Zilch. Zero. So Telia held up her hand to keep him quiet. "No, no. So you walk around here, like you've been walking around here for the past year, eyeing her ass like it's Ghirardelli's chocolate.

She's been walking around here dating men who were better left locked into whatever computer site they came from; but every time you walk into the room, her whole body stands to attention."

The door creaked again. Telia didn't even bother turning to see who had joined them. "Not now."

The door closed again.

"I gave you my bestie on a platter. And believe me; she knows she's been set up. The one thing I was banking on, the "keep me out of the dog house" plan, was your giving her an orgasm or three. She seems sweet, but she's sharpening every knife in her place right now and practicing her slicing technique."

Brandon's stupid ass opened his mouth again.

"Shush it!"

"You spent more effort on that Succubus than you are on my friend. And she's worth a thousand Susans. I'm going to ask what the fuck are you doing?"

Brandon clamped his lips. Telia waved her hand. "Go ahead. You can speak now."

"These things take time," Brandon explained.

Telia pressed her lips together. Time. Shit. Fuck and Damn. Brandon's right. These things take time. He had it. She didn't.

"I can't leave her with just anybody," Telia confessed. "Maybe if Dan wasn't .... I mean if I knew that he'd...," Telia collapsed on the couch. "We don't have time. You have to make every second, every interaction, every word count with her. I know you want her, and she wants you too. Why the hell are both of you being so damn stubborn when it comes to this?"

Brandon sat down next to her and pulled Telia against his side. "What if we aren't meant to be? "

Drawing back, Telia's eyes begged him for an answer. "You never once said that you didn't want this to work. You've always said you didn't *think* it could work. When you touch her, hold her, how do you feel? If you tell me you feel nothing, I get it. I'll back off. I'll try to get her and Remy together again."

Brandon's body stilled like someone had frozen him in time. Telia dared not to even breathe. So much depended on the next words that fell from his lips.

"No way. Fuck Remy. Echo belongs with me." Releasing a breath, he whispered, "We kissed. Telia, the lightning."

Smiling with a relief she didn't realize she could feel, Telia agreed. "I get it. Dan's arms are the same way."

Brandon tensed. "Before you go any further. He's my best friend—and a man. I don't need details."

Telia's giggle ended with a snort of laughter that caused Brandon to grin.

Brandon turned, his eyebrows peeled to his hairline. "What was that?"

Telia allowed a full laugh to break free. God, it felt good.

Brandon and Telia leaned back and watched Dan. Brandon cleared his throat before asking, "So how are you feeling?"

Telia tried to shut her eyes against the tears that immediately formed from that common question. "I feel like if I start crying that I'll never stop."

"What can I do?" Brandon inquired.

"Do you know the movie *Dirty Dancing*?"

Brandon's face scrunched in confusion. "You want me to rent you a movie?"

Punching Brandon in the arm, Telia continued, "Maybe I should trade up for someone who actually listens."

He grimaced, but didn't snap back with a retort.

"Patrick Swayze had really bad knees, a football injury or something. That jump and landing from the stage at the ending we all know and love was going to be horrifically painful. No getting around that. And you know what he did?"

"He got a stunt double," Brandon attempted.

"He made sure the cameras were rolling, and he jumped his ass off the stage."

"And the analogy is …?"

Telia wiped the tears from her cheek and sat up straight, extracting herself from the warmth of his body. "He died of pancreatic cancer. He knew long before the world did, but he didn't cry about it; didn't whine about anything. Well, he might have. I wasn't living with the man. He worked for as long as he could … lived for as long as he could. So that's what I'm going to do. I'm going to Swayze this bitch."

Brandon's smile formed slowly, as if it was on its own time delay. "Yeah. You wouldn't do it any other way."

"What's that supposed to mean?" Telia held up one finger. "Never mind. Don't tell me. I'm going to take it as a compliment. And I only have one thing to say to you."

Brandon paused, "Of course you do. What is it now?"

Telia playfully tapped his nose. "There's no place like home. Get your ass off this couch and go get your girl."

Brandon tried to stare her down, but she was a flight attendant. This was not her first stare-down go round. He stood. "Yeah, yeah, yeah." He paused when he got to the door. "For the record, I think you're amazing."

This man was still talking? "If you don't get your ass out of here …"

CHAPTER 34

To Echo, sleep was as elusive as sunlight in the middle of a snowstorm. So she stewed. Telia wasn't answering her phone. The kids, who were always good for a distraction, were with Remy. Brandon, well, the last thing she wanted to do was think of Brandon.

However, every time she closed her eyes, she could see him. Her body was screaming for her to call him and/or do him. Her body screamed for the sex. Her intimate areas were betraying her, their loyalty to their own satisfaction—selfish naughty bits.

No matter how much she tried to convince her body that Brandon was bad, she kept getting a tingly sensation in her nether regions. Her nether lips pulsating in need, and they wouldn't be happy until they were wrapped around his monolith.

However, she didn't know if she was ready for that.

If it was a sex thing, maybe. But every minute they spent together allowed him to worm deeper into her senses: the way he asked about her parents, really asked about them, who they were, not just that they were gone; the way he stayed day in and day out, present because Dan and Telia needed him to be; the slow way his smile crept in, as if it had all the time in the world to express happiness.

Maybe she should stick with the sex. Sex is easy. Now she toyed with

Sierra Kay   **167**

the emotions that change who you are, shift who or what you may become. Now she toyed with the emotions that mattered.

Plus, there were so many *what-ifs* that could go wrong. Their lives were entwined tighter than ivy on a chain link fence. The ripple effect of a failed relationship between the two of them would swallow everyone like a tsunami. Apparently, she was the only person in the world who realized that fact. A quick glance at her overdone attire brought home that Telia had pimped her out like she owned a diamond-encrusted cup and a cane—Don Juan style.

Echo stared down at the purple velvet bustier; pushing her cleavage up to her chin and thinning out her waistline, making her appear strip-pole-ready. How often did she get a chance to dress like this, with full professional makeup?

She extended her garter-encased thighs to the ceiling, enjoying the extension provided by the heels. There should be a law that women had to dress like this at least once a year, because even to herself she was hotter than Halle Berry on a red carpet and felt more confident than she'd felt in years.

However, Echo knew the illusion Telia crafted wasn't reality. Reality included dead parents, comas, babysitting, and a man that if he wasn't her godchildren's godfather, she'd be climbing faster than that rope in gym class. And then what?

She practiced a few of the moves that she'd learned a few hours ago. None of them would do her any earthly good alone in a mirror.

Just as she got to the dip, her bell rang. The clock on her iPod said the time was close to midnight. No way was she answering the door.

The incessant knocking that followed the bell had her grabbing for her robe and running for the door. *Oh, my God. What if?*

Launching herself at the door before a neighbor complained, she viewed Brandon through the peephole. Her heart rate elevated. She immediately yanked the door open, "What happened? Dan?"

Brandon's eyes bugged before he responded, "Dan's fine. No change. He's fine."

Echo collapsed against the door, holding her hand to her heart, willing it to slow down. She couldn't take this.

Brandon squatted in front of her. "Echo? Echo?"

If her eyes connected with his, the stress of this week would gush out in tears. "I just … Next time phone first. This is …"

Brandon led her away from the door, locking it behind him. He guided Echo to the couch and sat down and pulled her onto his lap. She relaxed on him, as he stroked her back with strokes that seemed to make everything that had her so tightly coiled seep away.

The tears she tried valiantly to hold in fell anyway. Her body shook with the emotion that she'd held back for days. Why couldn't life be easy? Why couldn't everyone just live happily for eternity? Why couldn't she keep her emotions in check?

Brandon whispered in her ear, "It's okay. It's okay. I'm sorry. It's okay."

When her tears turned to mere sniffles, Brandon shifted her to the couch. He leaned over and removed the stilettos. "Lie back. I'll warm some milk for you."

Chuckling, Echo lifted an eyebrow. "Is warm milk the official prescription, doc?"

The mention of doc, reminded Echo of the pain constantly on the outskirts of her emotions. Telia had taken time for granted. She hadn't realized that forever could literally be years, hours, or minutes.

Standing, she grabbed Brandon's hand and pulled him toward the bedroom. Fuck a glass of milk. And double fuck Susan. She wanted Brandon tonight.

CHAPTER 35

Echo's eyes darkened. Her shoulder straightened with resolution. She stood and tried to pull Brandon up. He knew her decision before she lifted herself off the couch. Even as the devil was break-dancing on his shoulder at the chance to make love to Echo, Brandon's mind closed the door on the very thought.

Yes, seeing her in the corset had him so hard he could jackhammer through his zipper. But this was Echo: Echo, who was mourning the passing of her parents, terrified of the prospect of Dan not making it, jobless, and quite possibly needing sex as a lifeline.

Sex between them didn't need to be a lifeline. It should be a celebration, exultation, not a distraction.

He resisted the tug of her hand. She turned and read the no in his eyes. Brandon's heart fell to the bottom of his chest when her eyes shattered in pain.

"Why don't you leave then?" Her throat thickened around the words, indicating how hurt she felt by his rejection.

"Why would I leave?" He needed her to understand. If he left now, the possibility of them would wither on a vine.

"You don't want to be here … with me. You knocked on my door after 10 p.m. What else could you possibly want?" Brandon nodded. She spoke the truth. He knocked on her door at midnight, which is prime booty-call hours.

At the Touch of Love

If sex was all he required, there were plenty of doors that would open for him. He wanted to be with Echo.

Standing up, he eased his hands around her waist and pulled her towards him. Her body gave off the sharp scent of her desire. Leaning down, he gently placed his lips on hers. A brief connection of their lips wasn't enough. He sunk into the kiss. The more he engaged, the more he wanted.

Kissing Echo was the best bad idea he'd had in a long time.

Pulling back, he placed his forehead against hers. No matter how much he wanted her; he didn't want to be that dude, the one that took advantage of a situation.

"Echo, what's your favorite color?"

He understood why her forehead wrinkled in confusion. He might as well have asked her the theory of relativity.

Echo winked at him. "Purple, can't you tell." She stepped back so he could admire the way her body appeared in the purple corset. As if he needed her to step back. The image of that outfit embedded itself deeply in his memory like a seed in a garden.

"Oh, yes, I can tell." He expelled a deep breath. "So what's your passion?"

Echo merely raised her eyebrows.

Brandon slapped himself on his forehead. "No. I mean I know you're a data analyst by trade, but does that excite you?

Echo nibbled his chin. "Brandon, you excite me. We are alone. And I'm fierce and wet and want you." Echo brushed her lips across his chin as she explained, "Now what are we going to do about that?"

Brandon stepped back. "We are going to talk."

If it didn't pain him so much to step back from Echo, he would have laughed at her expression.

He lowered her hand down to his crotch, and her expression registered shock. "Let me be clear." He explained, "I want you so bad that I might need two ibuprofens to walk out of here tonight."

Echo leaned in. "So why won't you let me take care of you?"

Brandon rubbed his thumb along her cheek. "The physical would be easy, but where would we be in the morning?"

Echo smiled. "Asleep?"

Laughing, Brandon agreed. "Please, we would probably be on Round 5; but that's not the point. The point is, if I want something real, something different, then I have to be real and different."

Echo couldn't believe her luck. But then again, this is how her life worked. "Are you going to be a girl about sex?"

Brandon lifted one eyebrow. "I think you've felt that isn't the case."

"I mean, can't we just enjoy sex?" Echo licked her lips, and she evaluated his body. "Have a good workout? Sweat out the sheets a bit?"

"Okay," he conceded. "How has that worked for you in the past?"

Echo grumbled.

"I didn't hear anything."

Echo conceded, "You know how that worked for me in the past. I'm single, aren't I?"

Echo continued to stare at Brandon, but he didn't even blink. "You're serious," she said with wonder lacing her voice.

Brandon nodded. Serious, yes; dead below the waist, no. If they didn't start talking about astrology soon, his body would veto his mind's good intentions and go for it.

"Fine," Echo sighed. "Let me change out of this."

As Echo headed to the bedroom, Brandon went to the kitchen. He heard drawers opening and closing as well as Echo muttering. He can only imagine the names she was calling him.

Hell, he was calling himself the same names. He didn't dwell on it though. For Echo, he wanted to do the work.

He placed a cup of milk in the microwave. After taking it out of the microwave, he added a touch of honey. By the time Echo returned wearing gray, long-sleeve pajamas, he handed her the cup.

He settled onto the couch and gently pulled Echo down until she settled into him.

"So I ask again, what's your favorite color?"

"Purple," she grumbled. The midnight quiet of her building left a void. The slight sounds of her refrigerator could be heard, if they listened hard

At the Touch of Love

enough.

"Fine." Echo begrudgingly asked, "Tell me about your G-Ma."

Pain exploded in his heart, as it did every time someone mentioned his G-Ma. He felt his body stiffen. He knew Echo felt it too. She probably also felt his hard-on deflate.

Echo turned. "Never mind. Tell me something else."

He couldn't say he wanted them to know each other and yet not talk about one of the most important people in his life. That's unfair. "G-Ma was fantastic … for me. My mother still says that she doesn't know who that particular lady was. The lady that raised her was stricter than a psych ward straightjacket.

"My G-Ma told me a story once: She had two brothers, right. And some bullies were chasing them home from school. They're running and screaming. And she was the oldest, and her mother was at work. They were her responsibility.

So she grabbed the closest thing to her on the porch, which was the empty milk bottle awaiting the milkman, and whipped it at the boys. Beaned one right in the head. Sent him home crying. But he left her brothers alone. Guess it worked."

Echo laughed out loud. "Man, I would've loved to see that. Sounds like she was a boss."

Brandon smiled. "Yes, a boss and a realist." With that story, there was a crack in his memory of his grandmother. Still an amazing amount of pain, but the belief that maybe he would be able to think of her one day without overwhelming pain sprinkled in. Hope blossomed. Echo gave him hope.

She slowly sipped on her warm milk, and he felt her body loosen. He kissed the top of her head.

Echo snuggled deeper into his arms. "They never said that death would be this difficult. Your life shifts completely in one day, just one day and your whole support structure is shattered."

Brandon closed his eyes as he rubbed her arm. "You can never prepare for it. How could you?"

"True," Echo yawned, "but the very people we miss are the ones who made us strong enough to survive missing them."

"Look at you," Brandon whispered in a voice so soft she barely heard it, "all philosophical. Can I ask you a question? What would you have done differently?"

Echo's head tucked into Brandon's underarm, but she replied, "Maybe believe in my strength, instead of succumbing to my depression. I'm starting to get Telia's point about wasting my time. And I hate when Telia's right. What about you?"

Brandon didn't even hesitate. "Save my G-Ma, any way that I could. That's pretty much it. Just save her."

"Did you ever think that maybe the reason God took her when He did, and she left when she did, was to save you? maybe save you the pain of having to deal with her illness? Take my story, for example: If my parents died at home, while I was away at school, no one would have known for days. If they were on vacation, it would have been weeks." Echo snuggled deeper.

Brandon gently rubbed her arm. "Logically, you managed to make all the sense in the world. Yet, you still mourn them so heavily. How can those two co-exist?"

Echo's breathing deepened before she responded, "Logically, people die all the time. We all have to do it sooner or later. But some days, I just miss them so bad it's like someone kidnapped me and plopped me down in an alternate universe with nothing familiar—except Telia, of course."

They let quiet sweep over them, as sleep pulled them into its warm embrace.

CHAPTER 36

As soon as Echo and Brandon entered the room, Telia grabbed Echo under the premise of getting coffee. Even Brandon recognized that as a thinly veiled excuse to gossip. Brandon smiled, as the petite, bubbly, brown-haired nurse explained that they were taking Dr. Dan for tests. Within a few minutes, two nurses transferred Dan to a gurney and pushed him down the hall.

Silence crept its way into the room and settled as if it planned to stay for a while. Brandon felt comfortable again. This was a far cry from the constant beep of the heart monitor. It gave him time to reflect.

Echo. The more they talked, the more enamored he became. Her wicked, sharp tongue. Very sarcastic. Brandon smiled.

Brandon walked over to stare out of the window, not enjoying the solitude, but hoping Dan got closer to waking up.

The door opened and Brandon turned, smiling thinking Telia and Echo returned. They hadn't.

In walked the stiletto-heeled, red-bottom-wearing ex-wife. One day, he would need to be the one taking the x-ray. This woman must have a tracking device embedded deep under his skin.

"Heeeyyy," she sang, with balloons trailing her.

When she noticed the empty bed, she raised questioning eyes to

Brandon. "I wanted to stop in and say hi."

"Tests." Brandon stroked his chin in thought. "I do find it interesting that you managed to sneak in when Telia wasn't here."

Susan didn't respond, but placed the balloon bouquet on the bedside table. "So do you have my check?"

"Wow. Straight to the point," Brandon stated.

Susan dragged her hand through her hair. "What's the problem? It's not like you don't have it. Pretend we are still married, and hand over the check."

Brandon plucked a tissue from the container. He gently twisted the end and twirled it in his ear in an effort to rid himself of the wax that must be blocking his hearing.

"Did you just say, pretend we are married?" Brandon cleaned the other ear. "Didn't I pretend enough when we were actually married? Pretended to be happy? That's why we're divorced."

Susan's eyes narrowed as she folded her arms under her breast. "You didn't pretend half as much as I did, baby."

Brandon closed his eyes and prayed for patience "You do know you need money, don't you. You don't insult people that you need."

Susan plopped down in a seat. "Brandon, why do you have to make it so hard? You pretend as if you want me out of your hair; and yet, you ensure that I stay in it. Miss me, don't you?"

Brandon couldn't believe her gall. "You cheated on me."

Susan glowered. "You're the one who filed for divorce. I never wanted a divorce."

Brandon questioned, "You really expected me to sit by while you had sex with another man.

As she stared at her nails, she added, "You could have watched."

Brandon didn't bother to respond. Their relationship had become a few highs sprinkled with way too many lows.

By the end of their relationship, Brandon worked at sex—it was nowhere near the enthusiastic coupling it had been when Susan was trying to reel him in.

By the time he understood that ending things would be better all around, it would've been easier to pop a Viagra and let Susan bounce on his dick, until she finished whatever gymnastics she considered a good time.

Susan's unimaginative, repetitive routine meant he ended up imagining another woman. Eventually, Echo became his go-to fantasy. Even back then, he'd wanted to taste the sugar promise of her lips. Brandon developed his skills to get Susan off as soon as possible, to get her off him as soon as humanly possible.

Susan snorted. "This temporary cash infusion has never been a problem before. It's her, isn't it? You were sniffing around her when we were still married."

"Don't even try," Brandon exploded, before lowering his voice. "Don't even try to pretend that I was unfaithful."

The previously bubbly nurse cautiously opened the door. Relief flooded her features. "Oh, Dr. Hall, it's you."

Susan turned around, eyed the nurse from tip to toe, and dismissed her. "Please give my husband and me some privacy."

"Ex-husband," Brandon interjected before the nurse retreated out the door, "ex."

Susan's lips lifted in a feral smile. "Brandon, go ahead and give in. Life will be easier for all of us, if I don't have to tell that bitch that you're 'dating' that you killed your own dearly departed grandmother."

Telia and Echo chose that moment to walk through the door. All the seconds of the year, and it was that second that they wanted to return from the cafeteria.

Echo's eyes widened as they locked into Brandon's. He could see Telia's eyes tighten. "First, where is my man? And second, I thought you'd exed this heifer from our lives."

CHAPTER 37

Echo's head ping-ponged between Telia and Susan.

Susan sneered at Telia. "I came to see, Dan."

Telia folded her arms. "I'm sure you did."

"I'll tell my comatose husband that Brandon's ex-wife dropped by," Telia smirked. "I'll be happy to."

Susan opened her mouth, but left without another word.

"I don't know how you did it, Brandon. I feel like I need an extra shower just being in the same room. Right, Echo?"

Brandon wasn't saying a word. Echo couldn't make herself turn from his eyes. What did happen to his grandmother? She knew she had Alzheimer's and she died. That's about it.

Step by step, Brandon closed the distance between him and Echo. "Babe, I didn't … I couldn't kill my grandmother. My G-Ma." He embraced Echo. "Don't look at me like I did. Please."

The dark-haired nurse came back. "Dr. Hall?" Brandon peered at her. "Your wife?"

"Ex-wife," he corrected.

"Yes, well, the lady that was just here is cursing out this old lady that bumped into her."

Brandon didn't as much as move. "Call security."

At the Touch of Love

The nurse responded, "We did. She's cursing him out, too."

Brandon squeezed Echo for good measure and followed the nurse outside the room.

Telia slouched in the chair and glared at Echo. "I can't believe you are going to believe that trick over Brandon. Dr. Brandon Hall killed his grandmother? Really? They were so close, at one point I thought he came out of her vagina."

"No," Echo whispered. "The last time at Dave and Buster's she said something like that. I know it's Brandon and you trust him, but he could be a Lifetime movie waiting to happen."

Telia responded, "You went to the repast. You helped to comfort the man. TYou truly believe he'd kill his grandma—any grandma. Remember?"

When she walked into the Ellison residence prepared to babysit; only to find out that the children had a play date and they expected Echo to actually attend the funeral, she felt bamboozled, led astray.

She hated funerals. Well, everyone hated funerals. She avoided them, always being busy when the very idea of someone's funeral came along.

After attending the double funeral of both her parents in college, she figured she'd clocked enough hours at gravesides.

After the funeral, the family went back to G-Ma's house. Echo, Telia, and Dan blended in with the mourners—all the mourners except for one.

Echo stared out of the kitchen window, watching Brandon alone in the backyard.

Telia came up behind her and wrapped her arm around Echo's waist. They both stared as Brandon in a dark blue European cut suit with black shoes, stood by the evergreen tree line with his head bowed.

Telia sat her head on Echo's shoulder. "He's hurting."

No shit. The death of Brandon's grandmother kept Brandon shrouded in an impenetrable curtain of pain. Echo recognized the feeling similar to how she felt after her parents' death.

Ahh, Echo mused. *That's why she was there*. Echo knew about death, pain. What she struggled with is surviving it. Every day it was her good morning kiss and her goodnight prayer.

Telia pushed Echo. "Talk to him, please."

Echo turned. She didn't want to revisit pain. Her life was built upon the foundation of it. However, if knowing this, Telia still dragged her here, Brandon must be in a horrible place.

Echo closed her eyes and inhaled air into her lungs, as she walked up to Brandon. The pain he shrouded himself in insinuated itself into the deep layers of her mood. Now she understood why everyone left him alone. Dealing with their own pain at the loss of his grandmother, plus his, had to be overwhelming.

As she came closer, she didn't bother with pleasantries. "It won't help, you know."

Brandon turned and Echo gasped, his eyes broken and searching. Is this how she appeared after her parents' funeral? Lord.

"Echo." Echo watched as he valiantly tried to pull himself together. Like shattered glass blowing in the wind, he'd never be whole again. He continued, "Thank you for coming. If you don't mind, I need a few minutes."

Echo placed her hand on his arm. "It doesn't help. The 'could've, would've, should'ves don't help."

Brandon held up his hand. "Listen—"

"Just give me one minute and I'll leave," Echo pleaded. After seeing Brandon's nod, she continued, "I'm a professional mourner, a card-carrying member of the Depression Club. I know what you're going through more than anyone else.

"I know you're thinking of all the things that you should have done differently. All the things that you should have said. If you were just there…"

Brandon's head snapped up. Echo plowed ahead. "But everything happens as it should. The police ruled it an accidental overdose of her medication. She was having a good day. Dementia. I can't imagine what you or she or anyone else went through dealing with that."

Brandon took a moment before continuing, "But I was the one she trusted the most, the one she depended on the most. This should never have happened."

Echo tried a different tactic. "So you'd prefer if she was here on earth with you instead of enjoying her reward in heaven? Is that what you're saying?"

Looking shocked, Brandon backtracked. "No, I didn't mean that. I

At the Touch of Love

meant—"

"You meant you'd rather see the disease ravage her mind rather than her go this way," Echo challenged.

Brandon stuttered and took a step back.

Echo stepped forward and touched his arm. "You loved her."

He nodded.

"That's all anyone can ask. You loved her."

Brandon pulled Echo into his arms. "So how did you qualify for your Depression Club Card?"

Echo threw back her head and laughed. "That's a depressing story for a different day."

Glancing up, Echo extracted herself from his arms. "Susan's coming. I don't know which scene she's planning, but I won't participate. I would like to think I have a bit of dignity to not fight at a funeral. However, if she opens her mouth the wrong way, I don't know if I'll be able to control myself."

Now, sitting in Dan's hospital room she had to admit, Brandon appeared as if he'd welcome it if the ground opened up and swallowed him whole the day of his grandmother's funeral. She witnessed the pain radiating from him. He didn't resemble a murderer. But then again, neither did half the men in Lifetime movies.

CHAPTER 38

Echo kneeled in front of Telia's bowed head. "Tee?"

Telia's lashes swept open, while the rest of her body remained perfectly still. Her eyes flashed so hot you could see the heat glowing from Telia's skin.

Echo shuffled back while Telia rose out of the chair. "I am fucking exhausted. Damned tired." Telia stalked. "Susan? You're going to believe Susan over Brandon."

Echo eyed the door, anticipating whether or not she could make it out. Telia shifted. Echo couldn't get to the door before Telia snatched her back. Echo would have to run her straight over to have a chance at the door. Now for each step Telia took, Echo retreated ... away from the door.

Even now, with Telia's exhaustion, Telia poised to whoop some ass, and Echo happened to be the only other person in the room.

Holding up her hands, Echo attempted to calm Telia. "I didn't say he killed his grandmother. I'm just ..."

"You're just making excuses so you have a reason not to put your heart on the line," Telia spat out through clenched teeth.

"Girl, you need some rest." Echo tried to reason with Telia. "When Dan comes back from his tests, I'm going to have Brandon take you home to get some sleep."

Telia folded her arms, leaned on the frame of the hospital bed, and

At the Touch of Love

waited for a spell before saying, "I don't have time for your shit, Echo—not one second of one minute. Get it together."

Echo's jaws clenched.

"I can't. You can't," Telia started.

Echo sighed. "Now what?"

Telia's head snapped up. "You know. I have never done this to you. Every time you've needed me and, even when you didn't even know you needed me I have dropped everything, including my husband and kids, to run and be by your side, to prop you up, to drag you back out to life. But now, I need you."

Yeah, right. Telia never needed her. Their relationship was balanced between Echo's need and Telia's desire to give. Echo yawned. "What can I do? Pick up your dry cleaning? Oh wait, you have people for that."

"I'm dying. I'm fucking dying," Telia screamed. The words slammed into Echo like a punch in the chest, and the jabs kept coming as Telia whispered, "Cancer. I have terminal pancreatic, and I'm dying."

Echo didn't realize she moved until Telia held up her hands. "Don't. I need to get a lot out, and I can't do that if you touch me. If you hug me, I will disintegrate into a thousand pieces."

Echo wanted to break down to her knees; but if Telia stood through this, then so would Echo.

"Until this day, I have propped you up when you fell down or apart. But that ends today. Today and the rest of the days forward, you will be here for me and mine. I need to know that my family will be taken care of, and the only person I know who will take care of my family the way I would want them taken care of is you."

"Telia, I—"

Telia held up her finger. "No, I'm not done. Your only job from now on is to be here for me—and for my children. That's it, in any way that I dictate."

Echo's bottom lip trembled. Lord, the woman resembled Shelley so much it wasn't funny.

"So a couple of months ago, after my first diagnosis, I met this lady on a flight," Telia remembered. "And we got to talking. She told me all these things that happened in her life—bad time, after bad time. Her premise for life was that it was a string of unfortunate events, and then you die. And for her, that might be true.

Telia's face lit up, as an epiphany of light shone from under her skin. "I got to thinking, and I was like, she's right. Here I am with stage-four pancreatic cancer that they're saying is terminal. And I was so down."

"The next day, I'm back at home, and I'm bathing Shelley right before I plan to read her a story and put her down for the night. She's all up in arms about her bedtime. So I told her, 'I know. Life is hard.'" Telia chuckled. "Do you know what my five-year-old told me?"

Echo huffed, but she didn't respond.

"Plain as day, she said, 'Not for me, Mommy.' That five-year old knew, without hesitation, that her life was damn good, even with the thing she hates most hanging over her head. And this woman, at whatever age she happened to be, didn't see it."

Telia's unfocused eyes stared into the floor tiles. "And I gazed down at this incredible child, one I never thought I'd have, with a man I thought I'd never love as much as I do. I knew I wouldn't get the opportunity to see my Baby Bug grow into an amazing woman; but God could've taken me out of the game yesterday, last week, last year. But I'm still here."

"And," she continued. "If Dan had listened to me when it came to birth control, then this amazing little person wouldn't be in my life." She grinned.

"He thinks I don't know that he knocked me up on purpose. But what he doesn't realize is that I wasn't being too diligent about taking every precaution to not get pregnant. I wanted him. I wanted his child. I wanted to give him everything I could, I just …" She shook her head, trying to stem the tide of emotion rushing through her like a mighty wind. "Not the thing he wanted most."

She glanced at the engagement ring, and then lowered her hand to her side in order to lock eyes with Echo, who wrapped her arms around her midsection in a personal hug. "Do you know how lucky we are? I have found my soul sister from another mister in you. You're amazing—a bit emotional and prone to fits of depression, but amazing nonetheless. We have amazing times together."

The phone rang, but Telia ignored it. This moment was too vital to break.

"I have two amazing children, who will contribute unimaginable things to the world. I have found the love of my life in Dan."

Wonder laced Telia's voice, "And he actually gives me orgasms. Do you know there are women in this world who never have orgasms? How sad is that, to go through life wondering what something as miraculous as releasing all thought for the moments of pure feeling? How do they fake that, if they never had it? Every time Dr. Dan lays it down, he lays it down."

Echo giggled and her eyes glowed with humor. For a moment, Telia could picture Brandon doing the same for her friend, by wiping away the sadness, by showing Echo how much she is wanted, loved, and cherished. There was no greater gift than love, and she wanted that for Echo more than anything.

Echo stepped forward. "Telia how could you not tell me? How could you go through this without me?"

Telia merely stated, "Your birthday."

Echo held out her hands as if weighing a scale. "My yearly birthday depression versus your life. No comparison. How are you feeling? What are you thinking?"

"I don't have long in this world. Does that bother me? Yes. Does it depress me? No matter how hard I try, sometimes it creeps up on me and smothers me like a wool blanket," Telia paused.

Neighbors strolled past Echo's door, and their laughter rang out loud and clear. It took everything in Echo to remain still, to not take Telia in her arms and not cry so hard that snot came out of her nose.

"Listen. You don't have a job. Who gives a fuck? You don't have to work. Your home is paid for." Telia listed Echo's blessings on her finger: "You're learning how to love an incredible man, who puts those little butterflies in your stomach. I know, because I've seen the way your eyes soften when you look at him. You have a family. It's not the family you were born to, but you have me and Dan and Shelley and Rocky, Remy, and even Brandon. But they won't hold you up if you can't or won't do the same for them. If I'm not here and you lock yourself away, you'll just be one hermit-assed heifer.

Echo's body trembled with the effort it took to remain silent. "That's the promise that I need from you. I need you to hold up the people that I leave behind. It's been a glorious ride. I need you to step in and not be me, but remind them of me. I need you to do the things that I won't be able to do myself—not the cooking or cleaning—the living."

Echo inhaled and let out a long, slow breath. Every word brought a different kind of pain.

"Because, Echo, I can't stay for you," she whispered. "I would if I could. I would stay for you, for my Dan. for my kids. Hell, honestly, I'm not picky. I'd stay for the wino that lives under the bridge on Wacker and Lake. But I can't. The best I can do right here and right now is to make sure everyone whom I love is as prepared as I can make them for when I'm not here."

Each breath shuddered out of Telia's chest, as if it had to first force its way past all the hurt resonated in the words she had just spoken. "See those," pointing to a pink and a blue journal on the bedside table. "I spend time every day writing notes to my babies. There are teardrops on so many pages."

Echo shifted to her other foot and broke Telia's spell. Telia apologized. "Sorry. You can speak now. How do you feel?"

* * *

Echo felt as though she'd been slammed in the chest with a hammer. No matter how many times Telia tried to lighten the conversation with her special brand of humor, Telia's words squeezed uncomfortably into every corner of the hospital room, smothering Echo like cotton.

How did she feel? Like she needed two emergency inhalers and a steroid mainline. Air. She needed air.

How often does a best friend say, "I'm dying, but I don't have time for you to fall apart because I have to focus on living?" *What can I say to that?*

Echo's bed called to her like a siren in the middle of the ocean. *Echo you can hide here. You don't have to face Telia. I'm here for you, even if she won't be.*

But if Telia Arthur had the balls to stare death in the face and say, "Bring it on," Echo's days of hiding out when life overwhelmed her were over. That was for people who had the luxury of having a Telia.

Squaring her shoulders, she merely responded, "Whatever you need.

At the Touch of Love

I've got you."

Telia's shoulders visibly relaxed and so did the worry lines on her face.

"By the way," Echo snorted, "Of course, Shelley's life's great. Every time she bats a lash, there's an adult at her beck and call. Hell, she circles shit in her toy catalog and conveniently leaves them for someone to find, and it miraculously appears. She has an army of one in Rocky, who thinks she hung the moon. Her life *is* damn good. I swear, if I wouldn't have to go through high school twice, I'd switch places with her in a heartbeat."

Telia threw her head back and laughed. Closing the distance, she pulled Echo into a hug. They clutched one another, both crying and pretending not to.

Then several moments passed before Telia pulled back. "Okay, we have work to do."

Oh, brother.

"Brandon." A new light appeared in the twinkle of Telia's eyes.

CHAPTER 39

The staff returned Dan to the hospital room. They didn't have the results from his tests yet, but Dan's coma remained. So the rest mattered little to Telia. Echo made her excuses and insisted on taking an Uber home, which made sense. Telia knew she'd given her a ton to think about. She'd give her time—at least a little time.

Telia grabbed her cell phone and noticed Remy had called. Picking up on the first ring, he answered, "It's about time. I called you this morning for an update."

"The same. Let me speak to my babies."

Remy paused, "You must be more exhausted than you let on, Lil Sis. The warden picked up the kids before I could get a spoonful of cereal into them this morning."

Although her tone remained calm, her mind screamed, "The warden? Christoff?" So Mrs. Ellison planned on getting her time regardless. Telia yelled bye and rushed out of Dan's room, heading over to Mrs. Ellison's house.

Telia stormed passed the blond-haired maid, Rachel, who opened Mrs. Ellison's door. Mrs. Ellison sat primly on the edge of the pink floral couch, which held center stage in the vacuous drawing room. "Where the fuck are my kids?"

The way Mrs. Ellison's eyes widened with surprise made Telia's anger

At the Touch of Love

dissipate, replacing it with the naked fear that was reflected in Mrs. Ellison.

Mrs. Ellison responded in even tones. "What do you mean where are the kids?' You were supposed to have the kids. You've spent the past few days playing hot potato with my grandchildren and now you've lost them. You've lost the babies."

Telia shuffled back. "Oh, my God. Oh, my God. Remy said ... Remy." Her chest tightened; she struggled to breathe as thoughts crashed into one another. "Remy."

Mrs. Ellison ran around the white wood coffee table and grabbed her shoulders. Telia felt nails digging into her skin. Mrs. Ellison shook her. "Remy ... what? What did Remy say?"

Telia closed her eyes and willed her breathing back to normal. Shelley and Rocky needed her. They had no one else. "He said Christoff picked them up."

Mrs. Ellison covered her mouth with her hand and took two steps back. Telia heard Mrs. Ellison whisper, "Oh, no."

Telia glared at Mrs. Ellison. "So once again, where are my kids?"

Mrs. Ellison walked back to the couch and sank into the cushions, her eyes darting back and forth as if she were watching a movie in her head. "I didn't ask him to. He just ..."

Frustration rammed into Telia's heart, causing it to beat against the ribs of her chest. Her hands curled into fists. This bitch had five seconds to produce the kids before Telia karate chopped her ass.

Finally, Mrs. Ellison met her eyes. "They're safe. He wouldn't harm them."

"Wait." Telia's mind began to put together the puzzle. "You didn't tell him to pick them up?"

Mrs. Ellison stood. "Not directly." She walked quickly over to an intercom. "Tell Christoff I need to see him."

A voice responded, "He's not on the property, ma'am."

Telia opened her mouth, but stopped when Mrs. Ellison held up her hand. "Find him and tell him I need him."

The nameless voice responded, "Yes, ma'am"

Mrs. Ellison leaned her head against the wall for a few seconds before the starch showed back up in her spine. "I told you yesterday that I expected the kids at my house today. He just made sure that happened. He tends to be efficient that way."

Telia couldn't believe the gall or the calm exhibited by Mrs. Ellison. "By kidnapping them? He kidnapped my children."

Mrs. Ellison paused and shifted her head to the side. "I wouldn't use that particular word."

Telia couldn't believe the sounds that flew from Mrs. Ellison's mouth into her ears. "These are your grandchildren, and Christoff took them to who knows where without permission. Kidnapping. Abducting. Snatching. What word would you prefer?"

A tentative voice came over the intercom. "Ma'am?"

Mrs. Ellison depressed the intercom. "Did you find him?"

"Well, ma'am, he described the environment as hostile and said to tell you that the children are fine."

"Shit," Mrs. Ellison muttered before responding to the intercom. "Bring me my cell phone. It's in the office on top of my desk. There is a file there. Bring that as well."

Telia folded her arms. "We should call the police."

"No!" Mrs. Ellison shouted before calmly adding. "Dear, the children are fine. Christoff said so."

"Why aren't you more upset? I'm not quite understanding what I'm missing."

Mrs. Ellison inhaled deeply, as if she were trying to control her own emotions. "The kids are safe with him."

"Why? Because you pay him?" Telia snapped. "Someone else could have paid him more."

Telia wanted to break something—a lamp, a chair, Mrs. Ellison's neck. Even as her heart raced, she didn't have any evidence that the children would come to harm with their grandmother.

True, Brandon warned her; but besides being cold and creepy, to her recollection, Mrs. Ellison had never done anything criminal. Although Christoff could also be described as having the same level of warmth as Count Dracula, she didn't have proof that he'd hurt the children either. This could just be a power struggle.

When she first called her lawyer about the money, she asked him about custody. The only way her children could be taken away from her was if she was incapable of taking care of them. Right now, that wasn't the case.

Mrs. Ellison continued with her statement, "No, I'm saying he's loyal because he is. This has nothing to do with his paycheck," Mrs. Ellison enforced.

"I'm calling the police." Telia raised her phone.

"I wouldn't do that. If he thinks it's hostile now, how hostile will he believe it will be with blue and red flashing lights?" Mrs. Ellison inquired.

"I don't give a shit," Telia responded. *Crazy ass family.*

A dark-haired maid, Chelsea, raced in with a cell phone and file before scurrying right back out of the door.

"It's not about money with Christoff. It has never been. He's proved his loyalty. Saved me. Sometimes from myself."

Mrs. Ellison eased closer to the window and dialed a number. All Telia heard her say was, "Christoff?"

Telia paced. Of all the time for Dan's family to get aggressive with their crazy, why now?. Brandon had been right at the beginning. Christoff would never have pulled this shit if Dan was awake.

Telia pounced. "Is he coming? Is he bringing the kids?"

Mrs. Ellison responded, "Maybe if you leave for a few hours, I can get this resolved easily. Keep this within the family."

Tension remained in the room. Each minute raised it another notch. Telia finally walked to the salmon-colored chair on the right side of the couch and collapsed into the chair. Finally, tears streamed down her face. She heard a soft ripping sound before a tissue appeared in her hand.

"After my parents died, I went into a mourning period, which included pain medication pills." She breathed. "Christoff saved me from an overdose. Got me into rehab. He's the one who took Daniel to his father's house."

Telia interrupted, "The police. We need to call the police."

"Christoff is loyal."

"If he was loyal, he would have left my kids with Remy," Telia screamed. "How can you be so sure about him?"

Mrs. Ellison turned and paused. "The same way you're so sure of Daniel, dear. He loves me."

"That doesn't make me feel any better about this situation." Rose nodded. She didn't expect a different reaction from Telia. Telia's phone rang. She snatched it, panicked. "Hello? Hello!"

"Ms. Arthur, can you come back to the hospital? Dr. Dan is starting to react to stimuli." Now, she's being forced to choose between her children and her husband.

Telia disconnected the phone. "It's Dan. Something's happening."

CHAPTER 40

Rose sat next to Telia on the couch. She didn't touch or hold her hand. "In all the years that you've known me, Telia, have I ever put my son in danger?"

Telia didn't respond. Mrs. Ellison kept talking. "I know you and I don't get along. I know that Daniel and I struggle. But I will never hurt my family."

Telia still didn't move.

"I promise you, I will use every resource I have; and I will get the children back. By the end of the day, this will be a bad memory." Telia and Mrs. Ellison locked eyes. "While you may not want to admit this, I am a mother, too."

"Go to Daniel. I'll get the children." Rose read the pain in Telia's eyes. She literally couldn't be at two places at one time. So Rose played her trump card. It wasn't as if the children were in Timbuktu. Christoff would never go too far without her. He didn't trust anyone else to protect her.

Rose blew out a breath. She called in the house staff. They all lined up in the living room. She needed loyalty, and she suspected at least one of her staff wouldn't follow directions.

"Rachel, you're fired. Your suitcase and your severance check are by the door." The resounding gasp of the rest of the staff reverberated around the living room walls. The staff loved Rachel, but so did the children. That made

Rachel dangerous. Rachel may ask questions; and right now, Rose couldn't afford less than complete loyalty.

As Rachel edged toward the door, Rose walked the line of her staff. "If anyone ever questions any decision I make, you will be following right behind Rachel. You're dismissed."

She heard the staff muttering and turning to wave at Rachel as she walked out of the front door. Rose strolled over to the bar and poured a glass of wine before calling down to the gate.

Security responded and Rose declared, "Miss Arthur is leaving the property. She no longer has access to the front gate anymore. Matter of fact, neither does my son." Covering all the potential bases would serve her well.

A half an hour later, Christoff walked into the room. Rose stood. "The children?" He nodded toward the door, "They're with Charlotte."

He asked, "Telia?"

"She's gone. I told her that I never lied to her, and I still haven't. I told her I'd have the children by the end of the day. I never mentioned that she'd have the children."

Christoff chuckled.

Rose questioned, "Did you have someone call posing as the hospital?"

Christoff replied, "No. Why?"

"That's why she left. I thought you had someone call," Rose explained. "I thought it was a stroke of genius."

Rose laughed and leaned her body into his. "Well, we will call that divine intervention. Now we have the Dobson money, and we have the Dobson heirs. There's a private jet with our name on it. Where should we go?"

CHAPTER 41

Echo sat in the lukewarm water in her bathtub. Her initial very bubbly, bubble bath now had a thin floating cover of bubbles like moss on a lake.

Every time it cooled, she'd release some water and add more hot water into the tub. She didn't want to face the world. The world could suck it. Her best friend was dying.

Echo didn't even know what kind of treatments she sought, or anything. All she knew was that one day Telia wouldn't be on the other end of the phone.

She could lose another fourteen years mourning Telia, until the kids were grown and she was etched in their memories as crazy Titi Echo, who lived alone with five cats, three dogs, and a ferret that she named Captain Crunch.

Or she could find the strength to figure out how to stand beside Telia to ease her transition, to be her friend.

Echo heard keys jangling at the door. "Echo," Brandon's voice. Wait, he didn't have a key. Damn trusting Telia.

"Echo?" Soon he made his way to the bathroom and folded his arms in the doorway.

Echo closed her eyes as her head rested against the bathroom tile. "I don't know why I lock the door."

Brandon smiled. "I have Telia's key."

She hated him right now and, at the same time, she wished he was in the tub with her with his arms wrapped around her.

"Did you know?" she turned and scrutinized him. "Did Dan tell you … about Telia?"

Brandon didn't meet her gaze, but then nodded.

Echo peered over at Brandon. Somehow his confident swagger caught a slump. "Yes, I knew."

Inhaling to ready herself for bad news, she questioned, "How long does she have?"

"Don't know." Brandon shrugged. "She doesn't want her days to be a countdown to death."

"Incredible," Echo scoffed as tears tracked down her face. "That's so Telia."

Brandon reached in the tub. Batting his arms away, she said, "No. No. Leave me alone."

Brandon lifted her out of the tub and her body's wetness soaked into Brandon's shirt. He stood her up to drape a towel around her, before lifting her into his arms once again.

Again, Brandon placed her on her feet. Taking the towel, he gently swiped the water from her skin. Echo wrapped her arms around her body, trying to contain the pain. Brandon lifted one arm then another, patiently. After he dried her body, she crawled into her bed. He pulled her back against his body.

Warm air swirled around them as the heat drove May's chill from the air. That and silence served as their background music until Brandon spoke. "Tell me, when your parents died, did you know it was coming? Did you have some type of premonition? A crystal ball?"

Echo shook her head. She didn't know if this served in his mind as a pep talk, but usually one didn't cheer someone who was upset about death by talking about more death.

"What were you doing when they died?" Brandon inquired.

Echo fought against the desire to ask him to leave. Asking stupid questions was not the way to her heart or to ease her mind.

She hesitated for a few seconds before she responded. "I was partying. Okay. I was partying while my parents were dying."

Echo struggled to get free from his embrace, but he held firm.

"What was the last thing they said to you."

She froze, blinking as she thought back and said, "For me to work hard and have fun."

"Your parents wanted you to be happy, to glorify in this amazing life." Brandon tightened his grip a bit more. "Tragedy does mean an end, but it also should give a renewed energy for each and every day that we have."

Echo laughed. "You think I don't know that. But sometimes you feel how you feel."

Clearly, he wasn't done, because he persisted as if she hadn't said a word. "If we mourn Telia's living, we can't rejoice in each day we have with her—or that I have with you, or you have with me.

Your parents gave you strict instructions to work and have fun. You can't do that mired in the past, or being fearful of the future. You can only do that living moment to moment."

Echo turned over and popped him in the head. "Did you listen to me? Sometimes I feel how I feel. Right now, I'm depressed. I just found out my best friend has terminal cancer.

I reserve the right to wallow for a while. But at the end of the day, she's my sister and she needs me. As my dear friend, Telia would say, 'Let's Swayze this bitch.'"

Brandon's chest shook as he chuckled.

Over the years, Telia gave Echo strength through the bond of their friendship. Today, Echo felt as if she could handle whatever curve balls Telia's condition threw at her. She'd just ask herself, "What would Telia do?"

Funny thing was, she had lived through the worst. She knew she could survive the death of a loved one. She already survived the death of two loved ones, and she didn't drown.

Granted, she trod water for longer than she probably should have; but that's irrelevant.

She knew what pain felt like. She knew she'd come out on the other side. She did it then, and she'll do it now.

Relishing the feeling of Brandon's arms around her, Echo realized that she'd survive Telia's transition not just because she could absorb strength from Brandon, but because she'd already absorbed it from Telia.

CHAPTER 42

Telia peered over at the bedside clock, glowing with numbers that displayed 3:00 p.m. She had been at the hospital for an hour. Although she could hear the low murmur of conversation in the hallway, her immediate companions were the heart monitor, Dan's breathing, and her thoughts.

"Dan, do you think Brandon went back to Echo's?" Telia mused aloud. "I told her about the cancer." She paced the floor, worried about Echo, the kids, Dan.

Telia gently laid back in Dan's bed with his hand encased in hers.

"Remember our first time? Three weeks into dating. Well, three weeks and one day. I still say you left your phone on purpose to get me to your house. But you hold fast to your story."

Telia stroked the fingertips that were a little puffy from all the meds floating through his body. His fingers were cold. Not freezing cold, but she was used to Dan's hand warming hers, not the other way around. She rubbed his hand between the two of hers.

Those hands. The first time those talented hands roamed her body was a beautiful thing.

The night they entered Dan's house. "This will only take a minute, Telia. Come on in."

Telia's three-inch heels clicked against the dark grey slate tiles in the hallway. A stand-alone coat rack was off to the left side. Dan shrugged out of his coat. "Do you want to take off your coat for a minute?"

Telia smirked, "No, thank you."

Left his cell phone, my ass. Telia mentally kicked herself. She should've stayed in her car. Absolutely, shouldn't have left the car.

Dan rocked in place. "Would you like a tour?"

"No, thank you." Telia knew where house tours led—to a bedroom. and bedrooms led to sex. She wasn't new to this.

As if reading her thoughts, Dan grasped her hand and said, "No bedrooms. Only public spaces." His warm hand engulfed her slightly chilled ones and pulled her into a family room. She didn't resist.

The slate tiles from the hallway spread into a dark, masculine room with a dark gray leather couch placed on a white throw rug. *The fellas watch football on a white throw rug?*

He tugged gently on her arm and led her upstairs. Unlike the very masculine colors that decorated the family room, the upstairs was much lighter with the palest gray paint and teal and yellow accents. It wasn't her color palette, but it wasn't college furniture either. So she gave him points for that.

"Okay, here we have the living room, dining room, and kitchen." Dan guided her to an expansive, open concept space. Wide windows allowed sunlight to pour in during the day; but now, all she could see were his neighbors in their living rooms across the courtyard. Did no one believe in blinds, curtains, or shades anymore?

Dan pulled her towards another set of stairs. "I want to show you something."

Third floor equals bedrooms.

"Is it your phone because that's why we are here, right?"

Laughing, Dan continued to tug. "Trust me. One more stop. Public spaces only."

"Umm-hmm." Telia didn't get to her age without many a man trying to show her any and everything in their bedrooms: views, art, trophies—both metal and skin.

Dan shifted and brought her closer to him. Leaning down until their breath mixed, "I won't take you into a bedroom even if you beg me."

Laughing, Telia allowed herself to be taken up the next flight of stairs, but they didn't stop. They kept going until they reached a door leading to the roof. Dan flipped a couple of switches, opened the door, and bowed, "After you, my lady."

On the rooftop, Telia was awed by a tent set up as she pulled back a flap, she was met with warmth on a downright freezing Chicago night. Cars passing on the street and teenagers walking down the sidewalk provided ambient sound. The beautiful twinkling lights of downtown spread across a skyline that was all towering skyscrapers backdropped by distant stars and the occasional beacon from an airplane. Telia was literally on top of the world.

Christmas lights were sparkling along the top of the tent, providing a glow that made the space as romantic as a moonlit night on a private isle. Soon soft music was being piped through hidden speakers.

The warmth spreading through Telia had nothing to do with the fact that she had on a wool coat. Dan's arms. Being in Dan's arm, she felt …. it was indescribable. Comfortable and intense at the same time. All of these emotions tangling in her body. She'd never felt like this and didn't know what to do with it. A part of her wanted to run for the door, down the three flights of stairs, and out into those six inches of snow that Mother Nature bestowed on the windiest city in the world.

Instead of running, she pulled away from Dan's chest. His eyes. Her reflection in his eyes rooted her in the spot. In the intensity of those deep blue orbs, she felt beautiful, special, his.

"Telia?" those eyes of his questioned her stare.

She leaned in and gently pressed her lips against his. As she drew back, his lips curved in a smile. Telia's lips tingled, yearning for a deeper connection. This time, she drew his head towards her and deepened the kiss into something that withstood the progression of time.

Try as she might, she couldn't get close enough. She never wanted any man so much that the want transformed into a need that immersed her mind, drowning all conscious thought leaving her body alone to make all relevant decisions.

Her body sang, "Hallelujah."

Dan broke the kiss. His breath challenged in an effort to stay normal. His eyes questioning again. "Telia?"

Telia placed her finger against his lips. "Shhh." She'd met more than one man that said one word too many and had her drying up faster than the Mojave Desert in the middle of a sandstorm. She needed to stay in this moment, extend it to its satisfying end.

Taking his hand, she eased him towards a lounger and gently pushed him until he sat down. She slid out of her coat, unwrapped her sweater, and shrugged it off her shoulder. The heaters, which he had strategically placed around the shelter, battled the Chicago breeze for supremacy.

Dan encircled her waist. His hands warming her against the chill. His eyes still questioning. Telia's stare pierced through the question; and as she removed her bra, hunger replaced the question in his eyes. Those hands splayed against her ribs, drew her towards him.

The door opened and a squat nurse slid into the hospital room. Telia's memory of that evening swirled away in a haze of reality. The nurse, a different one than she'd seen in the last few days, checked Dan's vitals on one hand. Telia held fast to Dan's other hand, sustained by the warmth of being with him that day so many years ago.

The nurse gave Telia a cursory nod, but did not ask that question that so many of them couldn't refrain from asking.

Telia stared at the nails that needed a trimming, the square tips. These hands had given her a lot of pleasure over the years.

"Dan, I don't think I told you, but that was the day that I decided that you were mine. I don't know what came over me. I've never been the aggressor. That night, I didn't want sex." She dismissed that thought with a wave. "Well, obviously, I wanted sex, but even more I wanted you. All of you, every square inch."

Telia placed his hand by his side. She trailed her fingertips along the curve of his face and the scruffy beard on his chin. Leaning in, she whispered, "I have a secret for you. I loved you that night. Possibly from our first date. Since we didn't wait the allotted one month to have sex, I did wait the allotted month to tell you that I loved you." A soft shimmer blossomed in Telia's soul.

A smile played with the edges of her lips as she tried to articulate what he meant to her. "You are the greatest blessing of my life. Without you, there is no Shelley, no Rocky. Without you, the laughter isn't as free and easy. Without you, my intelligence isn't challenged. Without you ... without you, I'm not me."

Telia raised her eyes to the ceiling. "God, this is hard. Because I pray that without me, you find your way back to you."

Telia's breath hitched and tears gathered in her eyes. But they didn't stay there. They rolled down her face gently dropping on Dan's cheek. She used her thumb to wipe his face clear. "We didn't have enough time, not enough time at all. I feel my body betraying me, Dan. Damn it, I feel it shutting down. I feel weaker. But I'm not giving into it. This cancer better be ready for a fucking fight."

Turning, she gently touched his face again. "You're my miracle. This life with you has been my miracle: not enough, maybe more than I deserve."

She leaned against the armrest of the bed. Amazed at the man who chose to love her and how well he rose to that challenge, his lips called to her. She leaned in for a gentle touching of lips and then another. Resting her lips on his, until she realized, their lips weren't resting. His lips sought hers out. She kissed him again, and his lips moved up to meet hers, deepening it.

Pulling back, shaking with an effort to contain the emotions ricocheting through her spirit, Telia dared to seek Dan's eyes. Those beautiful blues were staring back at her, a lift in the corner of his mouth. "T."

"Nurse." Telia screamed, caught between laughs and tears, "Nuurrse!"

She grasped Dan's cheek and kissed him again.

"Christoff," Dan's voice rasped.

"You want Christoff?" Telia couldn't comprehend. Why would he want Christoff?

Shaking his head, he whispered. "The accident. Christoff ... caused ... the accident."

No. No. No.

"Christoff has the kids." Blackness clouded Telia's vision, as she felt herself falling to the ground.

CHAPTER 43

Rose peered out of the window. Christoff eased behind her and wrapped his arms around her waist. She leaned into him, trying to decide at what point he would become useless—not this soon.

Turning, Rose peered into Christoff's eyes. The intensity of his feelings lay in his focus on her, on her wants and her needs. Right now, she needed to get the hell out of dodge

"So where would we be safe?" she asked.

Rose's manipulation of Christoff became complete.

Shadows appeared behind Christoff's eyes. "There's something I need to tell you, Rose."

"Yes?" Rose snuggled deeper into his arms. They really didn't have time for this, but Rose realized early in her life that you have to believe the fantasy that you're selling. Right now, she was selling that Christoff had her heart. And that's fine. He could keep her heart as long as she retained control of her mind.

"You know, Dan's accident?" Rose chuckled. How could she not know Dan's accident? The timing of it was perfect. It allowed her to lay out her plans.

"It wasn't an accident."

The words left Christoff's mouth, but they couldn't be right. "Pardon?"

At the Touch of Love

"It wasn't an accident," he repeated.

Rose took two steps back. Of course, it was an accident. The police said only one car was involved.

Thinking back. She hadn't seen him after she dismissed him. He appeared again when he drove her to the hospital. How did he know before Telia called that Dan needed help?

As she pulled back, Christoff continued, "He hurt you. He shouldn't hurt you."

When did Christoff become a one-man retribution squad? Rose's mind raced. She hadn't factored in this wrinkle. So proud of everything she'd accomplished, she didn't scrutinize the gift of her son's accident.

She transferred control of the money and kept moving; relishing in the fact that his highness and his highness's girlfriend would have to come to her for money, not the other way around. But this? Trying to kill her own son?

"I ran him off the road."

The words rattled around the room before coming together again in her ear. Did he just say? What?

Those words couldn't have come from Christoff. Yes, she wanted the kids. That wasn't a secret to anyone, but how? Why?

"What happened?" Rose knew better than to ask for clarification. What she knew now would be enough to put her in jail. She put additional space between herself and Christoff.

"I followed them to Cold Stone. After he left, I pulled in front of him and slammed on the brakes. I saw his face in the rearview mirror when he swerved to avoid me, but by that time I was driving again."

Rose miscalculated, severely. Christoff almost murdered her son. And if he woke up anytime soon, Christoff would be going to jail. And she wouldn't be too far behind.

Trying to keep her voice calm, she said, "You tried to kill my son."

So Christoff was crazier than Sam I Am, smoking catnip from a peace pipe.

Everything she did with the money had documents. It told the story that would allow them to escape free and clear—but attempted murder?

"Christoff!" she searched his eyes for some type of explanation of why he ran her son off the road. But that would require logic.

"He can't speak to the woman I love that way. It wasn't right. You shouldn't have to beg for money. It should be yours." Christoff beamed. "Now it is."

In the years that she had known Christoff, he rarely smiled. He remained solely focused on keeping her safe in whatever manner she required.

Now he's beaming. Crap. Now she's wondering exactly how deranged Christoff was. Now when everything finally fell into place, she realized, Christoff would never go quietly into the night.

Rose's plan revolved around his compliance. But he had already been off script by putting Dan in the hospital. What if her grandchildren had been hurt? What then? Given the provocation, he'd probably kill her and then dress her dead body in new clothes every day like a doll and prop her up across the dinner table with a plate full of food.

She felt Christoff staring at her, awaiting her reaction to the news that he damn near killed her only child. Rose settled back into his arms. Her mind screamed for her to run; but if she did that, she'd leave the children. It was better to not give Christoff thoughts of harming them. She needed to keep the lid of Christoff's crazy jar shut tightly.

At the Touch of Love

CHAPTER 44

Brandon's cell phone buzzed. He answered and shot up. "Get dressed." He shouted at Echo. She jumped up and threw on underwear and a jogging suit.

"Dan's awake!"

Echo jumped up and down. "Yes, Yes, Yes."

"But Mrs. Ellison and Christoff kidnapped the kids."

"Oh, shit," Echo exclaimed.

And just a few days after the first high-speed drive to the hospital, Echo again found herself holding tight and praying. This time her mind wasn't held hostage to the fog of memory. She felt sharp and ready to fight for her godchildren.

They rushed into Dan's room only to find Remy already there, banging away on his computer, and Telia lying on the couch with an ice pack on her forehead. In another chair, a bulky gentleman squeezed into the hospital chair.

Echo ran to Dan's side, hugged him before rushing to Telia. Telia announced, "I fainted. Can you believe it? Full out fainted. They wanted to admit me. Fuck it. I'm not going to be locked in a hospital when my babies need me."

Dan sat up in the hospital bed, eyes a deeper blue than Brandon had

Sierra Kay

207

ever seen.

Brandon shook his friend's hand and gave him a half hug. He sent up a prayer of thanks for his recovery; at the same time, he wanted to rush over to Mrs. Ellison's house and snatch the kids back.

"So." Brandon scanned the room as if trying to figure out what was going on. "Are the police on their way to Mrs. Ellison's house?"

Remy replied first, "Not yet."

Dan nodded to bulky dude. "Meet Sidney, my head of security."

Brandon paused and reviewed his mental Rolodex. "You have security?"

Telia piped up, "Apparently, we have security, because I know Sidney as frequent flyer dude. He was on a lot of my flights. I figured he just flew a lot for work," Telia scoffed. "Apparently, Dan hired him to watch over me. Ask Dan how they know the children are fine. Ask him."

Brandon exchanged a look with Echo. His curiosity begged him to comply. "So, how do you know the children are fine?"

Telia answered again, "Because apparently, the Disney princess watch that my baby wears all the time is a security device. They can even listen in on what's going on in the room. Right now, my kids are playing store with Charlotte."

Brandon nodded at Echo. He refused to be in this cluster alone. Echo narrowed her eyes, and Brandon focused more intently. "Who is Charlotte?" Echo asked.

Telia glared at Dan, who finally responded, "Well, Charlotte is on staff at Mrs. Ellison's house."

"And," Telia answered, "She's on Dan's payroll. I may be the only one who didn't know that Mrs. Ellison wasn't to be trusted alone with my kids. I thought Christoff was the culprit. She was so damn convincing."

Brandon eased onto the corner of the bed to process the precautions Dan took with his family. He had more questions, but it already seemed as if Telia was five seconds from blowing her top. Understandable, to know you'd been followed everywhere you went and didn't even know it. Dan clearly hired top-notch security.

Dan sighed and rubbed his forehead. The nurse glared at all the people, but she didn't suggest they leave before asking Dan questions on how he felt. She checked his pulse and checked the machines before leaving.

Brandon knew there were too many people in Dan's room. "Should we go?"

"Why?" Dan asked.

"Because there are clearly too many people in this room," Brandon replied.

"I'll have as many people in my room as I want. There is a little plaque in the main hall, downstairs with the Dobson name on it." Dan settled back. "They'd like to keep that contribution channel open. They wouldn't dare suggest you leave."

Brandon asked again, "So what's the plan exactly?"

Sidney's deep voice grumbled, "Remy here is in charge of transferring the money back over to Dan as quickly as possible."

"Oh, yeah." Telia announced, "I forgot to add that my brother manages Dan's bank account, not the Dobson money. No, Dan has his own millions."

Remy interrupted, "I kept trying to tell you, but you were always too busy."

"Whatever," Telia responded. "And this money is totally separate from Dobson money. Dan's dad saved the majority of his alimony and child support. Told Dan that Dobson money came with enough strings to choke a sane person. Dan uses it to pay for the security that he has stalking his family."

Brandon peeked over at Dan, whose eyes were lifted to the heavens. Echo patted Telia's hand before saying, "It's great that Dan is awake, isn't it?"

Telia glared at Echo with so much fire she should have disintegrated instantly. But she grumbled, "Yes."

Dan smiled, "I know you missed me, baby."

Telia glared, "I did miss you. And I'll probably be over-the-top excited once I get to the bottom of the lies."

Dan placed his hand over his heart. "I didn't lie."

Brandon winced and mumbled under his breath, "Bad move, partner."

"So you think because I didn't think to ask you if you were having me followed that it was okay? Lies of omission are still lies. Who knows what else you lied about? We're like King- Midas-rich. That would have been useful information."

Dan's lips quirked. "Well, technically, I'm King-Midas-rich. The kids are rich. Remember, you didn't want to marry me. So you are still a jobless pauper. Shame really. So much potential."

Telia heaved a pillow from off the couch toward the bed. It landed on Dan's stomach, causing him to whoosh out his next breath.

Telia folded her arms in satisfaction. Brandon needed to pull the tension out of the room. He didn't juggle, had no jokes, not that he felt anyone wanted to hear jokes.

Remy finally spoke, "Okay. Great. I just need to find somewhere to print these documents, get Dan's signature, and get someone at the bank to freeze Dobson accounts." Remy cackled, "Mrs. Ellison is going to be so pissed."

Brandon closed his eyes for a mere second before they popped back open again. "I told you a while back about this weird guy who seemed to be everywhere I went. You convinced me it was a coincidence. Was he your guy?"

Dan threw up his hands. "What is everyone's issue? You're safe. Drop it. Focus on the kids."

Brandon turned to Sidney. "If you're so good at your job, how did Christoff get that close to Dan; and how did he and Mrs. Ellison end up with the children?"

Dan raised his hand. "Charlotte's at my mom's house to watch for money moves. My coma threw everything into the air."

Brandon contemplated what was happening. It overwhelmed him. He couldn't imagine Telia's feelings. No wonder she was acting like she could portray Sybil in a Broadway production. Her children were in the hands of a man who tried murder once already, and they had no clue how to get them free safely.

CHAPTER 45

Echo gathered Telia in her arms and let her cry it out. It seemed as if every two seconds Telia showcased a different emotion. *Is this how psychosis begins?*

Rocking Telia, Echo emitted what she hoped were soothing noises. Tears still rolled down her cheeks, but the sobs shuddered internally versus wailing externally.

Dan mused aloud, "I always knew she'd go for the money. That's what she truly wants."

Echo couldn't wrap her mind around the fact that Mrs. Ellison received access to the accounts while Dan was in the hospital. "Why did you transfer the money to her in the first place?"

"It's a clause in my grandfather's will. My grandfather died on the golf course when I was ten." Dan responded. "They made me executor of the estate. Can you imagine?"

Dan's eyes portrayed worried, sad, and exhausted, but he kept talking. "I can only transfer it to a Dobson. Shelley and Rocky are way too small. Hell, I was too small. The weight of that. Grandfather ensured I was as ready as any could be, but the learning curve.... Let's just say for the sake of argument took a whole hell of a lot. "

Echo rubbed the crease on her forehead. They could rehash the past and the will until the cows came home, but she was with Brandon. She wanted a plan. Action.

Echo spoke first. "What do we need to do?"

Brandon and Dan exchanged looks. Remy responded without removing his eyes from his computer. "Working on it."

Brandon turned. "Where are the police? The FBI? I don't know about private security forces. But somehow I expected a full-on command center set up in Dan's room."

Dan pointed at Remy. "That's it."

Echo walked over and kissed Remy on the cheek. "I thought you were a financial planner."

Remy laughed. "Dan hired me years ago. He knew his mother … well. We've prepared for this."

Brandon asked. "How do you prepare for your mother stealing your children?"

Dan pressed his lips together. "I didn't plan for her stealing the kids. I planned for her to try for the money."

Echo walked over and pressed her lips to Dan's forehead. "You were in a coma. Nothing you can do about that."

Even though Dan's body still appeared weak and there was still bruising around his face, his eyes sparkled in anger. Many times over the years, she felt Mrs. Ellison underestimated Dan.

This would be one of them. Echo wondered if she knew Dan woke up. If she did, she would know that her claim on the money would end. How and when would she find out about Dan? And what would she do about it?

"If we can catch her in this act. Kidnapping. She'll never have access to the money again—mainly because she'd be in jail."

Having loved her parents so fiercely, Echo didn't understand this soap opera of a life. "You'd put your own mother in jail?"

Dan's eyes snapped. "For kidnapping my kids? I'll put her on the ground."

Something wasn't aligning with Echo. "Let's say Remy shuts down the money line and so the kids aren't as important to them.

"Then what?" Echo asked. "When Remy cuts off her access to the

At the Touch of Love

money, what happens to the kids?"

CHAPTER 46

Even nestled in Christoff's arms, Rose knew no peace. Her mind revved like a race car on the starting line. Next steps. Although she forced her body to be languid, her mind raced.

She lifted her face and kissed Christoff on the neck. "Let's get out of here. I'm thinking United Arab Emirates. A little sand in our toes. And no extradition."

Christoff smiled again. Did his eyes always widen when he smiled, giving his face a manic façade? Is that why he did it so rarely? Did it matter that he resembled Satan himself? She had found a man who would kill for her. Isn't that what every woman wanted?

Rose eased out of Christoff's arms to the intercom. "Charlotte, come to the living room, please." Rose glanced over her shoulder, instructing Christoff, "Wheels up in an hour."

Christoff nodded and left as Charlotte entered. "I need you to pack a bag for the kids. Summer clothes. Make sure you pack one for yourself."

Charlotte questioned, "For how long?"

"How long?" Rose repeated. Since when was it proper for Charlotte to question her? "Until I say we are coming home."

Charlotte's eyes darted towards the door. "Will Mr. Christoff be joining us?"

Rose's mouth opened then closed. Anger percolated beneath the surface, but logic weaved its way in as well—always the damn logic. Servants didn't question. But then again, someone should. What was she doing? How much was she willing to risk, and for what?

If this was the best she could do, maybe her father was right. The best thing she ever did was leverage her pretty to marry Daniel Sr. Here she was taking her only heirs out of the country, with a man who could have already killed them once; and, given the right circumstances, wouldn't hesitate to try it again.

Everybody had a line they wouldn't cross. Even though Charlotte's impertinence sent anger gliding beneath Rose's surface like a crocodile through a swamp, she'd found her line. She should have recognized it before. At the end of the day, she was a Dobson. Daniel was a Dobson. Shelley and Rocky were Dobsons. Christoff was not.

"Charlotte, change of plans. Get the kids out of here." Rose rushed, hoping the urgency in her voice would push Charlotte to move faster. "Take them to Telia at the hospital, St. Augustine. Move quickly and quietly, but move."

Rose felt the tension slithering up her neck before Christoff's black loafers re-entered the room.

"You know, for someone who demands loyalty, you have so little of your own," Christoff's deep voice rumbled through Rose.

Over the years, she had heard every inflection in Christoff's voice. His voice, no matter the level of anger, never brought fear percolating through her system like coffee on a stove. Today, it did. The difference was, this was the first time she'd stared down the barrel of a Glock.

"Charlotte, go!" Rose urged.

Charlotte didn't leave. In fact, she insinuated herself between Christoff and Rose. How the hell did this twit ever get hired? She has yet to follow one single instruction.

Rose walked around Charlotte, glaring as she passed. As if she needed protection from Christoff.

"Christoff, what are you doing?" Rose inquired.

"You said you loved me?" Christoff asked it as a question, when mere seconds ago he believed wholeheartedly.

"I'm just letting the children leave. I'm staying here with you," Rose explained, hoping that the crazy that Christoff revealed hadn't completely taken over.

"But we're a family." Christoff's brow furrowed. "We have to raise them. When Telia dies, we're all they have."

"You're lying, Mr. Christoff. I don't like you anymore. Tell him, gran—Mother Ellison." A trembling, angry voice spoke from around the corner, "My mommy is not dying. I want my mommy."

Shelley stalked into the room, pulling Rocky behind her, and stomped on Christoff's foot. Rocky's eyes were wide with fascination, as if he felt this was a room to avoid. Shelley leaned in with determination.

Rose closed her eyes. Other women had grandchildren who stayed in front of televisions or video games. Rose created a complete toy room for Shelley and Rocky, with every possible toy in every catalog. Where were they? In the middle of adult conversations, which, in this instance, put them in the middle of a gunfight.

Yes, Dobson blood showed. They didn't cower even to a maniac with a gun, although Christoff quickly lowered his weapon when they entered. Rose had been right about Shelley. She would be glorious, if she survived.

Rose stepped closer to Christoff. "Let Charlotte take the children to the playroom." She kept eye contact, hoping he would see pleading in her eyes and not rebellion.

While a part of her wanted to end this without going to heaven, hell, or jail, a greater part of her was pissed off because Christoff was off script. Still, all he had to do was follow the plan; but no, he had his own plan. Thanks to him, one or both of them could be clanging tin cups across cell bars in the next twenty-four hours. Yet, she couldn't focus on how he ruined everything. He needed to feel her love, or he would kill them all.

The shifting of Christoff's eyes indicated his confusion. As Rose reached Christoff, she touched his face. "The children, let them leave." Rose grazed his cheek with the back of her hand. Christoff nodded.

"Children. Right now, go into your playroom and stay there until either

At the Touch of Love

Charlotte or I come to get you," Rose demanded.

"But Mother Ellison? Christoff said—" Shelley began.

"Now! Your parents won't like it if I tell them you didn't listen."

Through her peripheral vision, Rose saw Shelley pulling Rocky with her out of the room. The shuffle of little feet became more and more distant.

Although it chaffed, Rose did what was expected. She smiled at Christoff, as she muttered, "Thank you."

Christoff's lips pressed against the top of her head. "In all the years I've known you, I've seen every emotion you've had. I've never seen gratitude. Except …" Christoff rubbed his chin back and forth on the top of her head, "Except when you wanted something from your ex. Then you displayed more emotions than Halle Berry had husbands. But you never meant it."

Rose played with the fingers on his free hand. "I mean it now."

"Do you?"

Rose lifted her eyes to peer into Christoff's.

Christoff's smile didn't reach his eyes this time. "You'll never know how much I loved you."

Loved. Past tense. Oh, shit.

As Rose lowered her head, Christoff pointed the gun at her abdomen and pulled the trigger so quickly all she had time to do was inhale before the stench of her own burned flesh reached her nose.

The bullet's impact pushed her away from Christoff. As blackness rimmed her vision, a shot rang out from behind her. Charlotte's legs spread, gun drawn, smoke wafting. Alive. Children safe. Rose closed her eyes as her body continued its journey to the marble floor.

CHAPTER 47

Telia didn't know her heart could stop in her chest for three whole minutes and not kill her, but that's what she felt when she heard Shelley's voice enter the room with Christoff and Mrs. Ellison.

When Shelley told Rocky they were going to follow Miss Charlotte, Telia screamed at them to stay where they were. However, Shelley couldn't hear them.

When the children found Charlotte, and Shelley challenged Christoff and unfriended him, Telia felt faint again. This time she didn't have the luxury of passing out. Her children's lives hung in the balance of the next few minutes.

Dan's heart began racing so much that the monitor beeping increased, causing nurses to enter the room, but it quickly quieted as everyone prayed for the children's safety.

When Charlotte called the hospital room, minutes after Shelley made it safely to the toy room, everyone sighed relief.

Except Dan, barely above a whisper, he asked, "What about my mother? Where is she?"

The phone fell silent. Even the incessant beeping seemed to pause. Charlotte, the ultimate professional informed them, "Christoff shot her. She didn't survive her injuries."

Dan translated, "Died. She died."

At the Touch of Love

Telia wanted to walk to him. A part of her mind knew she should embrace her husband, absorb his emotions. But that part was buried under the anger she felt for her children being in that situation in the first place, buried under the emotional exhaustion of the last four days. Her hands shook with the adrenaline pinging around her system.

How did they expect Telia to feel about the woman who threatened to kidnap her children? She was doing her best not to dance around the room to that song from *The Wiz*, "Brand New Day." She didn't have mourning in her.

Once Charlotte disconnected, Remy raced from the room to deal with the business side of death. Sidney paused at the door. "The press and police will be all over this. We can handle both, though the police will want to talk to you, I'm sure. I'll guard the hospital door until a backup comes, and then I'm heading over to the house. By all means, please stay in this room."

Telia rose. "I'm going with you. I'm going to my kids."

Sidney held up his hand. "Charlotte may have already left with the kids. It will be better to stay here until they get here." She couldn't stay here. In her mind, she wanted to scream, cry, and climb the walls. Pacing in this cage was a bad move. However, it was the only move she had.

"I have a house that no one knows about," Dan explained. "We'll make arrangements to go there tonight if we can."

Although Echo and Brandon barely breathed, she could feel their presence. She told Echo that she should trust her feelings for Brandon, which meant she had to trust her feelings for Dan—or risk being a hypocrite.

Before this, she existed in the bubble of his love. Now the bubble popped, and she had bruises from the fall.

At some point, the hits had to stop coming. At some point, this nightmare had to end. But every revelation added another punch to her overburdened psyche.

Her babies could have died, twice. The children she cared for and nurtured in her womb could have been snatched away. She didn't even know they were in danger. Dan did.

They had bodyguards following them, every step, every day. She didn't even know they were needed. Hell, bodyguards infiltrated his mother's staff. Her life included the word infiltrated, used in the correct context. Dan knew.

Yet, he didn't bother to share. He didn't bother to tell her what it meant to be his. He didn't feel it necessary to share this part of his life. And now he expected her to traipse off to his secret hideaway house. How many other secrets did he have?

Telia turned slowly with her eyes closed, grasping the handrail of the bed. "You lied to me. Every day, for years, you lied to me."

Echo and Brandon immediately rose from the couch making excuses before heading for the door. When she passed, Echo rubbed her arm. Telia didn't want to be comforted. She wanted, needed for this to be over.

She wondered if this was how her father felt when her mother told him about her affair. Anger pushed through her bloodstream like steam through milk in a latte. But also she felt that pulsating pain so deep that the only reason Telia's legs didn't collapse from underneath her was due to her grip on Dan's hospital bed.

Dan held up his hands. "Whoa. You never wanted to know about the Dobson side of life. So I didn't tell you. I didn't lie. You didn't ask."

"Lies of omission are excusable at ten years old. By the time you hit twenty, that logic doesn't wash. In what scenario would I not want to know that my children were so rich that their own grandmother would kidnap them?"

"But she tried to send them back here."

Telia scoffed. "Really? The fact that they're okay justifies the fact that a man that I thought was an overly attentive businessman traveling my route turned out to be a bodyguard. Well, no, Rachel and Charlotte are bodyguards. He's the head of your security detail."

"I protected my family," Dan shouted. Telia didn't even recognize the man on the bed. Didn't even know who the hell he was.

"I need air." Telia walked to the door. When she opened it, a man, with arms so big it was a miracle his suit didn't rip like the Incredible Hulk's when he flexed, blocked her path.

"I'm sorry, ma'am, but it would be better if you stayed in the room until we can get you all out of here."

Although she nodded, her eyes shone with unshed tears. "So this is my life? "I'm sorry ma'am, but … you have to stay in a room with a liar and possibly cheating man who has another house that you knew nothing about, so that we can protect you."

"Don't you dare." Dan snapped, sitting up in his bed. "I've never cheated on you."

Telia challenged. "How would I know?

Dan hollered, "My mother just died, I'm two seconds out of a coma, you're coming at me with this 'you lied to me bullshit.' Well, another reason it sucks to be with me is that the media is going to bite into this story like a steak. So, yes, you're going to get a lot of I'm sorry ma'ams. If you want, I can arrange for your 'space' at a separate location."

Telia glared. "Where will my babies be?" Dan simply stared at her.

"Right. They'll be with the man who can 'protect them,'" Telia mocked. She collapsed in the chair by the door before adding. "I'm being inconsiderate. I'm sorry for your loss."

Telia didn't feel sorry. She didn't feel anything now. Numbness replaced the spurt of anger.

"Telia—" Dan attempted.

"No! If you say something, I'll say something else. And I'm sure it will be the absolute wrong thing. So let's just let it ride for right now."

"I love you," Dan's eyes plead in support of his words.

Telia sighed. "That's the thing about lies. Now every word is filtered through that history." Telia didn't have the mental acuity to filter fact from fiction.

All she knew is that the past four days revealed she didn't know nearly enough about the man she decided with her heart to spend the rest of her life. "This doesn't settle well in my gut. And I fear, more than you can imagine, that it may never settle well; and I can't say what that means."

Shelley pushed the door open shrieking, "Daddy!" She jumped up on the bed. Rocky screeched as well, holding out his hands for Dan. As the children settled on the bed, Shelley started her story. "Daddy, Mr. Christoff isn't my friend. He said Mommy was going to die. So I stepped on his feet. And Mother Ellison made us go to the playroom. And Charlotte brought us here. We went through the garage. Mother Ellison has a lot of cars."

Telia felt Dan's eyes on her, but she didn't raise her eyes to meet his. Finally, she ran her hand through her hair. "Baby bug, that's a lot. Your dad hasn't been well. Let him rest."

"Mommy," Shelley whined. "He's been asleep forever."

Sidney came through the door. "Ok, people, here's the plan. We have to move you within the hour."

Telia refused, "We can't move him. He needs medical care."

Dan folded his arms. "One thing that my mother taught me is money provides solutions."

CHAPTER 48

A cool summer breeze wrapped itself around Brandon, as he examined the Chicago skyline from the Ellison's' rooftop desk. He should be spending all summer up here, sipping on Dan's secret stash of scotch.

The tinkling and giggling from the open windows, along with smooth jazz, formed the background to the evening.

A month after Dan's release, Telia arranged for a party at the Old Towne residence with their closest friends. Dan, Telia, Echo, Brandon, and the kids spent much of that month at Dan's hideaway, which ended up being another mansion, of course. But this one was in Winnetka, with plenty of land for the children to run around.

Apparently, Dan bought it after medical school, when he was considering trying to live his mother's lifestyle; but it never fit him.

Now he rented out this palatial ten-bedroom lakefront house. Brandon understood Dan's rationale. After a few days of losing everyone in the house, they all agreed to stay within one wing.

The around-the-clock medical support Dan hired began to have less to do with his issues than Telia's. Brandon almost snorted his breakfast out through his nose, when Telia told Dan if she saw one more doctor on her vacation, she'd dislocate his kneecap. The doctor remained, just not in Telia's view.

Now they were back. Brandon saw the cracks in Telia and Dan's relationship, which they were trying to fix. Love still existed, but so did an underlying tension.

Next week, Brandon and Echo planned to return full-time, so that Brandon could resume work, while Dan and Telia would disappear again away from the watchful eyes of the media.

"So this is where you've been hiding," Telia exclaimed as she opened the rooftop door. "Are you avoiding Susan?"

Susan harassed them until she got an invitation. Dr. Phillips showed up as well, with a different date. That's not why he hid on the roof deck.

"No." Brandon shuddered. "That's just a convenient side effect of hanging out up here."

Telia chuckled, but it didn't flow the way her free laughter normally did.

He walked over and touched her forehead before she swiped his hand away. "How do you feel? Tired? In any pain?"

Telia sighed. "Before you get out your spinal tap, the pills Dr. Dan gave me are still working."

Dan found a combination of pills that made Telia more comfortable with her condition: less pain, more energy, or at least more than other patients he'd seen with pancreatic cancer.

Dan spent a fortune, literally, trying to find a cure for Telia's condition; but he hadn't used her for a guinea pig. Although she still tired easily, she seemed to be holding up well tonight.

If the frown on her face wasn't due to pain, what was it? She clutched a clear plastic storage bag with an envelope inside.

His eyes rose and connected with Telia's. "She knew you didn't kill your G-Ma." Brandon closed his eyes. Only one person accused him of killing his G-Ma. She kept coming back like a boomerang on a merry-go-round. Maybe it was time to clear the air or at least his conscience.

"What do you have there, Telia?" He pointed, as Telia's fingers slid up and down the zipped closure.

"Just a letter I found." Breaking eye contact, she peered at the cityscape. "It's beautiful tonight, isn't it?" The jazz melody seeped through the house. "I love this song."

At the Touch of Love

Brandon felt in his bones that this conversation would be one he'd rather walk through hot sand on the equator, wearing a plastic jacket, than to have. But then again, that could be the problem. If he shut it down the first time, it wouldn't keep coming up. "And where did you find the letter?"

Telia stared at her shoes, rocking back and forth on her heels. "Susan's purse."

Brandon snorted. "So what? It just fell out?"

Telia's eyes defiantly glared at his. "Well, it was in my house, on my guest room bed."

"And you went through all of your guests' purses?" he inquired.

"Do you want to hear about the letter or not?" she demanded. "Never mind. Forget it. Thought you'd want to know." Telia turned on her heel with a stiff spine.

Brandon inhaled a deep breath. His heart beat against his chest. He didn't know what the hell Susan had found, but if Telia thought it important enough to bring it up in the middle of a party, maybe … just maybe. "Wait, Telia." Not that she had taken one step other than to turn around.

Telia slowly turned, holding the letter up to him. "It's yours."

Brandon paused. He reached out, but then clenched his hand into a fist. It wasn't his business. This was beneath him. Wasn't it?

"I shouldn't. That's Susan's," he explained.

Telia shook the bag. "No, actually it's yours. It's addressed to you. It's written to you. It's from G-Ma."

Brandon's legs didn't hold him upright anymore. He collapsed on the edge of the chair. Settling back into the deep white cloth cushion, his hands over his eyes.

"Usually when Susan arrives at parties, she's the first to throw her belongings at the staff like they work for her." Telia explained, "Tonight, she held on to her purse as if she didn't want to let it go. She seemed off. So the minute she left it, I saw why.

Telia continued, "It was meant for you to have. Susan must have stolen it."

Brandon willed the strength to read G-Ma's handwriting, but even now wiped the perspiration from his hands onto his black slacks.

Telia put her hand on his shoulder. "Do you want me to get Echo?" she inquired.

"No. No." Brandon insisted, "I don't want Echo to hear ... or see. She's having fun. Leave her be."

"Okay." Telia bit her lip, gnawing, looking more unsure than she had in any moment they had ever shared.

Brandon motioned to the chair across from him. "I knew G-Ma planned to kill herself."

Telia gasped. "But the letter said."

"Yeah." Brandon leaned his head against the back of the chair. "She probably wrote my get out of jail free card. G-Ma always covered all the bases."

"But Brandon ..." Telia started.

"I didn't kill my G-Ma. That much is true. But I knew she didn't want to live like that, die like that." He mumbled, "Fucking family."

"One of my cousins filmed her on a bad day. Bastard posted the video. It's one thing to know that you're losing it. It's quite another to witness something that you don't even remember; witness your memory loss; witness not knowing the people you love the most and seeing the tolerant sadness in their eyes." Brandon whipped his plastic cup and watched as the scotch spiraled out. "Mother fucker."

Telia's eyes widened as droplets narrowly missed her.

"Shit," Brandon exclaimed. "I'm sorry. It's just ..."

Telia placed the letter on the table between them. "You should read it."

Brandon stared at the letter, but he couldn't will his hand to retrieve it.

"She asked me to be there when she did it. She asked me to hold her hand. You know, I've been a part of the transition of strangers that didn't make it off the operating table, people I didn't know, didn't love. How could I let my G-Ma die alone? But I didn't believe in what she was doing. So how I could be there?"

Telia leaned in and whispered, eyes wide, "What did you do?"

"I hired a nurse. Someone to be with her every minute of every day." Brandon shook his head, emitting a mirthless chuckle. "God, how she hated that. Told me it made her feel like an invalid. But on a bad day, she wasn't alone."

Telia's forehead wrinkled in confusion. "If someone was always with her, then how did she take too many meds?"

"I didn't know that she occasionally had the nurse run errands. She called me over." Brandon's voice cracked. He exhaled slowly, "I was there, holding her hand as the life seeped from her body. And …" His body shook as he tried to maintain his composure. Telia came over and held him.

He pulled back, because if he sank into the comfort she provided, he'd be crying all night. He needed to push through. To ease the sour ball of guilt weighing, poisoning his core. To … to … He stood, giving Telia the seat and settling in on the table.

Telia reached out to touch his knee.

"And I left her there, because that's what she asked me to do. And we both knew that if I stayed that I might lose everything." He let out low breaths.

"What did she take?" Telia inquired.

"She didn't tell me. She Googled it. She learned how to kill herself … from Google." Brandon stared into the night, seeing nothing, hearing nothing. "I hoped she would forget. Crazy, huh, what people with Alzheimer's remember?"

Telia sighed. "Oh, Brandon."

"I don't even know if she made it into heaven," Brandon admitted. "She did commit suicide after all."

"Well," Telia admitted. "I know what I'd say if I was your grandma and good old St. Peter stopped me at the pearly gates, questioning me about suicide being a sin."

Brandon felt that he probably shouldn't ask, but curiosity tickled his tongue. "What would you tell good old St. Peter?"

Telia beamed her best 500-watt smile. "Suicide's a sin? Sorry. I forgot."

Laughter shot out of Brandon's mouth, as if his tonsils were slingshots. He immediately clamped his hand over his mouth. "I'm serious, Telia."

"Yeah, I know," she acknowledged.

Brandon turned and picked up the letter, flipping it over and over in his hands. "It means nothing. It absolves me of nothing. I let my G-Ma die."

Telia grabbed his hands. "She made the decision."

Brandon shook his head. "I let my G-Ma die. Knowing Susan, this letter was to Susan like a red flag to a bull."

"That doesn't mean you have to spend your life paying her off," Telia demanded.

Brandon thought he could, but Susan would get more and more demanding. She had nothing—no proof, only a suspicion. Suspicion is not evidence. Life could be difficult, but not impossible. And now that he had the letter, Susan had even less.

"No. I'm done paying her any more than the judge required." Brandon grabbed the letter. "That's probably why she has the letter here. This is the first time she's seen me since we went incognito. She's just sidetracked by her beau, Dr. Phillips, and his new boo."

"Yeah," Telia responded before touching his arm. "When you're ready, come back and join the party."

Brandon nodded and turned to leave the rooftop. "Please don't tell anyone. I want people to believe it was an accident. That was G-Ma's last wish."

Telia smirked. "I'll take it to my grave."

Brandon stopped. "Don't do that. Don't."

Telia's eyes clouded with confusion.

He continued, "You remind me of G-Ma in a way. Your life causes everyone around you to bask in this amazing ripple effect of love. When and if that's no longer the case, the effect will be felt at least three times as hard and in reverse."

He touched the top of her head. "It's nothing to be cavalier about. I know that's your coping mechanism. But you matter, to all of us. And you should know."

"You are killing my party high." Telia snarled with mock anger. "Now get out of here before I start to cry.

She swiped her index fingers underneath both eyes. "Didn't your G-Ma ever tell you not to ruin a girl's makeup?"

"Gosh. Another rule? Isn't it enough that I open doors for womankind?

At the Touch of Love

I swear, you all are never satisfied."

Telia chuckled. "If you think opening doors is all you need to satisfy a woman, then you have a lot to learn, young Jedi."

Brandon pulled Telia into a hug. "Thank you for listening, understanding."

Telia's hands tightened around his waist. "Thank you for trusting me with your story."

Brandon laughed. "Hell, I thought you might pickpocket me if I didn't come clean. I'd rather give you a story than a credit card any day."

Telia slapped his arm. "And I won't even tell you that you need to tell Echo. Tonight, at least."

CHAPTER 49

Echo stood in Telia's living room, wearing a floor-length cream column dress, which she swore made her butt appear as if it had its own zip code. It served as a contrast to Telia's silver dress, which captured the light and threw it around the room with wild abandon.

The thirty-odd guests, dressed in their finery, milled around and danced to the music the DJ played, clearly enjoying the benefits of the open bar. Telia Arthur knew how to throw a party.

The wait staff mingled, sharing nibbles and white wine. Telia refused to eat colored food when she wore light colors. The first date with Dan, when she spilled paella on her white outfit, cured her of that particular ill. With Echo's light-colored dress, she was forced to the same colorless diet.

Echo nibbled on a carrot stick. Even though her stomach threatened to grumble loudly for a steak, Echo tried to be neat with this beautiful silk creation. She daydreamed about a hamburger, with mustard and ketchup dripping over the side. The table did have some chicken wings, but she'd need to eat twenty of them to make a dent in her hunger. Plus, she'd yet to find a neat way to eat chicken wings. She'd have to go all in or go hungry.

As the most recent guests entered, Echo turned fully towards the snack table. However, her shoulders tightened, as the tension level in the room continued to rise. Susan refused to leave when Dr. Phillips came in with his date. Each minute that passed while Dr. Phillips was smiling and gazing into the eyes of another woman, who appeared to be at least ten years younger than

At the Touch of Love

Susan, caused Susan's spine to stiffen.

Remy idled up and gave Echo a half hug. "Hey, lil sis."

She leaned into his hug. "Remy!"

He perused the room. "Good to see you all. Pretty busy month or so. How's Dan handling Mrs. Ellison's death?"

Echo thought about the time they'd spent at the country house: the shadows that darkened his eyes; and the spark created by Shelley, Rocky and Telia. "I think he's doing okay, making it. Tee says he's trying hard to grasp the good days and hold on tight."

"Sounds like good advice." Remy nudged her. "Maybe someone else should take it."

Echo stared at him. "Are you trying to hide a lecture behind a casual conversation?"

Remy gave a half smile. "Not my fault you're hearing a lecture in a casual conversation."

Echo laughed. "Well, you'd be surprised. Next year, I'm going on vacation for my birthday. My parents loved to travel. So I'll pay homage to life, instead of wallowing in death. How's that for growth?"

Remy's smile grew. "I'd say that's pretty damn good. The facial tissue industry may have issues, since their sales will drop so significantly."

Echo punched him in the arm.

Laughing, he added, "But that sounds amazing to me. I'm glad."

They turned and perused the dance floor to see Susan in the corner glaring at Dr. Phillips.

"So how did Susan get on the guest list? Telia can't stand her, and she's your man's ex. Matter of fact, why is Dr. Phillips here?" Remy questioned.

Echo threw her head back in a laugh. "Dr. Phillips is now Brandon's best friend for getting him out of his marriage," she explained. "Now Susan kept calling Brandon and Telia, trying to finagle an invitation. We already knew Dr. Phillips RSVP-ed with a plus one; and since Susan called, she clearly wasn't the one."

Remy sighed. "Ah. I get it."

"Yeah," Echo continued. "Telia said she gets what she deserves for trying to be where she knew she wasn't wanted."

"That sounds like Telia," Remy sighed. "No matter how much I tried to instill the high road in her, she slips back low every now and then."

The music shifted from slow jazz to pop. They turned around to see Dan bopping around the living room/dance floor. While he and the beat of the music clearly did not have a close and personal relationship, he seemed to have fun.

"So, Echo," Remy challenged, "I dare you to have a dance-off with Dan."

Echo snorted. "I will wipe the floor with good old Dr. Dan and send him upstairs to cry in his pillow."

"Well, what he lacks in skill or talent, he does make up for in enthusiasm."

Brandon and Telia descended from upstairs. Telia immediately started grinding on Dr. Dan, who laughed as he tried to keep up.

Brandon came over and shook Remy's hand.

"Brandon, we've been challenged to a dance-off," Echo declared, without taking her eyes off Remy. He didn't know who he messed with. She happened to be a semi-professional video vixen.

Brandon glared at Remy. "A challenge, huh. Well, Remy, it depends. What are the terms?"

Remy thought before declaring, "The winner gets a private chef for the weekend."

Brandon stroked his chin, as if he was deep in thought. "If the chef is Echo, the deal's off."

Remy and Brandon laughed together, which brought Dan and Telia over to their corner. Dan shook and shimmied in front of Echo, while pulling her to the dance area. Telia grabbed Remy and Brandon. Remy proceeded to out-dance them all, declaring, "Don't let this pretty face and impeccably cut suit fool you."

CHAPTER 50

Brandon leaned against the wall, chuckling as Remy tried to teach Echo and Telia dance moves from the 80s. Remy must have studied under Kid or Play, because he had every move highlighted in their movie, *House Party,* down pat. The animated trio's antics were keeping him entertained.

"Where have you been hiding all night?" a familiar voice whispered in his ear.

An arm snaked its way around his waist. Of course, Echo picked that moment to turn around and stopped mid-laugh, which caused Telia to turn as well. The thunder represented in her face let him know it was past time to deal with his ex-wife.

He held up his hand and nodded, trying to convey that he'd handle the situation. Although neither of them appeared happy, they let Remy distract them by introducing some breakdance moves into his repertoire.

He unraveled Susan's arm from his waist and walked away. "Follow me." He heard her heels clacking behind him, as he walked up the stairs to the guest room, where the coats hung on a mobile rack and the purses were lined on the bed. He thought about closing the door, but thought the better of it. No need to let Susan's imagination wander the wrong way.

Susan glanced around the room and eased herself down on the bed, crossing her legs. "Babe, do you remember the first time we were at Dan and Telia's house?"

No way would he walk down memory lane with Susan. Hell, he'd take a Google Map reroute two hours out of the way before going down memory lane with her. More giggling from downstairs left him impatient to return to the party.

"Nope," he responded, squelching any further questions.

Susan's face fell. "What the hell is wrong with you?"

And the fact that she asked indicated how clueless she was. "You. You are wrong. You've been wrong since day one."

"Come on, we had good times once." She ran her tongue over her lips. "We could have good times again. Why don't you close the door?" She actually batted her eyes and patted the bed. He wanted to turn to see if anyone else saw this tired play. He didn't know if she had developed amnesia when it came to their divorce proceedings, or if she really thought she was that irresistible—with her "boyfriend" on the arm of another woman one floor down.

Susan stirred nothing in him but contempt. These days, Brandon fed off the sweet laugh that wafted up the staircase. Echo. But he couldn't build on his foundation with Echo until he closed the chapter on Susan; that is, until he shut the door so firmly on her financial wrangling that the knob broke off and left her on the other side without any more openings.

His G-Ma was gone. She'd made her decision. He hated her decision, but G-Ma wouldn't want him held hostage by Susan's nonsense. That's why she wrote the suicide letter in the first place, to protect him.

Time to stomp Susan like a roach. That's the only language some people understand.

"Listen, I'm not giving you a damn cent more than what the judge ordered. It's done. The bank is closed. Financing rescinded." Brandon's voice increased as he continued, "I just don't give a shit.

"Matter of fact. You and I could see a penny on the sidewalk at the same time, and I would snatch it from you before you could think to bend over," he clarified. "If I found out that you won the lottery, I would sneak through your window and shred the winning ticket before you could make it to the bank. You could have saved for years for a life-saving operation and needed a last nickel to fund it, and that last nickel wouldn't come from me. In other words, fuck off."

At the Touch of Love

The more he spoke, the more Susan's face turned an odd shade of purple. She jumped to her feet, "By the time I'm done with you, you won't be able to prescribe Orajel®."

"How do you propose to do that?" his voice returning to its normal pitch.

"I have my ways," she cackled. "You'll be sorry."

"About what?" Brandon leaned against the door jamb, as if he didn't have a concern in the world.

"You'll see." Susan snatched her purse from the bed and her wrap from the coat rack. "You'll be begging to write me a check tomorrow." Susan elbowed him out of the way, but paused when he began speaking.

"I'm calling my lawyer on Monday. It seems there are some assets that you forgot to mention in the divorce proceeding. Like the insurance policy that you took out on G-Ma. May be legal. May not. But I'm sure the court would love to know about it."

Susan began to shake.

"Oh, and don't forget the significant amount of jewelry that you didn't disclose during our divorce. Those count as assets.

"You wouldn't dare."

And because he couldn't resist. "Just so that you're aware. Mail tampering is a felony. Let me hear one note of one word whispered about me or my G-Ma, and you'll be in handcuffs so fast, you'll think it's one of those bondage porn movies you watch."

"What do you mean mail tampering?" Her eyes widened as she wrenched open her purse. She rustled around, but it was so small she had to realize as soon as she opened it that G-Ma's letter was missing.

"You stole the letter?" she shrieked. "You went into my purse and stole the letter?"

"How could I steal a letter that was addressed to me? How does that work in a court of law?" Brandon countered.

Susan's mouth opened and closed several times, but she didn't have a response.

"I was willing to pay you to leave. You should've just moved on." He waved her away. "Get the hell out of here before I get one of those beefy goons from Dan's security team to escort you out, because I have better things to do than waste another second of my life being infected with your fungus."

Susan huffed her way down the stairs. He felt the tension raise down the stairs and the murmuring after she left.

As he turned into the hall, he almost ran into Echo. "Were you checking on me?"

"Nope," she smiled. "I needed to use the facilities."

"At this minute." Brandon didn't appear convinced. "Right."

"Nature and all. Plus," she added as she encircled his waist with her arms, "I didn't know if I needed to beat her with a shoe or not. Telia offered, but I was a safer choice. Telia probably wouldn't stop."

Laughing, Dan pulled her in closer. He leaned down to kiss her. "I saw you down there trying to keep up with Remy. Since you're in the mood to learn, I have a few moves to show you later."

"Oooh. Can't wait." Echo shivered with anticipation.

Brandon pulled out of her arms and propelled her towards the stairs with a lingering caress of her rear. He couldn't wait either.

Hours later, the last guest left and the cleaning crew remained. Brandon clapped Dan on the shoulder while Dan smothered a yawn.

"Don't you have staff to manage the staff?" Brandon joked.

"Funny." Dan's droll look made Brandon laugh.

"Excuse me, Mr. Ellison?" the petite brunette stated. "Sorry for interrupting, but we're all done."

"Here you go and thank you," Dan responded, handing over an envelope.

As the young lady hustled to the door, Brandon began inspecting their work. "Dude. You don't even know if they did a good job. You're supposed to go over it before you pay them."

Dan waved him off and walked towards the stairs. "I'm so tired that I don't care about anything but my bed."

Brandon trailed him. "I'll get Echo, and we'll get out of your hair."

However, when they reached the bedroom, the sight of their women, each snuggling a child and their hands clasped made Brandon pause. It was all

At the Touch of Love

he could do not to shed a tear. Even Dan gave a suspicious sniffle.

After a bad pantomime, they walked back into the hallway. Dan whispered, "You can't take Echo home, not tonight. Did you see that shit? That was the sweetest thing I've ever seen. Telia with Shelley and Echo with Rocky, who just might replace you if you're not careful."

Brandon glared. But truthfully, he had to agree. The scene was too perfect. Instead, he whispered, "We should get a picture."

Dan nodded. "It'll have to be overhead, which means your goliath ass will have to take it."

Pulling his phone from his back pocket, Brandon muttered, "Fine."

As he got into position and took that first photo, he realized something and pulled Dan back out of the room.

"Dude," Dan exclaimed. "If we keep going in and out of there, they're going to wake up."

"I want to be in the picture, too."

Dan squinted. "You want to be in a picture with my wife and kids?"

"Don't make it sound sketchy," Brandon warned. "Listen, when we remember this night with them sleeping in there, don't you want to be part of the story."

"Someone has to take the picture," Dan insisted.

"Where's that thing Shelley had tonight," he said, gesturing a sign that signaled something long and thin. "The one she was running with when she almost poked my eye out."

Dan snapped his finger. "The selfie stick. Let me try her room."

He hustled down to Shelley's room and came back with the selfie stick. Brandon walked into the room and pretended to go to Telia's side of the bed until a strong arm by Dan stopped him in his tracks. Chuckling silently, Brandon walked over to Echo's side and eased himself on the bed. Both men froze to make sure no one woke up.

Then Brandon eased down as Dan took a few shots of him facing the camera. Then he pretended to be asleep, hoping Dan got a shot of that as well.

As Echo snuggled closer to him, he relaxed just for a moment. He really wasn't in a hurry to leave. He'd just rest his eyes before he went to either of the kids' room.

Just for a minute.

CHAPTER 51

Telia woke up with a familiar tingle in her stomach and butter soft lips pressing their way against her head. She felt in her bones that it wasn't morning yet and with Shelley sleeping beside her, she knew Dan wasn't trying to start something.

He shifted as she stirred. She lifted her eyelids just a little to see Echo and Brandon sound asleep on the other side of the bed. Well, Dan clearly wasn't getting any with everyone all in the bed together. This was not HBO.

Dan whispered, "Hey."

Smiling, she shifted towards him, "Hey, you're going to wake everyone."

Dan waved the others off, as if they were inconsequential. "Look, babe."

As he showed her the photo that was taken at some point during the night, she fought to keep her breathing regular, but she couldn't stop the tears from collecting in her eyes. She loved every single body that was currently dancing with the sandman in her bed.

This time when she was barely awake, she didn't have the wherewithal to "Swayze" it. She could give in to the thought that she was dying. She could give in to the limited time she had with her family. She could give in to the tremendous blessing and curse that embodied her life.

Blowing out another breath, she laid her head back down on the pillow.

Dan placed his head on top of hers. "We did good. We have a kickass family."

Telia smiled and recited her favorite passage from Maya Angelou's *Passing Time*.

Dan whispered, "This isn't passing time. This is living life, Sweetie, glorious life."

All Telia could do was nod. She tried to silence the voice in her head that constantly clamored with the reality that she would no longer be a part of this collective. But she was here today. Today was a moment. Dan's accident showed them the fragility of those moments. The need to collect as many as she possibly could before … before.

Telia sank into Dan so tightly their bodies would have blocked the sands of time.

Even though the sun hadn't roused yet, Telia tried by sheer will to keep her eyes open for as long as possible, to etch the feelings of this moment so deep in her soul that it would traverse with her to the other realm.

Telia couldn't contain the joy increasing with each beat of her heart. "I don't want to be mad anymore or carry anymore of the bullshit from your mom one more day. Life's too precious. Marry me."

Dan's face puckered in confusion. "But you don't believe in that piece of paper."

Telia licked her dry lips. "But you do. And I want that for you. For us. All of us." She grinned, giving him a sly wink. "Plus, you've been freeloading off my love for too long."

Dan chuckled into her hair. "First time I've ever been called a freeloader."

Telia shrugged and whispered back at him. "Well, if it fits …."

Dan nibbled her ear. "Where's my ring?"

"Layaway."

"Layaway? What's that?" Dan pondered. Telia elbowed him until he let out a soft laugh and responded, "Any day, anytime, anywhere."

Telia nodded as her body demanded she finish the sleep she started. As she drifted off, her illness was no longer an albatross weighing every step, every breath. She loved him, and she would be totally his in every way. For

At the Touch of Love

now …

She was air.

At the Touch of Love

Hi Reader,

Thank you for spending time with *At the Touch of Love.* If you enjoyed it, please consider leaving a review.

Stay abreast of new books and giveaways from Sierra Kay by following me on social media platforms.

Website: sierrakay.com
Facebook: authorsierrakay
Twitter: @sierrakay1
Instagram: authorsierrakay
BookBub: Sierra Kay
GoodReads: Sierra Kay

Until next time , be well.

Sierra Kay

At the Touch of Love

www.ingramcontent.com/pod-product-compliance
Lightning Source LLC
Chambersburg PA
CBHW020059180626
46812CB00006B/2392